TO KILL A KING

HOLLOWCLIFF DETECTIVES BOOK 2

C.S. WILDE

Join the Wildlings to keep up to date with the latest on C.S. Wilde and participate in amazing giveaways. Also, you'll get a FREE copy of BLESSED LIGHT, an urban fantasy romance novel!

CHAPTER 1

Somewhere in the past...

As an assassin for the League, Bast loved nights like this. The overcast sky blocked any shred of moonlight, drenching the forest around him in a thick penumbra. It was a great advantage for an assassin, but a bad omen for many night fae, since most nightlings drew their powers from the moon. Contrary to most of his people, though, Bast's magic didn't come from the light.

It came from the darkness.

Le infini nokto drin wu hart—The endless night inside him.

The darkness that filled his veins and his essence, the power exclusive to the royal house. Some called it a curse, others a gift, but it didn't matter in the end. Magic didn't explain itself, it simply was.

Believing a moonless sky could be a bad omen was stupid —all omens were—except, this time, a grim sensation pricked Bast's chest. The kind of grievous feeling that preceded a point of no return; the same sensation that overcame him moments before he'd killed his first victim.

Funny. Bast had been only ten back then, but he'd assumed he would always remember the face of his first kill. The horror in their eyes, their screaming and crying, their futile begging. Yet, five years later, he couldn't.

Halle, Bast couldn't even remember who he'd killed last week, and what they'd tried to offer in exchange for their lives. It was always the same—wealth, favors, sex, powerful spells...

None of it mattered in the end. Death couldn't be bargained with, and Bast *was* death.

"Take your time," Leon whispered beside him as they assessed the villa, hiding behind a dense row of bushes. "Be mindful of your surroundings. Not everything is what it seems."

Bast narrowed his eyes at his oldest brother.

Leon had wavy hair trapped in a low pony, but a few loose curls framed his face. His eyebrows were as dark as midnight, and his skin a tone lighter than Bast's own.

One could say Leon resembled Father, but their eyes were different. Father's were cold and blue; Leon's warm and pink like Mom's. And where the king was brutally cruel, Bast's big brother was caring and kind.

Also, overprotective.

A modest grin cut across Bast's lips. "I know what I'm doing. There's a stunning spell around the house, but it's weaker there." He pointed to the garden's far left. "With a shield, I could cross it without trouble. I'll be seen, obviously." He turned to the guards on the upper right, middle, and center of the roof. "But I can take them all with my blade."

Which was the most fun way to kill, really. Using just his magic drained Bast's energy and slowed him down. He was much quicker, more efficient—unstoppable, actually—with a blade.

"From then on, it's about eliminating everyone inside the house," he continued, patting the sword strapped to his belt as one would pet a faithful hound. "That's what the bounty said, yes?"

Leon stared at him, a mix of shock and pride running behind his rosy eyes.

Yes, Bast was a youngling, but he wasn't *any* youngling. He was a fucking prodigy with the highest kill rate in the League. Master Raes himself said he out-performed his most experienced assassins. In fact, Bast had such a talent for bloodshed, that his friends had given him a nickname.

Yattusei—Death-bringer.

Slowly, Leon nodded. "Yes, your plan is solid, but you don't have to go ahead with this. I've always believed you were too young to—"

"Ignore him," Corvus interrupted from behind Bast. The *shig* wore the same onyx battle leathers they did—the League's uniform. He leaned against a tree trunk with arms crossed behind his head, his eyes closed as if he was relaxing by the freaking beach or something. "Leon is jealous of what you can do, little *Yattusei.*"

Little Yattusei?

Corvus was only six years older than him, that *suket.*

There were five Night Princes: Leon, the big brother— literally, since he was stronger and taller than the rest of them—Benedict and Theodore, the twins; Corvus, the prick; and Bast, the perfect. Then came Stella, their half-sister, but she didn't count since their father never acknowledged her.

Stella was five, but already understood that faeries hated her for being the king's bastard, *and* for being half-werewolf.

Such a cruel thing for a five-year-old to know...

Even Bast's brothers hated her. Theodore himself often

3

showed his dislike for the "cute aberration," which meant a lot, considering he was a monk.

They could hate her, though. *Halle*, the entire Lunor Insul could hate her, as long as they knew Bast would kill anyone who dared lay a finger on his sister.

In fact, *that* had been his first kill. The assassin Father sent to kill Stella when she was just a baby.

Bast had beheaded the *shig*, then barged into the throne room and threw the fae's head at Father's feet, if only to send a message.

It was incredible how memories could resurface out of nowhere...

"Thanks for the useless input, *baku*," Bast snapped at Corvus.

Baku meant fool, or moron, depending on the intonation, but Bast weighted the syllables equally so it meant both.

Corvus chortled, but didn't open his eyes. "Just being honest."

"You're distracting him," Leon pointed out bitterly, then turned to Bast. "Focus on the mission. Father himself commissioned it, so we cannot fail."

Leon and Corvus were also a part of the League of Darkness, as Father had once been, and his father before him. The twins, however, had chosen to break family tradition. Ben enjoyed the tomfoolery and endless fuckery that came with the job of being a rich prince, while Theo dedicated his life to worshipping Danu.

Ironic that the two looked exactly the same, yet behaved like complete opposites.

Bast frowned at Leon. "Who are we killing, by the way?"

"You know better than to ask," the wrong brother replied from behind them.

Bast focused on Leon. Corvus might be right, but Bast would only take Big Brother's word for it.

"I have no clue," Leon admitted. "Certain bounties are so secret, we can't know who we're killing. It seems that is the case tonight."

"Which is why daddy dearest asked the League to kill everyone in there," Corvus scrambled closer. "Well, he asked *you* specifically, Bast. Which boggles the mind, doesn't it? To ask a child to murder at least…" he narrowed his eyes at the villa, "… two faeries and three shifters."

Bast gritted his teeth, trying to channel his anger as Master Raes had taught him. Use it in his favor; control it before it controlled him. It was awfully hard sometimes, especially when it came to Corvus.

"I may be young," Bast snarled, his tone ice and stone, "but don't forget the name I've been given."

Grinning, his brother arched one silver eyebrow at him. "Aren't you a child wonder, *little Yattusei?*"

Bast shrugged off the tease, then crouched, building momentum in his legs. "See you on the other side, *bakus.*"

He jolted toward a tree trunk, hiding behind it, before speeding closer to the back patio—all the while, his magic enveloped him in a shield. As Bast crossed the stunning spell, he felt a light fizzling on his skin, but nothing more.

"There!" one of the fae guards on the roof shouted. The night was dark, but not enough to mask Bast.

As his shield vanished, he grabbed two cursed daggers from his cross belt, and flung them at the faeries above him. Cutting through the guards' weak magic shields, the blades pierced their foreheads right in the middle.

"If an opponent goes down, make sure they don't get up." One of the many valuable lessons Master Raes had taught him.

The fae's bodies crashed down onto the lawn with a harsh thump, their arms and legs twisting in unnatural ways.

Even under the darkness of a moonless sky, Bast could discern them as Father's soldiers, nightlings with a duty to enforce Tagradian law in Lunor Insul, guided by the Night King himself. Yet, these soldiers were rogues.

Why did they desert?

No time to figure it out. The third guard, a wolf shifter, jumped from the roof. His landing—a proper crash, actually —shook the ground.

Night guards aligning with wolves?

Not impossible, but unlikely.

Standing tall atop his hind legs, the *shig* had to be at least three times bigger than Bast. The wolfman's claws sharpened as slobber dribbled down his jaw. Muscles bulged underneath his thick black fur.

"*Halle*," Bast grunted under his breath as the wolf joined both claws.

He jumped back right before the beast wreck-balled the spot where he'd been standing not a moment before, leaving a hole on the ground.

Without hesitation, Bast unsheathed his sword. The sleek blade glinted slightly, even underneath the cloudy weather.

He dodged another attack from the wolfman, then swung his arm up. The blade cut across the werewolf's neck effortlessly, opening a long, bloody gash that drenched his midnight fur with red.

Stepping back, the wolf gasped, slamming his hands over the wound.

Shifters in general had a penchant for healing quickly, so Bast had to make sure this one wouldn't bother him again.

Plunging his blade into the wolf's heart, he twisted it once before yanking it back.

The shifter's eyes rolled to the back of his head, his legs caved in, and his body hit the ground with a loud thud. The massive wolf then morphed back to his human form, because, well… he was dead.

Turning to the bushes, Bast flipped his brothers the

middle finger, even if he couldn't see them. Yet, another of Master Raes' teachings invaded his thoughts.

"Do not rest until the deed is done."

Good advice, as always.

Bast faced the villa, and a sphere of darkness shot from his hand toward the glassed patio doors, shattering them into a million pieces.

He stepped inside.

The place was eerily quiet, but Bast was called *Yattusei* for a reason. His shadows and stars were stronger than his vision, so he closed his eyes.

A dim presence reverberated against his magic. It came from the top of the stairs where a werewolf waited for him; Bast could feel him stamped to his darkness.

The beast had the high ground, so Bast couldn't go to him. Instead, he shot a blast of magic upwards, and it pierced the floor next to the wolf.

A fair warning.

Growling, the wolfman jumped to the base of the stairs, and another shifter, this time a leopard, joined from the living room. Two giant, bloodthirsty beasts, ready to rip him in two.

Bast didn't panic, but he did fear. As Master Raes said, a fae without fear was a fool, but a fae in panic was dead.

Concentrating on the advantages he faced, he took a deep breath. Bast was smaller than they were, which made him faster. Also, he had a shitload of magic.

This battle was as good as won.

He lunged forward. So did the beasts.

Dodge. Turn. Pierce. Slash.

As it turned out, he didn't need to use magic. His blade had been enough, as usual. Falling limply onto the floor, the shifters' bodies started to change back to their human forms, sticky red pooling underneath them.

7

In the stillness of the night, Bast heard whimpering coming from a room on the second floor. This seemed to be the remaining presence in the house.

The last kill.

Gingerly going up the stairs, he avoided the hole his darkness had pierced on the second floor.

Stifled cries came from behind a white door, and Bast couldn't tell why dread filled him as he turned the door handle.

He had ended lives before, both innocent and guilty. Mothers, fathers, daughters and sons, brothers and sisters, all for the League. *Yattusei* didn't care about the bounty's past, only their inevitable end.

So why did he hesitate now?

Opening the door, Bast gasped, his lungs failing him. "Idillia?"

Father's mistress took him in, her black eyes filled with shock, as she put down the knife she was holding. "Bast?"

"Why are you here?" Looking around, panic set deep into his chest, and Master Raes' teachings vanished from his mind. "Where's Stella? Is she all right?"

Recognizing his voice, his half-sister burst out of a closed cabinet, and wrapped her tiny arms around his legs.

"Basti, Basti!" she cheered, giggling with a pure happiness inherent of small children. "Bad *manies* are after us, but they can't beat you! We're safe!"

Bast's throat became awfully tight.

He was the bad *manie.*

Sheathing his sword, he placed a hand over her head. "Of course you're safe." Tears pricked his eyes as he turned to Idillia. "Father wants you and Stella dead."

She scratched the back of her neck. "Not exactly old news."

"I know, but he left you alone after I killed the assassin he

8

hired." Bast figured that joining the League, and throwing an assassin's head at Father's feet would've done the trick. Apparently, he was wrong. But what had changed? And more importantly, why did he demand Bast kill them?

He knew why, of course. That sick *malachai* would call it a show of faith. Everything was a show of faith when it came to that prick.

"I want to leave Lunor Insul," Idillia stated. "Stella and I can be happy in my home borough, Lycannie. But your father doesn't want his shame to be known beyond the island. His pride is too great."

A certain hurt took over Bast. "I've always protected you both, and you've always been well cared for in Lunor Insul. Why would you take my sister away without telling me?"

Shame flickered in her eyes. "It's not that. You pay for our food, our home, Stella's private lessons, all with the money from your bounties. It's a heavy burden for a chi—"

"If I'm old enough to kill, then I'm old enough to be considered an adult," Bast snapped.

"Fair enough." She raised her hands. "But growing up here, Stella will always know hate. I don't want that for her."

Chest tight, he looked down at his little sister, who buried her face in his legs. Yes, he loved her. Yes, he wanted her nearby, but he also wanted what was best for her, and Idillia wasn't entirely wrong.

"Sometimes, loving someone means letting them go," the wolfwoman quietly added.

Bast tapped Stella's head, and she stared up at him with big blue eyes incredibly similar to his own. Big baby eyes filled with tears.

"You up for this?" he asked.

Stella nodded shakily. "I don't want to leave you, Basti… "

Forcing a smile, he caressed her chin. "Everything will be fine, Baby Sis." He turned to Idillia. "I'll figure something out,

I promise, but don't take my sister away from me. She's the only thing—" his voice failed him. "If you stay, father won't try to kill you and Stella. So, stay. Please."

Sighing, Idillia stepped forward and put a hand on his shoulder. "Staying isn't the best for her. Here, she'll always be a bas—"

"Don't."

"Say it, Basti," Stella mumbled, tears in her voice. "I'm a basta—"

"Quiet," he snapped, knowing Stella didn't understand the weight of the word, the trouble it entailed, especially in Lunor Insul, where adultery used to be a crime punishable by death—usually of the female and child.

Thank the unification for banishing that.

"Give me a couple of days. With any luck, father will recognize Stella as his own." It would be impossible, but Bast had to find a way, otherwise he'd lose his sister.

"Don't lie to them, Sebastian." Corvus' voice rang from an empty spot near Idillia—he must've used an invisibility spell.

Bast didn't have time to react; his brother had already appeared out of thin air behind Idillia, and slashed her throat.

Gasping, Stella's mother stared at Bast as she stumbled back, collapsing on the wooden floor. Fur instantly began to spread atop her skin, since shifters healed quicker in their beastly form.

"Step away from her!" Bast bellowed as Stella's screams swallowed the space. She pushed against her brother's legs, attempting to run toward her mother, but Bast kept a tight grip on her.

He couldn't let her get close to Corvus.

"Save mommy!" she howled, but Bast couldn't help Idillia and protect Stella at the same time.

Keeping his focus locked on Bast, Corvus bent down and

slammed his sword into Idillia's chest, twisting the blade just like Bast had done to the shifter guard.

The sound of meat being slashed wasn't new to him, but this time, it clawed at his ears and ripped his soul.

Idillia stopped moving, and the fur retreated into her skin.

"Mommy!" Stella fell to her knees. "Mommy, no!"

"I will fucking end you, Corvus," Bast gnarled through gritted teeth, his fangs sharpening, and his darkness filling him up to his head.

"I did you a favor, little brother." Taking a cloth from his belt pouch, Corvus cleaned the blade. "Now, you can keep your bastard sister. You should be thanking me."

The sick *shig*!

Heart wrenching sobs escaped Stella while she crouched on the floor, her wailing piercing Bast's chest.

"You killed her mother in front of her!" A storm of night and stars bloomed from Bast's body, black lightning crackling around him, making the walls shake. "She's just a child!"

"So were you when you murdered an assassin to save her." Corvus observed his brother's crackling magic without any interest. "I'm not scared of your wrath."

"Burn in Danu's hells," Bast snapped, unsheathing his sword. He pulled Stella to her feet, pushing her against his left leg, his grip tight on her.

Corvus studied Stella's little, sobbing, form. "Whether you want to face it or not, your sister is living on borrowed time."

"Enough!" Leon shouted from the door.

Fuck! Bast had forgotten to guard his back.

Leon had been kind enough not to attack, and Bast appreciated the show of mercy, but he slammed his spine against the wall nonetheless. His cloud of night aimed at Corvus while his blade pointed at Leon.

Big Brother watched him closely. "You may be *Yattusei*, but you do realize you can't take us both, yes? We're trained assassins."

"Fucking try me," Bast barked, holding Stella fiercely to him.

Leon shook his head. "Father gave us a mission."

"And you're finishing it over my dead body!"

"You've always loved Stella more than your own blood." A certain bitterness coated Leon's tone. "Why?"

Burning tears streamed down Bast's cheeks as he realized he might defeat Corvus and Leon, but not in time to save Stella. Her death would render this entire fight pointless. His entire life, too.

He was so screwed.

"She *is* our blood! She's better than all of us!" His voice cracked, fear once again turning into panic.

Master Raes would be so disappointed...

"Bad, evil princes!" Stella cried, but was smart enough to stay close to Bast.

With a heavy sigh, Leon rubbed the bridge of his nose. "Father hoped you'd follow through. I suppose since the mother is dead, the child won't go to the continent. I don't want your hate, brother, so I propose we consider the matter settled."

"How will you convince Father?" Corvus asked him. "He wanted them both dead."

"I'll find a way."

"There you go, stealing all the fun as you always do," the prick grumbled, shaking his head.

Leon sighed in exasperation. "Why are you always such an asshole, Corvus?"

"Because it's fun, brother."

"So, it's agreed?" Bast interrupted, still wielding his sword at Leon and his night at Corvus. "Stella may live."

"Father will be furious," Corvus warned.

Well, he wasn't wrong.

"If you weren't Master Raes' best assassin *and* under the League's protection," Leon said carefully, "the king would have killed you a long time ago for defying him. Nevertheless, he will disown you for this, rest assured."

"If he doesn't banish you from the island," Corvus added.

"He won't," Leon countered in a threatening manner. "Our brother will remain in Lunor Insul, so will his sister. He simply won't live in the castle with us anymore. Knowing Father, that should sort the matter, at least for now."

Still sobbing, Stella watched her mother's lifeless body. "Mommy…"

"Don't look, Baby Sis." Bast put a hand over her eyes before facing Big Brother. "So be it. I never cared about the throne."

"I know…" Leon nodded to Idillia's body. "Remember, Bast. The moment you leave the League, you're on your own, and no one, not even I, will be able to protect you."

CHAPTER 2

MERA CLOSED her eyes and listened to the ship's hull breaking through the waves below. A warm, giddy joy spread in her chest as she imagined herself down there, underneath the hull, dashing across the ocean.

Utterly careless. Utterly free.

It was a beautiful dream, but a dream nonetheless.

When she opened her eyes, her fingers dug deeper into the Nightbringer's metallic railing. Being aboard a war vessel designed to kill schools of waterbreakers was a cruel irony. Mera had once feared these spiked, dark-metal ships when she was little.

Now she was aboard one.

She didn't have a choice, really. Sailing was the only way to Lunor Insul, the night fae Island. Bast could've flown them, but they were carrying three sets of luggage with the basics, plus some necessary equipment. Also, before she could have asked him, he'd claimed, *"I'm not a beast of burden, kitten."*

So there she was. Aboard a freaking Nightbringer.

The point of a warship sailing on safe waters was lost

on her. No mermaid could ever cross the forbidden zone and survive to tell the tale. Unless they were the water-breaker who impregnated Sara Hyland; the male called Poseidon—a siren with a god complex, who had overcome the magic within these waters. The magic that should've consumed his flesh, bones, and all that he was, yet he'd survived it.

Same as Mera.

Someone approached her from her right, but she didn't face him. Maybe if she ignored the dickwart's presence, he would go away.

"You think you're punishing me with your silent treatment," Bast taunted playfully, "but I find it cute."

She turned to him, and Poseidon in the trenches, she shouldn't have.

The wind tousled loose threads from his messy bun, his moon-silver hair resembling either silk or spider webs. Bast's face was made of perfectly straight lines, his smirk creating charming dimples on his cheeks.

To top it all off, the setting sun drenched him in a mix of pink and orange, turning the male into a freaking painting. Without meaning to, Mera blushed.

Damn her traitorous body!

"I'm not giving you the cold shoulder," she lied, her legs feeling awfully weak.

With that, Mera leaned over the railing and stared at the ocean, mostly to avoid losing herself in the living magnet called Sebastian Dhay.

'Beauty should be admired', her siren sang with a chipper tune.

Ignoring that horny bastard, Mera studied her own hands. "I don't trust you to do the right thing, Bast. It's shitty to say that about my partner, isn't it?" Sadness and anger created a strange mix in her chest. "You killed *everyone.*"

15

"If an opponent goes down, make sure they don't get up," he countered absently.

"That might have worked for an assassin, but you've been a Hollowcliff detective for a while now."

Bast had told her the truth once he'd been cleared for duty, a few days after the massacre at the Summer King's penthouse.

At first, Mera couldn't believe Tir Na Nog police had hired a former assassin as a detective, but she confronted Captain Asherath after Bast insisted on it. The red-haired fae had merely answered, *"Bast is my best detective, and he's been atoning for his sins. Do 'cut him some slack', as you humans say."*

So, that was that.

Glaring at her, a muscle ticked in her partner's jaw. "If I didn't know I'm a detective and not an assassin, my arrest rate wouldn't be the best in Tir Na Nog, would it? But those faeries... if they spoke about you, it would have been your death sentence."

"I was perfectly aware of that when I made my choice."

"So was I!" He ran a hand over his hair, nearly undoing his bun. "I'm sorry if I'm not as selfless or as righteous as you are, but my partner's life was in danger and I did what I had to do."

Mera opened her lips, yet found no good comeback. She tried, though, searching her mind as she kept there, her mouth half-open and a frown on her forehead, but it was useless.

"Sakala mi," he cursed under his breath as he hunched over the railing. "I didn't ask you to trust me. Our captains did. So you better do your job, *Detective Maurea*, and let *me* worry about my actions."

Her siren licked her lips. *'Oh, angry Bast is a thing to behold.'*

Mera rolled her eyes. She hated disappointing her siren

16

—*not*—but fighting with her partner would take them nowhere.

"Your intentions were noble," she begrudgingly admitted. "The execution was the problem, pun intended."

"I don't care." He raised a challenging eyebrow at her. "If I'm so terrible, why didn't you tell your captain? Why am I not behind iron bars right now?"

"Many reasons," she pondered. "I guess I didn't want to see you in jail for protecting me. It didn't seem fair." A grin hooked on the left side of his cheek, but she immediately raised a warning finger at him. "Just don't go berserk and kill a bunch of people again. Okay?"

Bast's scorching blue eyes fixed on her as he stepped closer. "So long as they're no threat to you, fine."

"I'm not a damsel in distress," Mera snapped, hating the flutter in her stomach that increased with his proximity. "We're here to protect and serve. Remember that."

"Always." Bast winked at her, then nodded over his shoulder toward the ship's faraway destination, where a patch of land the size of a thumb rose from the sea. "So, are we in this together?"

"Do I have a choice?"

His laughter engulfed her, as if Mera had told him a funny joke. "Not really."

Captain Asherath shouldn't have put Bast on this case. After all, he was the potential victim's son. However, he was the only nightling in the Tir Na Nog precinct, which made him the most qualified faerie to do this—and also the worst possible choice.

Asherath did ask her to keep him safe, not that Sebastian Dhay needed any help with that.

Suddenly, his hands lifted to touch her face, but Mera instinctively stepped back. "What are you doing?"

A certain hurt flashed behind his eyes, but could he blame

17

her for being on her guard around him? Bast was a trained assassin... and also her partner.

Ugh! Working with him wasn't going to be easy.

"I need to unleash the Faeish you learned in school from your mind," he said as if it was no big deal. "Most faeries who work with tourism speak English, but the rest of us prefer sticking to our ancient tongue."

A lot of Tagradians—shifters, witches, and humans mostly—visited Lunor Insul's crystalline beaches during summer. Mera had always wanted to go, but Ruth refused to let her near salt water.

A wise decision, really.

"I learned Faeish at school," she pointed out, "Didn't faeries learn English, too?"

"Of course we did, but you aren't exactly fluent in my language, are you? Unused knowledge is lost knowledge."

Check mate.

Lower faeries also visited the island, though light Sidhe from Tir Na Nog refused to step into Night Court territory. Vamps preferred Lunor Insul during winter, when it was foggy and rainy, though one vampire diplomat, a Mr. Charles Grey, had been living on the island for decades. He worked as a city auditor to the Night King's practices, but he hadn't reported an incident to Hollowcliff since... well, ever.

"Be that as it may," she tapped her temple, "you're not having a peek, buddy."

Bast studied her intently. "Kitten, this will make things a lot easier for you. Besides, reading minds isn't a stroll in the park for me. I can unleash knowledge you already acquired, and I can slightly blur memories that recently happened, but getting front row seat to what's going on in there?" He knocked on her forehead. "Not so easy."

The possibility of giving a partner she didn't fully trust a free pass into her head didn't please her, but if he was right, Mera would need fluent Faeish to interrogate their suspects.

"Fine." She raised one finger. "But no funny business."

Placing a hand over his heart, he bowed his head at her in a silent promise. Which didn't set her at ease, mostly because she wasn't sure if Bast's word was worth something. Not anymore.

Pressing his thumbs on her forehead, his other fingers dug on the back of her skull. Bast closed his eyes, going still.

Mera stared at him, waiting to feel something other than the warm sensation pooling between her thighs.

Why did he have to be so freakishly handsome?

"You need to relax," he noted, his perfect face deep in concentration.

Fine.

Closing her eyes, Mera let her shoulders drop before taking a deep breath. A long moment passed, but she felt nothing out of the ordinary.

"When are you—"

Bast removed his hands. "I'm done, *chichi.*"

"Seriously?" She opened her eyes, glancing at him dubiously. "I don't feel any different."

Chuckling, he crossed his arms. "You do realize I just spoke Faeish with you?"

No way!

"You never learned certain words, so you won't know how to translate them at first," he explained. "You'll understand the translation for others, but if their meaning is more complicated than in English, you'll perceive the original in Faeish faster."

"*Akka baku,*" she said then slapped a hand over her mouth. "I spoke Faeish. I'm speaking in Faeish right now!"

Bast laughed; an earthy, joyful sound that made her smile. "Yes, you are, *chichi.*"

She frowned. "What does *chichi* mean?"

"Kitten."

"*Malachai*," she whispered, but couldn't hold back the grin that spread on her lips.

Meanwhile, Lunor Insul grew bigger at the bow of the ship.

The island was simply enormous, a long and wide piece of land with three mountains spread in a line that cut through the territory. If she didn't know better, Mera might have confused it with the continent.

She finally understood why the locals called it Lunor Insul—the approaching port was shaped like a half-moon. Sunset drenched the island in an earthy orange and pink that quickly changed to purple. Slowly, lights began flicking to life at the base and around the mountains.

"If it wasn't for my mom," Bast confessed, observing Lunor Insul with a certain bitterness, "I wouldn't have returned."

His mom, the Night Queen.

For the little they interacted, she'd seemed kind, and yet... aloof. As if her mind and body didn't occupy the same place.

Mera had hoped Seraphina Dhay would've joined them in the Nightbringer, but she'd chosen to fly back to the island a day earlier. When Mera asked why, Bast's mother cast a bitter glance at the water. "Better death plummeting from the sky."

Distracted by thoughts of the queen, Mera barely noticed the spear that cut through the air, piercing the wooden floor right between her and Bast.

A miracle really, that it hadn't hit them.

Adrenaline shot through her veins as she whipped out her gun. "What the hell?"

"Danu in the fucking prairies," Bast grumbled before he sent a whip of darkness toward the sky.

A Sidhe clad in black fighting leathers flew above them, but he wasn't fast enough to evade Bast's whip of night and stars. It twirled around his body, and when Bast pulled, the fae crashed onto the Nightbringer's deck.

Mera thought she'd heard bones break, but the faerie didn't utter a sound. His wings disappeared into thin air.

The rest of the passengers—a group of crow-shifters with bleached hair—rushed toward the bow, ready to morph and take flight, but they probably didn't want to abandon their surfboards. So they waited.

Idiots.

Mera aimed at the kneeling faerie. She'd seen his uniform before… the assassin sent to kill Bast two weeks ago had worn those same clothes. Which meant this fae must be with the League of Darkness.

She gripped her gun harder. "Don't these *bakus* ever give up?"

The fae frowned at Mera, as if something other than the fact she was aiming a gun at his head had surprised him.

Ah, yes. She'd spoken in Faeish.

This assassin looked a lot younger than the last. He had lavender skin, and his white hair hung below his left ear, turning under. Like he was in a boy band or something.

He tried to break free from Bast's whip of night, but it was no use. Gritting his teeth, he forced himself up but nearly tumbled over. He tried again until he shakily stood on both legs.

"I'm draining your energy, youngling," Bast explained. "The more you fight, the more tired you'll become."

"This is your gift, *Yattusei.*" The young faerie snapped, sweat blooming on his forehead. "To consume, corrode, and destroy." Facing Mera, he glared at her. "He *is* death, human. You'll do well to stay away from him."

The image of Bast shoving a dagger through the previous

assassin's throat flashed in her mind, followed by the massacre at the penthouse. She shook off the memories, hoping her partner wouldn't repeat his ways, and yet, the boy's words stayed with her.

"He is death..."

"Tell me about it, kid." Funny that she'd called him kid when he might be a lot older than her.

"You're a child," Bast noted the obvious, his lips curling in offense. "Does Master Raes think so little of me?"

The boy stopped struggling and gave in to Bast's night, his chest heaving up and down with the effort. "You were once a child, too. That did not stop you from becoming *Yattusei.*"

Bast waved his hand in the air, dismissing the argument. "My lead is not one to be followed. Why did Master Raes send you?"

"He didn't. After Eckbach failed to return from his mission, I assumed you'd done something to him." His eyes glistened with tears. "I'm here not for revenge, as that is not the way of the shadows. I'm here, because I deserve an answer, *Yattusei.* My mentor must be mourned."

"Ah, he had a name," Bast answered coldly, a severity in his tone that seemed alien to him, and yet fitted him perfectly. "Mourn him all you want. It won't change the fact he's dead."

Lowering his head, the boy-assassin held down a cry. He hadn't shed a tear when he'd crashed onto the deck, yet Mera was certain he'd broken his foot—or at least twisted his ankle —but he cried now for his dead mentor.

Mera pitied the poor kid. Against her better judgement, she put her gun back in its holster.

"Go and inform his family." Bast's night retreated into his skin. "Weep for your mentor, but do not be foolish enough to try avenging him. Understand?"

The youngling nodded reluctantly.

"And tell Master Raes to lift the bounty, or I'll keep killing every assassin he sends my way. Do I have your word?"

"Yes," the faerie snapped, his nostrils flaring as he tried to balance on one good foot.

Bast didn't seem convinced. "Say it after me: *I promise I will not lay a finger on you, Sebastian Dhay, or the human woman accompanying you, and that I'll inform Master Raes as you requested.*"

The young Sidhe rolled his eyes, but he repeated the promise nevertheless.

A snap of darkness flashed between them, a thunder of void cracking through the air, which probably meant the promise was sealed.

A magic promise was no small thing. If the young faerie broke his word, he would be in a lot of pain. Possibly for the last time ever, depending on how strong he was.

The assassin's lavender wings blinked out of thin air. Like Bast's, they were scaleless and smooth. One of them hung slightly crooked, but it flapped well enough to ease him upwards.

The faerie nodded to Bast's uniform—white shirt, gray vest, and pants that made him resemble a dandy from the past.

An awfully captivating dandy.

"There's no running away from death, *Yattusei.*" The fae's wings kept flapping awkwardly behind him. "It's not merely your gift. It's who you are."

With that, he took off into the sky.

CHAPTER 3

THE HARBOR WAS MADE of marble and sandstone that matched the color of the moon on a clear night. Also, the place was *packed* with tourists.

Contrary to their elitist counterparts in Tir Na Nog, night fae welcomed all creatures to Lunor Insul. They encouraged visitors to come as often as they wanted, but on grounds of cultural respect, the Eastern and Northern territories—where most night fae lived—were forbidden to anyone from outside the island.

Once a fae, always a fae.

Walking down the ship's ramp, Mera stepped on the white sandstone floor. Only magic could explain why there were no boot marks on the surface or even a tiny speck of dust. The moon hung shyly in the purple evening sky, ready to take over when the sun finished its descent.

Walking ahead, Bast carried two of their suitcases while Mera dragged the third. "Come on, kitten."

She followed him through the vast harbor, dodging tourists and passersby as they went, until eventually, Bast halted on a sidewalk.

"Whoa," Mera mumbled.

Now that the crowd had dwindled, she could actually see across the street and study the town. Every white building rose from the marbled floor the way trees rise from the ground, showcasing smooth grace and tender strength.

Blue flowers decorated the window sills on some constructions, while others had silver swirls embellishing their façades. Some were round, others squared, but they all had pointy, teardrop-shaped roofs.

If someone could build houses on the moon, Mera figured they would look like this.

Lunor Insul town had a gentle kind of beauty, like that of clouds strolling on a summer sky, or rain pattering on leaves. It nearly took Mera's breath away.

Nightlings flew in straight lines parallel to the street, showcasing magnificent wings of different textures; scaled, smooth, and some even dotted. They dodged self-driving carriages and electrical vehicles; actual cars and buses imported from Clifftown, all packed with tourists and faeries.

Magic and technology together. It was a thing to behold.

When Bast signaled for a magic carriage, Mera thought she should ask him what had been on her mind for the past hour. There would never be a right time, anyway.

Taking a deep breath, she decided to go for it. "Why did the bounty hunter call you *Yattusei?*"

A big, snow-white carriage with golden embellishments and red padded seats stopped before them. The vehicle had no driver or horse, yet it didn't have an engine either.

Bast didn't answer her as they loaded their luggage onto the vehicle, and he didn't answer as they got inside.

"Will you at least tell me what *Yattusei* means?" she pushed.

Instead of finally giving her something, he bent forward.

25

"Take us to the precinct," he whispered to the carriage, and the vehicle jolted to a start before going on its way.

"Fine." Crossing her arms, she huffed. "Don't answer me, then."

Bast seemed fine with that, keeping silent and thoroughly ignoring her.

Mera was curious to meet the vampire diplomat tonight, since he was scheduled to show them the island's precinct—if one could call it that.

Lunor Insul was technically a part of Tir Na Nog, but the Night King reported directly to Hollowcliff, not the fae borough. And because the island was technically a township, it didn't have a proper precinct and officers like in the mainland, which meant Mera didn't know what to expect.

The carriage glided seamlessly across the smooth surface of the streets, dodging other enchanted and electrical vehicles, plus the occasional fae. Yet, as they left the western side of the island, the traffic thinned.

Their carriage went up a hill lined by thick forestry on both sides, slowly leaving behind the electrical cars and most humans.

Night fell fast around Mera and Bast. Flickering lights suddenly blinked to life around the carriage, floating above and around them like fireflies made of white light. Mera looked back to see an entire island consumed by these mystical lights, as if the stars had come down to twinkle *everywhere*.

"Wow," she muttered as she surveyed the city in the distance.

"Like what you see?" Bast asked from beside her.

Without facing him, she nodded, lost in the splendor that stretched across the island. "It's incredible…"

In Mera's experience, there were two sorts of beauty. The kind that stole her breath away, and the kind that revealed itself the more she studied it. Lunor Insul's was the latter, a quiet, shy sort of beauty that had snuck up on her until it became jaw dropping.

She whirled forward, and when her gaze met Bast, she gasped.

A soft luminescence glowed on his dark skin, as if someone had sprayed him with neon blue dust, especially across the bridge of his nose.

"Every nightling's skin reacts to the magic in the island," he explained, clearly noticing the surprise in her face. "Local flora and fauna also have it." He pointed to a bird flying past the faerie lights. Neon green patterns spread on its wings, as if the poor thing had been tribal-tattooed. The patterns matched the bird's radiating green eyes.

All around them, plants glowed softly with glittering colors—purple, yellow, green, red. The entire rainbow came alive as the sun vanished in this place, their shine intensifying the darker the night became.

She turned to Bast, not knowing what to say. Without thinking, Mera cupped his cheek, wondering if his skin would feel any different.

It didn't, of course, but his glowing freckles matched the bright blue of his eyes, and she realized then, that Bast was the epitome of beauty, at least to her.

Merciless and gentle at the same time.

His mouth hung slightly open, as if he admired her as much as she did him. Cupping her hand softly, he smiled. "I'm glad you're here. I'm not the religious type, but if I were, I would thank Danu for you, kitten." He leaned closer, his lips nearly brushing against hers. "Thanks for sticking around, even after... you know."

His words warmed her heart, her cheeks; the space between her thighs, too.

All it would take to complete their kiss was a bump on

the road. Mera never prayed, didn't believe in such things either, but she prayed for a bump, hoping some greater force out there would listen.

"I'm your partner, aren't I?" she countered playfully.

"Yes, and I'm the luckiest bastard in this damned world." He watched her lovingly. "Mera, I…"

The carriage slowed down, stopping before a roadblock—the border to the eastern side of the island.

Lowering her hand from his skin, Mera scooched to the side, a warm tingling burning underneath her cheeks. She couldn't decide if she felt relieved or angry at the interruption. Possibly both.

Silently, she watched the oncoming guards, two night fae with deep purple complexions and long white hair trapped in low ponies. The glow on their skin shaped neon pink and purple patterns similar to the bird's.

"So, your family runs Lunor Insul's entire security force," she remarked quietly while the faeries approached.

The Sidhe's fitted navy uniforms with silver details helped them blend in with the night, and the luminescence around the island.

"They do, yes. It's why there are no officers on the island, just the night guard. Whenever a detective is needed, we can fly from Tir Na Nog directly. Or take the boat." He winked at her.

"The government puts a lot of trust in your court."

"The island gets a hefty sum of tourism money." Bast shrugged. "It's in my family's best interest to guarantee everything flows smoothly with the continent."

According to history books, the Night Court had welcomed Tagradian intervention, and was one of the first to join the new government, either because they knew it meant progress, or because they wanted the light courts to shove it.

Probably the latter.

In return, they received the government's full trust. Recently, the light courts had lost most of their power, thanks to Bast and Mera, while Lunor Insul remained fairly independent—and as strong as ever. Which meant Bast's family was a lot smarter than the rest of the faeries.

She couldn't tell if that was a good thing or not.

When the guards asked for their documents, Bast and Mera showed them their badges. Nodding, the fae stepped out of the way.

"*Yattusei* means death bringer," Bast blurted quietly when the carriage rolled forward.

What a horrible nickname. It fit him perfectly, and yet, not at all.

"I don't enjoy talking about that part of my life," he admitted. "I was a different faerie then."

"Were you?" Nearly two weeks ago, he'd ended more lives in minutes than Mera had in all her years in the force.

Death bringer.

Exactly that.

"There's a difference between killing with motive, and killing to survive," he argued. "I've only done the latter since I came to the continent."

Deep down, Mera knew he was right, and yet, a part of her didn't want to face it; didn't want to admit that what happened at the Summer King's penthouse had been the best of all outcomes. That it had been a matter of survival for them both, and that she felt relief instead of guilt, though she'd never admit it aloud.

Better change the subject.

"Who's this Master Raes you mentioned when the fae attacked us?"

"He was my mentor and the head of the League. We must

29

pay him a visit tomorrow if we want to find out what's going on. We can't solve my father's *alleged* murder with assassins breathing down our necks."

He was right, of course.

"One more thing," he added. "I might need to use you as a last resource tomorrow. In case things go south."

"Oh, no, no, no. If I do something—"

"No macabre, I promise. Your glamour is gentle enough that they'll barely notice."

She narrowed her eyes at him. "I don't like this."

"You don't have to like it." He gave her an infuriating grin. "You just need to do it."

Prick.

Finally, the carriage came to a halt, and they got off swiftly. As soon as they had their luggage, the enchanted vehicle jolted to a start and drove away.

Mera observed the white, two-story house with a tear-drop roof. "This is it? It's small for a precinct, isn't it?"

Cocking his head to the right, he shrugged. "I suppose it will be enough."

Bast placed his hand on the wooden door and it clicked open.

The two-room area was dark, but Mera could distinguish a sofa in the precinct's waiting space, then a cell at the back of the second room. Two desks stood not far from it, with a coffee machine on the right, and a water cooler. Beside one of the desks, and blending perfectly with the dark, she noticed a medium-sized safe with a silver handle for locking confidential information or evidence.

Well, at least the basics were here.

Bast snapped his fingers and the faerie lights outside ventured into the precinct, passing through the closed windows the way ghosts would cross walls—if ghosts existed, that was.

Faeries were provided with electricity like the rest of Hollowcliff and Tagrad, so there was bound to be a light switch in there somewhere. Most fae however, preferred sticking to the old ways whenever possible. Bast himself could use a computer and a phone—Mera had seen it twice—but he wouldn't do it unless absolutely necessary.

The faerie lights did a great job at lighting the waiting room, though.

"Welcome." A creepy voice sprang from the back, near the cell.

Mera narrowed her eyes to find a shadow breaking through the darkness. Another form appeared beside it with neon-purple glitter sprinkled atop its skin.

"Of course it's the two of you," Bast grumbled as he willed the faerie lights toward the second room.

A vampire clad in a black shirt and business suit stood before them, alongside a fae with cropped graphite hair dressed in the same way. As if they worked for a secret agency from the movies.

The vamp had milky skin and short auburn locks. Dark circles lined his clear green eyes, making him look either tired or hungry, she couldn't tell which. His companion's skin was almost as light as his, though the rest of his features were remarkably similar to Bast's. Except for his hair, of course.

Mera pointed at the fae, then at her partner. "You're related."

"Benedict Dhay." He bowed at her with a hand over his heart. "But you can call me Ben. It's a pleasure to meet you, Detective."

"Indeed." Stepping forward, the vampire took Mera's hand and kissed it. His clammy, ice-cold touch sent shivers down her spine. "Charles Grey at your service, Detective Maurea."

"Thanks." She pulled her hand away, wishing she could wipe it on her jeans.

Some guys oozed bad business, and this vamp was a prime example. She didn't get the same vibe from Bast's brother, though, even though he'd told her Benedict was nothing but a philanderer and borderline alcoholic.

Appearances could be deceiving when it came to the fae.

"Thanks for welcoming us," Bast offered in a freezing tone before showing them the door. "If you will?"

"Ah, Sebastian." Charles Grey's smile reminded Mera of a hungry hyena. "It's good to see you after such a long time."

"Is it?"

"Of course it is, brother." Benedict stepped closer. "You're finally home."

"This hasn't been my home in a while." Bast crossed his arms, a clear sign any chance of a conversation between them was over. "Don't you two have a party to crash somewhere in the island?" Turning to Mera, he nodded toward the duo. "Charles and Ben are Lunor Insul's most infamous party animals. Alongside Corvus, that is."

Shaking his head in disappointment, Benedict blew and exasperated breath. "Why did I expect this would go any differently?"

"Because you thought I'd forget you're Corvus' lapdog," Bast snapped.

Charles watched her partner with a certain bitterness. "Good at holding grudges, aren't we?" He clapped his hands, faking cordiality. "Make yourselves comfortable. The access to the second floor is outside, through a set of stairs. You'll find two bedrooms, a kitchen and bathroom, as well as a small living space, all ready for your *enjoyment*." He eyed Bast and Mera in a knowing manner that felt icky. "Don't forget, tomorrow you see Prince Leon at precisely 9:00 a.m."

"Make that the day after tomorrow," Bast said. "I have personal business to attend first."

Ben's jaw hung, his eyes widening. "What could be more important than seeing your family?"

"Don't buy his act," Bast warned Mera. "He's a cruel jerk."

"Oh, I don't," she assured. "Your people enjoy playing games."

Raising one eyebrow at her, he smiled. "*My* people?"

"Yeah, you know." She motioned to his pointy ears and strikingly blue eyes. "Assholes."

Both Bast and Benedict chuckled, but her partner immediately scowled at his brother. As if they weren't allowed to share a moment, a laugh. Mera felt sorry for Benedict, even though she knew pitying a fae might be foolish.

"Corvus and I aren't these monsters you make us out to be," Ben grumbled quietly. "Besides, how are you any better than us, Bast?"

"I'm not," he countered point blank, yet his manner softened. "I'll explain everything when we meet again, I promise. Right now, you have to let me do my job." He turned to Charles Grey. "Speaking of which, are you here to represent Hollowcliff or my court?"

Charles blinked, as if he couldn't believe Bast had dared to ask. "I'm here for both, as they are one."

A remarkable save.

The vamp bowed at Mera, then narrowed his eyes at Bast. "I'll be seeing you, Detective." And with that, he left.

Benedict stepped forward, his jaw clenched and his eyes watering; eyes incredibly similar to Bast's own. "Have it your way, brother. As you always do."

Darkness enveloped him before he blinked out of thin air. One moment Benedict stood there, the next he was gone.

So, that was what winnowing looked like. Mera had asked

Bast once if he could do it, to which he'd replied with a dry as hell, *"No."*

Trying to stave off the headache coming on, she rubbed her forehead. "What a great freaking start, partner."

CHAPTER 4

BUILT ENTIRELY OF BLACK MARBLE, the League of Darkness differed greatly from everything else Mera had seen on Lunor Insul. Tall columns supported the square, three-story structure, which was surrounded by a vast green lawn.

Birds chirped from several willows and beeches, peppering the green fields, while night faeries milled about in black fighting leathers. Most of them held books and scrolls, while others lectured students in the open garden.

This place was more like an academy than an assassin's guild.

"I didn't know the League even existed," Mera mumbled to herself as they stopped before stairs that had to be made from the deepest void of space. "I'm a detective and I had no idea. I'd heard about House Fillanmore, but never about the League."

How could she have missed it?

The stairs led them to an outside porch that lined the façade of the entire construction. Pushing a heavy wooden door open, Bast took her to the inside of the property. "Don't be so hard on yourself. Most who discover the League's existence don't live for long."

Well, *that* didn't make her feel better.

At all.

They crossed vast ebony halls, with ceilings supported by tall columns. The entire setting reminded Mera of ancient temples honoring the old gods. Up above, an indoor balcony opened to the second and third floors.

"It shows the League's superiority," Bast continued. "House Fillanmore is reckless, which is why you know who they are." His eyes scouted for something as they moved forward, but Mera had no idea what it might be.

Completely alone, their steps clinked loudly against the marbled floor.

"Shouldn't an assassin's league be better guarded?" she noted.

"Trust me, we're being thoroughly surveilled."

Stopping to check, Mera found nothing around them. Either these assassins were extremely stealthy, or she was losing her mind.

"By the way," he whispered, "I would appreciate it if you employed that waterbreaker persuasion soon."

A low grumble escaped her lips. "You're using me."

"Absolutely." He frowned. "Shouldn't I?"

Ass.

Benedict's words rang in her mind. *"How are you any better than us?"*

In that moment, a striking female with ivory skin and straight, dark purple hair suddenly stepped in their way. She'd come from the left, too busy reading a book to notice them. She wore a long black dress with silver embellishments that matched her necklace and earrings.

The nightling looked proper, regal, and also outwardly beautiful.

"Karthana?" Bast asked, taken aback by her presence.

She stared at him with wide topaz irises, and the book immediately fell from her grasp. "Bast?"

Her mouth dropped open in an oncoming scream, but Mera was quicker. "We come in peace. No need to fear us, fae *kuata.*"

Sister? Seriously?

It sounded like a line from a bad movie from the sixties, but it worked. The glamour crawled underneath the fae's skin without her noticing it. Mera's magic wasn't meant to cause a brutal change in her behavior, just... assure her. Boost her trust.

Karthana's expression softened, and she swallowed back the scream. Her fingers scratched her own arm nervously while she stared at her feet. "What are you doing here, Sebastian?"

"Came to clear things up." Bast's Adam's apple went up and down as he watched her, anticipation whirling behind his blue eyes.

"You shouldn't have," she finally answered, still avoiding eye contact.

'I don't like the way he looks at her,' Mera's siren growled.

It was disturbingly similar to the way Bast looked at Mera, but she couldn't do much about it.

'Establish dominance,' her siren offered. *'Kiss him right here in front of her.'*

Shut up, Mera ordered.

"The vision I had..." Karthana's voice wavered. She seemed on the verge of crying. "I didn't mean to get you in trouble, but I saw you killing Father. I had to tell him, even if I suspected the vision had been faked."

Stepping forward, Bast wrapped his arms around her, and Karthana instinctively gave in to him, crying against his chest.

"It's all right." His lips brushed against the top of her head. "I came here to make it right."

A knot tied inside Mera's throat and fire went up her head. Without meaning to, her fists closed.

Karthana had been Bast's betrothed before he'd abandoned everything to go to the continent. The same female whose vision had sent a swarm of assassins their way, and Bast was hugging her!

What the fuck?

Being this kind to a possible suspect went against the death bringer inside Bast, but matched perfectly with the partner Mera knew. And she *hated* Karthana for taking advantage of that.

"So, even though you suspected the vision was faked, you sent assassins to take care of my partner, correct?" she asked, emphasizing the 'my' before 'partner'.

Karthana's head lifted, as if only then remembering Mera was there. She didn't step away from Bast, though.

He didn't step away from her, either.

"Her *father* did," Bast answered, regarding Mera as if she'd somehow crossed a line. "Master Raes leaves nothing to chance. It's why he guides the League so efficiently."

'That faerie better step away from him, or else...' her siren warned.

Mera's chest ached at the sight of Bast being so close to another woman, but she had to clear her head and focus on the issue at hand, so she tried to control the bitter jealousy thrashing inside her.

"Detective Dhay, we should handle this properly as part of our investigation." Mera's pleasant tone held a storm inside it. "Do let go of our suspect."

"I'm not a suspect!" Karthana cried.

"Karthy isn't trying to harm me." Bast's forehead wrinkled into an amused frown. His attention returned to Karthana, and he leaned closer. "Forgive my partner. She can be a bit temperamental."

Oh, fuck him. Fuck him very much.

"Detective Dhay, I don't appreciate your condescending tone."

"You're in trouble, Bast," Karthana pointed out, a gentle smile decorating her plump lips.

"With Detective Maurea? Always." He chortled. "It's part of the fun, you see."

"Excuse me," Mera growled more than spoke. Taking a steadying breath, she turned to Karthana. "Your vision has put my partner's life in danger, and consequently, mine. Forgive me for not being as trustful as he is."

"That's why we're here," Bast added. "Karthy, you know I'd never harm your father. He must know that, too."

'Karthy, Karthy, Karthy,' Mera's siren jeered. *'Ridiculous fucking nickname.'*

"We do, but Father abhors loose ends." The faerie shrugged. "Add that to the fact none of the seers we hired could see past the veil…"

"You have a lot of nerve, youngling," a voice rang from the indoor balcony on the second floor, right before a sword pierced the air toward Bast's head.

Instantly, a circle of darkness with twinkling stars came to life atop her partner, swallowing the sword completely, before it blinked out of existence as fast as it'd been created. Yet, Bast's expression revealed nothing as he looked up to the fae on the second floor.

Taking out her gun, Mera aimed at their opponent. "You're attacking Hollowcliff detectives. Stand down!"

The male, a Sidhe with sapphire skin who wore a simple black cloak, raised a white eyebrow at her, deepening the wrinkles on his face. His calculating light gray eyes pierced through Mera. "Who you are, or what you represent do not matter to me, human."

His white hair was trapped atop his head in a loose bun similar to Bast's, and Mera wondered if this was why her partner used it this way; to honor the faerie who now tried to kill him.

The old fae's hand lifted, and some twenty nightlings clad in black fighting leathers peeled off the walls.

The assassins stood around Bast, Mera, and Karthana in a circle, waiting for the final command. They certainly hadn't considered Mera and Bast a danger, or else they would've attacked sooner. Either that or the old faerie wanted Bast's head all to himself.

The fae, who was obviously Bast's former mentor Master Raes, glided down the stairs, and as he did, an assassin appeared beside Mera. Swiftly disarming her, the assassin made a face as he held her gun with his fingers, like it was a piece of radioactive thrash.

"Hey! Give it back!" she ordered.

"Once the matter is resolved. *If* it's resolved," he added, before returning to his previous position.

The ring of fae opened to Raes as he reached the base of the stairs. Regarding Bast for a second, he then pulled out a dagger from his robe and dashed forward, pressing the tip against his neck.

"Father, no!" Karthana yelped.

Damn it!

How Mera wished she had her gun...

"Are you here to fulfill my daughter's vision, *Yattusei?*" the old fae asked, narrowing his eyes at Bast's strained neck. "Let's see if you can top your master, you ungrateful—"

"Easy, *broer!*" Mera tried, pushing her glamour forward. "We come in peace." The magic wafted at him, but somehow it didn't stick.

40

"I'm not your brother." Raes frowned at her with confusion. "Do you have a mental problem, human?"

Certain supernatural creatures could resist her magic if they were strong enough. This certainly seemed to be the case with him.

Bast stepped away from Karthana with his hands raised, but Raes kept the tip of his dagger underneath her partner's chin.

Mera exchanged one glance with Bast, her message clear. *"Let me use the macabre..."*

He shook his head vehemently, before turning to the fae threatening his life. "I'm not here to fight you, Master. Do you really think if I were here to kill you, I would come through the front door, with a human to hinder me, and in broad daylight for everyone to see?" Bast motioned to the assassins around them.

'Hey! Not nice.' Her siren scowled. *'Also, not human.'*

"You know me better than that, Master Raes, after all, you trained me." Sighing, he looked straight into his master's eyes. "I would never harm you, and I'm going to prove it."

"How?" He scowled, but Bast's words seemed to resonate with him. "A vision such as Karthana's can't be a lie. We tried the seers. They found nothing."

"And still, we have struggled to believe the vision, Father," Karthana remarked, her voice almost too weak to be heard. "Bast is family."

"Family means nothing to this *malachai*," he snapped, disgust in his tone.

"That might be true," Bast admitted, "but you both mean something to me; always have, and always will."

Childish as it was, listening to Bast confess he cared about Karthana left a bitter taste in Mera's mouth.

"Lies," Raes hissed. Swallowing dry, he pressed the dagger slightly forward.

41

"Easy," Mera warned, though technically there was nothing she could do. Not unless she used the magic Bast had forbidden her to use.

"It's fine, kitten," he assured before turning back to Raes. "Your best seers couldn't peek past the veil, yes?"

"And?"

"Don't you find that strange?"

Raes cocked his head left. "You know the rules I abide to."

Yeah, better safe than sorry. He had made that perfectly clear.

"I'm alive," Bast pointed out the obvious. "You're the greatest assassin of all time, with an army of killers at your disposal. Devoted fae who could've ended us the moment we stepped inside, yet they let me hug your daughter, Master." Bast motioned carefully to his very lively self. "Which means you already gave me a chance."

"Maybe I don't fancy getting in trouble with the government." Raes raised his chin. "Seeing as you and your partner have become local heroes."

"That's not the main reason why I'm alive, and we both know it." Bast chuckled. "Naivety doesn't suit you, old Sidhe."

Was it wise to tell that to the guy with a dagger against his throat?

"I'm anything but naive, you thick-headed youngling," Raes grumbled under his breath.

A long moment passed, deadly silence filling the hall as Raes and Bast's gazes fought against each other, a mute battle storming between them.

"Fine," the old fae gave in, but he didn't move the knife. "Perhaps you're right."

"Good. Because I've asked the help of a friend."

As if on cue, steps echoed behind them.

Mera spun around to see a Sidhe with light pink hair woven into a low braid that cascaded down her back. She was clad in a cerulean dress with embroidered hems, golden jewelry twinkling on her wrists, neck, and ears.

"Mad Seer," Raes muttered.

Frowning, Mera rubbed her eyes, wondering if they might be playing tricks on her. "Madam Zukova?"

"It is me," she agreed in her Northern accent, her chin held high with a certain pride. The old fae stopped before them and spread her arms widely, making the golden bracelets around her wrists jingle again. "What can this seer do for you today?"

CHAPTER 5

RAES LED them to the second floor and through a long corridor, but kept his dagger at hand. It made sense, of course. As far as he knew, Bast could try to kill him—even if the old fae's heart told him it was unlikely, assassins didn't usually rely on their emotions.

If old hag Ursula had told Mother that Mera would kill her one day, the queen would have ended her daughter's life on the spot. Luckily, old hag Ursula was a sham, well, most of the time, anyway.

In any case, Raes loved Bast a lot more than Mother ever did Mera, though to Raes' credit, that wasn't a hard feat to achieve.

As they walked, Mera studied the corridor's walls, which were crowded with oil paintings of several old Sidhe standing stoic and proud. The portraits watched them with incredibly vivid irises, and at some point, she could swear the image of a thin fae with wrinkled skin and night-black hair had moved.

When Mera took a closer look, however, the picture seemed still, like any oil painting should be. Except, that lying on the floor next to the black baseboard, was her gun. Picking it up, she checked the cylinder.

The iron bullets were all there.

"What the…" Her gaze roamed the space, trying to find the fae who had taken her weapon before, but he was nowhere to be found.

Bast was already a few steps ahead, so Mera had no time to wonder before she was forced to pick up the pace.

"Not much has changed, Master," Bast noted, following Raes and his daughter.

"Nothing is the same, *Yattusei*," the old fae countered without turning back, a certain grief in his tone.

Karthana, who walked side-by-side with her father, shot Bast an apologetic glance.

"Perhaps," he agreed, "though I prefer to believe certain things never change." He winked playfully at Karthana, and the purple-haired fae countered with a sweet, adoring smile.

Mera's fists balled, her nostrils flaring.

'He's mine!' her siren growled.

Taking a deep breath, she unclenched her muscles. No, Bast wasn't hers, and now was not the time to lose it because of petty jealousy.

Tugging at Mera's hand, Madam Zukova pulled her backwards. "I don't need to be seer to realize there's much water under bridge, no?" she whispered, nodding at Bast, Raes, and Karthana.

"Tell me about it." Mera slowed down until there was a good distance between the two of them and the three nightlings ahead. "How did you get here?"

The mad seer nodded to her own back as if she had her wings on display. "I flew. Much faster than boat. Besides, Sebastian offered good money for consulting." A raucous chuckle scratched the inside of her chest. "Madam Zukova loves money."

"Well, thanks for coming," Mera offered truthfully. "Until this mess is sorted, we can't work our case."

"It is written," she assured. "I will help."

Mera certainly hoped so.

Raes stopped before a wooden double door carved with the head of a snake, and once he let them inside it closed shut.

Bookshelves that went all the way up to the high ceiling walled what seemed to be a vast study room. The floor, made of pitch-black marble as the rest of the League, had golden lines forming a circle in its middle. The word *'Impernokto'* was scribbled under the ring in shining cursive.

Empire of Night.

Stepping forward, Madam Zukova watched the space. After a while, she nodded to herself and tapped Bast's shoulder. "This will do."

Her hand motioned toward two velvet ottomans near a tall window, silently asking Karthana to sit. Nodding, Raes' daughter did as she was told.

The mad seer sat in front of her, then took hold of her hands.

"Deep breaths," she instructed, closing her eyes. "Focus on the vision."

"How did you get the mad seer here?" Raes whispered from beside Bast, close enough that Mera could listen. "If it weren't for her, I'd have you in the dungeons by now."

"I knew you'd listen to her," Bast countered, which wasn't exactly an answer. "She's rather famous in our world, isn't she?"

Our world? Mera thought Bast had left *that* world a long time ago.

Madam Zukova and Karthana stayed still and silent for a long while, until the seer turned to Mera while keeping her eyes closed. "This fae has strong feelings for your partner, yes?"

No surprise there.

Karthana inhaled sharply and tried to pull her hands away, but the mad seer held them tightly. "Not yet, child."

Bast gaped at Raes' daughter. "Is this true, Karthy?"

The frantic *thu-thump, thu-thump, thu-thump* of Mera's heart thundered in her ears, as molten fire rushed up her head.

"Bast..." Karthana's lips quivered. "It's not that simple."

"It never is," he croaked.

A cold, merciless void swallowed Mera from inside. Did Bast still have feelings for Karthana?

Did he love her back?

"There's another male." Madam Zukova rubbed Karthana's palms with her thumbs. "You are conflicted, and that's blocking my view of the vision. Choose the answer you already know. I must see beyond your fears and worries, yes?"

Karthana glared at the seer, but even in her anger she seemed too poised. Too... perfectly mild. Like a princess from a fairytale.

Eventually, she nodded and closed her eyes.

Deep breaths, Mera told herself. *Inhale. Exhale...*

She had no right over Bast's heart. Sure, they'd kissed before, and the simple memory of it turned her knees to jelly. They'd also shared a dream in which they'd had mind-blowing sex, but Bast was her partner, and that was all he would ever be. He could date whoever he wanted, and Mera had to be fine with that. If his choices left a bitter taste on her tongue, so be it.

Raes watched her with a hint of worry, or maybe curiosity—hard to tell which. Clearing her throat, Mera recomposed as much as she could, the fire in her dimming, yet still burning.

With a curt nod, Bast's former mentor returned his focus to his daughter and the mad seer.

Another moment of silence ensued, until Madam Zukova raised her head. "The vision was faked," she declared.

Raes' dagger dropped to the floor, and he took Bast in his arms, patting his back joyfully. "I knew it, youngling!"

"Yes, you did." He hugged back his master. "Otherwise I'd be dead."

"I see faerie who sent vision," Madam Zukova added, still deep in concentration. "I can reach him if you want."

Bast let go of Raes and stepped forward, his teeth grinding. "Absolutely."

Raging bloodthirst coated his tone, and Mera feared for whoever was on the receiving end of his wrath.

The mad seer's forehead crumpled as she hummed a tune deep within her throat. Slowly, a fog formed in the middle of the room, floating in the air. At first, it showed a blurred form against a lighter background.

"Oh, *jalls*," the figure grumbled from inside the cloud, its voice muffled.

The mist swirled and cleared quickly, revealing none other than Benedict Dhay.

Poseidon in the trenches, Bast had been so right about the asshole. Any pity Mera had felt for him vanished instantly.

"*Rae-henai!*" Bast snapped at the faerie, motioning to attack, but it was useless since his brother wasn't really there. He was just a projection.

"I can explain!" Benedict yelped.

"I don't believe that's necessary." Raes crossed his arms. "We'll be coming for you soon."

"Wait! Please!"

"Why, Ben?" Bast pushed, a string of hurt weaved into his

tone. "Why would you manipulate Master Raes and Karthana to send assassins after me? Do you hate me that much?"

"No, brother! We knew you could take them easily, and that Raes would never kill you—or at least, he would never try hard enough. To end *Yattusei*, one would have to try hard, wouldn't they?"

"Stop lying!" Bast barked.

"I'm not! We wanted you back in the island, and we almost succeeded! Then mom visited you, and our efforts proved pointless." He scratched the back of his neck. "In hindsight, the plan should've been a lot simpler."

"*Our* efforts?" Bast asked through gritted teeth, his fangs sharpening. His magic pulsed in invisible waves from his body; waves that banged against Mera's core. "*He's* behind this, isn't he?"

Ben swallowed.

He didn't confirm it. He didn't have to.

Karthana jumped to her feet, and for the first time, Mera glimpsed a dim fire burning inside her meek façade.

"Lies!" she argued. "Corvus would never—"

"He knew you wouldn't agree to it," Benedict told her. "That's why he asked me to do it. He couldn't bring himself to send you the vision."

"Of course I wouldn't agree!" she snapped. "You put Bast's life in danger!"

Stepping forward, Mera dared to join the conversation. "Ben, if you wanted your brother here, there were better ways to do it. Smarter ways."

"He knows," Bast gnarled. "But as you've said it yourself, kitten, my kind enjoys playing games."

Benedict shrugged slightly. "You can't blame us for having a bit of fun. If anything, we should earn points for creativity."

His definition of fun was twisted as hell, but Mera shouldn't be surprised. Faeries would always be faeries.

"You're aware this counts as attempted murder, right?" she asked, casually pulling a small notepad and pen from her jacket's pocket. "You're in trouble, buddy."

"What? For a silly prank? Detective, it was all in good, harmless fun! We just wanted our brother back."

"*Fuchst ach!*" Raes gnarled. "Fun? I lost one of my assassins because of your stunt, *malachai!*"

"I say good riddance," Benedict countered. "He clearly wasn't good at his job. Besides, assassins' leagues aren't legal, are they?" He shot a smug look at Mera. "I don't see you having a problem with that, Detective."

Bastard was right.

Rubbing the bridge of her nose, Mera sighed in exasperation. She was there to solve a potential murder, not waste time on Sidhe behaving like children.

"What do you want to do?" she asked Bast.

He glared at the cloud for a while, his fists tight and nostrils flared. "We'll deal with them tomorrow."

Benedict let out a relieved breath as his image slowly faded, and then he was gone.

"All good that ends good," Madam Zukova said as she tapped her legs and stood. Approaching Bast, she showed him her palm.

With a nod, he pulled a small pouch filled with coins from his pocket, and gave it to her. "As always, you delivered. Thank you."

Madam Zukova wiggled the pouch, then put it inside a pocket in her dress. "You must tell your partner eventually, Night Prince."

"I don't know what you're talking about."

"Tell me what?" Mera asked, stepping closer to them.

"The vow he made. It may not be today or tomorrow, but he'll tell you when it's time." Madam Zukova raised one finger at her. "Not before and not after. So do not push him, Queen of Waves and Dust."

Mera blinked. *Queen of Waves and Dust?*

The mad seer didn't bother sticking around to elaborate. With a wink, she left as swiftly as she'd arrived.

Turning to Bast, Mera crossed her arms. "Care to explain?"

Bast's lips pursed, and he shoved his hands in his pockets. "Not particularly."

"The mad seer's revelation changes things." Raes's scowl marred his azure complexion, his focus on her partner. "Do you reckon your brothers might be involved in your father's murder?"

"Those two idiots? Maybe. I certainly wouldn't put it past Corvus. Wait." Bast gaped at him. "You agree with Mom? You suspect Father didn't die of natural causes?"

He blew air through his lips. "I'm an assassin, youngling. I recognize unnatural death from a mile away. Your mother sensed this too, but she didn't want to worry your brothers. Besides, they're not detectives."

That's why she'd come to Bast. The Night Queen knew he found guilty people for a living, though Mera doubted Seraphina Dhay had suspected one of her sons might be the culprit.

Raes's attention turned to Karthana. "My dear, won't you show Detective Maurea our beautiful gardens? Sebastian and I have certain matters to discuss."

His daughter gave him a polite bow. "Certainly, Father."

Oh, hell no.

Stepping forward, Mera slammed both hands on her waist. "Excuse me. Detective Dhay and I are partners. Whatever you discuss with him—"

"I'll tell you later, I promise," Bast assured.

"Seriously?" Mera glared at him, then at Raes.

C.S. WILDE

Seeing they were adamant, she threw her arms in the air and stormed out of the room. She was almost half-way through the corridor when she sensed a soundless presence following her.

"No offense, but back off," she snapped at Karthana without looking back at her.

"Father said—"

Reaching the stairs, Mera pivoted on her heels, nearly slamming face first into Bast's precious girlfriend. "Let me be straight, *Karthy*. I don't like you, and I don't trust you. Your vision put us in a lot of trouble. Bast doesn't mind because he's clearly thinking with his dick, but I know better."

A furious blush rose to Karthana's cheeks. Fumbling with her fingers, the faerie avoided eye contact. "I-I'm truly sorry, but if you had a vision where a loved one was killed, wouldn't you tell them?"

Mera swallowed dry. If she'd seen someone killing Ruth in a vision, she'd make sure the bastard was six feet under before he had a chance to come close, or even explain himself.

Suddenly, what Raes and Karthana had done, their trust in Bast despite the vision, it seemed awfully… grand.

"It has all has been sorted now, Miss Maurea," she added. "We found the offenders, and I'm certain everything will be cleared once they speak to Bast."

"Don't call me '*miss*'. It's Detective." Mera went down the stairs, her soles clanking against the marbled surface, but Karthana kept following her.

The damn faerie couldn't take a hint, could she?

"I do have feelings for Sebastian," the *perfect princess* blurted after a moment, "but I would never—"

"Not my problem. Don't care."

Karthana stopped and took her hand as they reached the

52

base of the stairs, and at first, Mera wanted to jerk away, but something in Karthana's pleading violet eyes stopped her.

She hated how pretty *Karthy* was, though she fully understood why Bast liked her.

Pretty, kind, meek.

All things that Mera wasn't.

"*Detective*, Sebastian and I were practically raised together," she explained quietly. "We were promised to each other upon our birth. It was an auspicious union, and we remained together even after the Night King disowned him." She expelled a heavy sigh. "Indeed, I loved Sebastian, very much so. Once we reached a mature age, we became…" Her cheeks reddened to the color of a tomato. "… intimate several times."

A rush of annoyance took over Mera. "That's too much information."

"I apologize." She shook her head. "What I'm trying to say is that eventually, Bast left. My love wasn't enough for him."

"He had no choice," Mera said quietly.

Her partner had left his home, and the League, to follow his sister, Stella. If Karthana was bitter because of that, well, then she was an asshole.

Mera still remembered the day she and Bast left for Lunor Insul perfectly…

The wind tousled Stella's black hair into a thousand different directions as she hugged her brother, burying her face on his chest. After a long while, Stella stepped away, her lips forming a line.

"Be careful," she'd said. "They're your family, but they're cruel."

Bast kissed her forehead. "I know, Baby Sis."

When Captain Asherath called him to discuss some arrangements, Bast hugged Stella one last time before stepping away.

As he left, Stella stepped closer to Mera, taking her hands. A certain desperation thrashed behind her clear blue eyes; eyes similar to Bast's, but at the same time, so incredibly different.

"Promise me you'll look after him," she begged.

"Stella, I—" Mera's voice failed. Bast was the last fae on earth who needed protection.

"You're angry at him, I get that." Stella glanced back to make sure Bast couldn't overhear them. "He probably deserves it, but he needs you, Mera. More than he knows." Seeing the hesitation on her face, Bast's sister gripped her hands tighter. "If not for him, then for me. Promise me."

Shaking her head, Mera brushed a stray lock of hair from Stella's face. "I get why he never says no to you."

Why he'd left the protection of the League once he became an adult to follow her to the mainland; to try a new life for them both, even if it meant risking everything.

It was the eyes. Big, puppy eyes filled with innocence and kindness.

Boy, would she regret this...

"Fine. I'll keep your ass of a brother safe, even if it's the last thing I do. Happy?"

Giving her a beaming grin that warmed her chest, Stella pulled her into a hug. "Thank you, my friend."

Mera blinked, breaking away from her memories.

"I understand why Bast left," Karthana added from beside her. "I respect that, Detective, though I do not understand why he would abandon his entire life here to watch over a bastard sister."

Mera scowled, opening her lips to send Karthana to a nasty place, but the fae calmly raised her palm.

"Our ways and beliefs may seem odd to you, but they are what they are. Again, I do not understand why Bast did it, but I respect it. Letting go of him was immensely hard, and yet, not impossible."

A thought sprang to Mera's mind, and she narrowed her eyes at the fae. "Madam Zukova mentioned there was another male involved. That you were *conflicted*."

Karthana nodded. "When Bast left, it freed the way for

another auspicious union. The Night King and his advisors were most pleased, but I wasn't ready. I don't think I am, even after all this time..." she drifted off briefly. "However, as the years passed, I learned to care for my new betrothed."

No freaking way.

"You're getting married to one of Bast's brothers?"

"Yes." Karthana swallowed, her eyes glistening. "Not everyone understands my betrothed like I do, Detective. I don't approve of his methods, but I believe that deep down, he did what he did because he wished Bast would attend our wedding."

Mera stepped back. "Oh, shit."

As if on cue, the second floor rumbled so hard, that dust and marbled pebbles rained around them.

"I will fucking kill him!" Bast roared from the study room.

CHAPTER 6

RAES SAT before the study's closed door in a meditative position, his eyes shut. Crossing her arms, Mera stared down at him.

"You're in my way," she grunted.

"I know."

"I need to talk to Bast."

"I know that, too, but first, Sebastian must control his emotions," he said without opening his eyes. "If an assassin loses his temper he loses the battle, and make no mistake, Detective. This *is* a battle."

"Yeah, yeah." She raised one finger at him, which was pointless since he couldn't see her. "Except Bast is a Hollowcliff detective, *not* your precious *Yattusei*."

"No, my dear." He smiled peacefully at her. "He's both."

From a few steps behind, Karthana paced left to right, fumbling with her hands and mumbling under her breath. The faerie's anxiety weighed on Mera's shoulders like a giant boulder.

"Will you stop?" Mera snapped at her. "There's no point in doing that. You've already spilled the milk."

Karthana froze, her pouty lips quivering. Mera could swear she was about to cry.

Ugh!

Truth be told, Mera didn't dislike Karthana. She should, of course. Bast had feelings for her, and Raes' daughter alone had put them in a world of trouble. Also, she was marrying Corvus Dhay, the dickwart who'd put a bounty on Bast's head alongside Benedict. And still, if Mera felt anything for the faerie, it was pity.

"I warned her that the Night Princes would only bring her grief," Raes admitted quietly, as if he needed to explain Karthana to Mera. "Sebastian is hard as stone, Corvus sharp as a blade, whereas my daughter is soft and gentle. Yet, she's also her own fae, and does as she wills." He lifted his chin, eyes still closed as he chuckled. "I sense, however, that you might just be harder and sharper than them both, Detective."

Was that a compliment?

"Thanks. I guess." Pulling her badge from her jeans' pocket, Mera showed it to him—again, pointless, since his eyes were closed—but she figured she should try either way. "Keep stalling, and I might shut down the League of Darkness indefinitely."

He smirked. "The wind may howl, but the mountain does not move."

Before Mera could tell him to fuck off, the double door clicked open, revealing Bast. He stood on the threshold, watching them with a curious frown.

Jumping to his feet with the agility of an acrobat, Raes greeted him. "Have you conquered your wrath, youngling?"

"I have it under control. For now." He bowed slightly at Raes, then placed a hand on the old fae's chest. "Thank you. We'll keep in touch." With that, he took Mera's hand and went down the stairs, not bothering to look at Karthana or say goodbye as they passed her.

Against Mera's better judgement, she shot the faerie a sympathizing glance. That was all she could do before they turned on the corridor, and went down the stairs, leaving a grievous Karthana and her stoic father behind.

"That was rude," Mera said as they crossed the vast halls of the League, heading toward the green fields around the property. "It's not completely Karthana's fault."

"That fool is engaged to Corvus," he grumbled. "Being stupid is definitely her fault."

"You're angry." Halting at once, Mera jerked her arm away. "It's because you have feelings for her, isn't it?"

His chest rose and fell with an exasperated sigh. "I do, but not in the way you think."

"Elaborate."

He didn't. Instead, his silver wings blinked out of thin air, spreading mightily behind him. Giving Mera his hand, he huffed. "Are you coming or not?"

"Winnowing would be more practical," she pointed out, just to spite him.

Bast rolled his eyes, an impatient sound roaring inside his chest. "Not every Sidhe can winnow, as you well know."

"Why?"

"You must have a clear goal, and the resilience to get there no matter the cost," he explained, a muscle ticking in his jaw. "Which means that to winnow for the first time, one has to be desperate."

"And you've never been desperate?"

"I have, but winnowing also consumes a lot of our energy. The rare number of faeries who can do it, can't winnow more than once or twice in a row. Besides, isn't flying more fun?" He motioned for her to come closer. "Off we go. No time to waste."

A happy sensation swirled in her chest.

Bast had a point: flying was amazing. Mera had been

yearning to do it again for a while, and she wouldn't refuse the chance. Stepping closer, she let Bast take her into his arms. He easily lifted her, as if Mera was made of paper.

Holding onto the nape of his neck, she took in the musky scent near the back of his jaw. Desire pooled in her belly, but she quickly snapped out of it. "Let's roll, partner."

Bast shot her a mischievous grin before they jolted to the sky.

"Wohoo!" Mera shouted as they went, the wind whipping around her face and making her hair swirl in a thousand different directions.

The drop in her stomach only intensified when Bast looped in the sky, over and over again. A rollercoaster had nothing on this.

So much fun!

On and on they went until he stabilized, moving in a straight line, and giving Mera a moment to catch her breath.

Leaning slightly away, Bast watched her with warm blue eyes, his fingers digging on her skin, keeping her close.

So very close.

"It reminds you of the currents, doesn't it?" he asked.

She nodded eagerly, not able to hide the giddy smile that cut across her lips. Yet her jealous, petty siren kept poking at the back of Mera's mind, unwilling to stop until she got a clear answer about Karthana.

"So," she began carefully. "Your ex is promised to your brother, Corvus. It's normal to be angry, Bast. You obviously still love her."

He stared ahead, the loose threads of his bun swinging wildly across his face.

"I do love her," he finally agreed.

Being impaled by a spear had to feel better than this. Mera swallowed dry, her throat prickling as if walled by nails, but she tried to keep a comforting attitude. "You should tell her how you feel."

"As I said before, I care about Karthana, just not in the way you're thinking." He clicked his tongue in annoyance. "Do you ever listen, *akritana?*"

"Explain it to me, then."

"Look, Karthana loved me before I loved her, and even then, I didn't love her enough. It wasn't fair, kitten." He winced as if he'd tasted something bitter. "I hurt her when I left; all I ever did was hurt her, and still, she forgave me. She's the kindest, most understanding faerie in this world. It's simply who she is. Karthana can't help her own nature."

"That's really nice," Mera admitted, knowing that was also why she couldn't hate Raes' daughter.

Because Karthana was so damn nice.

"It is," he agreed. "But she's with Corvus now, and that scares me. My brother is no good to anyone, especially a sweet fae like her." He cocked his head to the side. "So yes, I love her for giving me her body and soul, for loving me when I couldn't return the feeling, but I could never be with someone as gentle as Karthy. And honestly? Neither could Corvus."

Funny. Earlier, Raes had told Mera the exact same thing.

"I hear you, but before we bring hell to your brother, how about we prove your father was murdered?" she offered. "Since Raes' assassins won't bother us anymore, we can focus on the case."

"I agree. My family has kept me distracted long enough." The sky reflected in Bast's irises, intensifying their blue. "So far, we only have my mother and Master Raes' assumptions. We need proof, or our case is bust."

"Hey, your father kept tight records of everything he did, right?"

"He had to. It was part of the agreement with Hollowcliff.

Actually, it was one of my forefathers' ideas during the unification. It showed transparency toward the continent. It's also one of the reasons why we have so much power in Lunor Insul."

Transparency built trust.

Not a bad strategy at all.

"If we find out what your father did during his last weeks, we might find out how he was killed."

Bast nodded. "Poison. Master Raes believes the killer used blue ivy. It fakes cardiac arrest, and it's untraceable once ingested. It takes time to work, though, usually one or two days, and it has a strong and bitter taste. I can't imagine how—"

"Something sweet," Mera blurted, the idea coming to her quicker than a breath. "It would have masked the taste. We need to find out what your father ate two days before he died. Especially the desserts."

"Would you look at that. Charles Grey was right." Bast's eyes shone with something wild and untamed. "We *will* be seeing him around."

Bast didn't bother to knock.

When he spread his hand on the wooden door, a cloud of darkness that resembled the night sky unfurled on the surface. Once it retreated, it left a big hole in its place.

Just like that, his magic ate a chunk of the door.

"Your night consumes stuff," Mera noted, analyzing the round gap the size of a grown man. "Where does it go to?"

"Beats me."

"Can your brothers do the same?"

"They wish." He chortled. "Their magic looks similar to mine, but it isn't the same."

She waited for him to elaborate, but he didn't. Mera wanted to prod further, and yet, she knew Bast. Pushing for an answer would get her nowhere.

He flicked the door open—what was left of it—and the hinges creaked shyly. As they went inside, the young assassin's words rang in her mind.

"This is his gift. To consume, corrode, and destroy. He is death."

Yeah, but *he* was also her partner.

Fresh air ventured through as they walked in, but Charles Grey's home still smelled stuffy, reeking of rotting blood and sweat. Pulled down curtains engulfed the place in an eerie dusk, which battled against the light that came from the opening behind them.

Poseidon in the trenches, the entire place was a mess.

Stacks of papers lay thrown around everywhere—the floor, the table, the sofa, and even near the kitchen sink. A crowd of glasses and cutlery lay strewn atop the dining room table. On the kitchen countertop, too.

If Charles Grey was the government's overseeing eye in Lunor Insul, then he must have gone freaking blind.

A groan came from the far left, behind a wall, where two forms reclined over a big futon, their limbs intertwined.

Bast and Mera approached to find the diplomat lying beside a dark-skinned male Sidhe with white hair, and green freckles glowing dimly on his skin.

Bast kicked Charles' shin, not harshly but not gently, either.

"Piss off," the vampire grumbled, burying his head in the nape of his partner's neck.

"Faerie blood can be addictive to vamps, and Charles has developed a particular taste for nightlings," Bast explained to her quietly. "Lucky us, there aren't many night fae back in the mainland, so my court basically controls his supply."

Mera nodded. "Control the supply, control the addict."

He tapped the side of his nose knowingly. "Charles has been in service for decades, but he never gave us a headache, even when the Night King's decisions went against Tagradian law. Such as ordering Stella killed."

"You're wrong," Charles slurred from the futon. "Diplomacy is about concessions. Finding a middle ground. So, thank you kindly, but I do my job just fine." Rubbing his eyes, the vamp begrudgingly sat up. "What do you want, Sebastian?"

"My father's registry from the week before he died, please. Also, a record of everything that was delivered to his room, and all daily menus prepared for him."

Yawning, the vamp pointed to a cupboard on the living room. "Third drawer on the left. Now, let me be." Dropping back on the futon, he curled up with the half-naked faerie.

Bast and Mera shrugged before going to the cupboard. Opening the drawer, her partner snatched three black notebooks as thick as bricks.

"Why don't Sidhe embrace technology?" she asked. "Even lower faeries, who could benefit a lot from it, keep being skeptical. I'm not saying you all should join social media and have phones, but using the basics would be nice."

"I've heard of high-fae becoming 'influencers' on your networks," he argued as he dropped the notebooks atop the kitchen's countertop.

True.

Bella Vina, a Spring Court Sidhe who resembled a living doll, earned crazy money for posting pictures on her Gartram profile.

Daring faeries like her, however, were the exception.

"Back in Tir Na Nog, we use laptops to file reports in the Tagradian mainframe," Bast added as he skimmed through the first notebook. "See? Not all is lost. Oh!" He snapped his fingers. "Sewage systems! We invented those, didn't we?"

Damn, he was right again.

Alfons Theodon, a banshee who worked as a city planner in Clifftown centuries ago, had patented his idea to the human borough for one dollar, as a thank you for welcoming him after being banished from Tir Na Nog—for stealing a locket from a rich Sidhe so he could feed his family.

"Those aren't the basics; they're downright necessities." Mera nodded to the notebooks. "Case in point, an electronic register would be soooo much easier to check."

"Give us time." Giving her a wink, he kept leafing through the pages.

For practically immortal creatures, faeries had plenty of time, though many humans used potions to prolong their lives nowadays. Ruth herself was two hundred going on fifty.

Mera suspected Professor Currenter had done this on a much bigger scale, since he was the only waterbreaker alive who'd witnessed the great war. Not even faeries lived for that long. Some said he was cursed with living forever; others, that it went a lot deeper than what the living could understand.

Snatching the second notebook, she brought it closer to the destroyed door—the only source of light in that hellhole —and scanned through it. After a long while, Mera found the records she'd been searching.

"Your father had no dessert the week before his death, and he always ate at the palace. He was more of a wine and cheese guy." She snapped the notebook shut. "Great. Just… great."

"Hmm." Bast raised his book toward the sunlight so he could have a better look. "Father received a box of chocolates from 'an old friend' on the thirteenth. He died on the fifteenth." He grinned to himself, which was odd considering this was about his father's murder. "It matches with how blue ivy works."

For the first time since they'd stepped on this island, Mera felt they were moving forward. "Bingo, partner."

"Did you bring the forensic kit your captain gave us?"

Oh, boy. This would not end well.

That vital diplomacy Charles raved about might come in handy very soon. "Are we doing what I think we're doing?" she asked.

Closing the notebook, he headed for the door. "Absolutely."

CHAPTER 7

Somewhere in the past...

KEEPING his back slammed against the building's brick façade, Bast balanced on the ledge. He glanced down at the steep fall beneath his feet, but for someone with wings, heights weren't exactly a problem.

Contrary to Tir Na Nog and Lunor Insul, shifter and human boroughs were concrete jungles.

Literally.

Their buildings resembled never-ending stone trees without crowns. Bast wasn't a fan of those high constructions that reached for the sky, but he couldn't change them, so why bother?

Right next to him, the window to his target's apartment reflected the full moon on the dark sky.

Halle, Bast hated when his target was a shifter, specially a wolfman—and not only because his sister was half-wolf. With their keen sense of hearing and smell, they could sense him coming from a mile away. It was why he could never surprise Stella, which annoyed him immensely.

As an assassin for the League, Bast had been everywhere in the continent, and Lycannie, the shifter's borough, was no exception.

For the past three days, he had used an amulet to mask his appearance while planning his target's death—a detective, and a damn good one, apparently. Not that it mattered, in the end.

Bast was the executioner, not the judge.

He had studied the wolf's habits, his favorite places and foods. Funny how Bast had gotten to know every borough in Hollowcliff while planning someone's demise. And yet, that was his favorite part of working for the League—meeting Hollowcliff's different citizens, eating their foods, hearing their music. A cultural melting pot, this land never ceased to amaze him. Enjoying what it had to offer made the unpleasant part of his job easier somehow.

Chilly wind blasted against him, and Bast cursed under his breath. He should've taken his sleeved fighting leathers, but his naked biceps turned Karthana into a horny beast, and he planned on meeting her after he was done here.

That should teach him to stop thinking with his dick.

From inside the apartment, a lock clicked, announcing the door had opened. Shouting and rumbling followed.

Maybe, just maybe...

"Hide, Michael!" a male suddenly yelled.

The wolf had caught his scent.

Shocker.

Bast threw himself against the window, cracking the glass into a million shards as he rolled into the place. Quickly jumping to his feet, he unsheathed his sword and pointed it at the wolfman who didn't resemble a wolf at all. *Yet.*

"I'll let you shift, Bruce," Bast offered.

It was the honorable thing to do. He'd followed the wolf earlier that night, and watched when his boss took his gun and badge. Yes, his target was unarmed, but luckily for him, Bast hated unfair fights.

"I can take you with these," the detective raised his fists, "*pixie.*"

With a chuckle, Bast shook his head. "You have to up your cursing game, *mate.*"

Bruce winced as if he'd been branded by a hot iron. "Witches say 'mate'. In Lycannie we say 'pal'."

"Ah, thanks for that, *pal.*" Hesitating for a moment, Bast frowned. "What do humans say?"

"Beats me. I guess something silly, like 'dude' or 'man'."

Bast raised his shoulders but kept his blade aimed at the wolf. "Maybe let's stick with Bruce for today, what do you say?"

"I'd rather not. You don't know me."

"But I do, Bruce. Detective extraordinaire, wolfman of justice." Bast strolled forward, observing his tacky beige suit and green tie. "By the way, you have terrible taste in fashion. Been meaning to tell you that for a while."

Bruce raised his brow. "Coming from the asshole dressed like a gothic condom, that's a compliment."

Bast couldn't hold the busty laugh that escaped his lips.

"Oh, you're funny, Bruce, and you've got balls. That's why you're in trouble in the first place, isn't it?"

"Life's about what we do before death comes calling." He dropped his fists. "You are with the League, so there's no point in fighting you. I'm tired, pixie. Real fucking tired of fighting the system and getting nowhere."

The 'system' had broken Bruce, that much was clear.

He'd lost his gun and badge today, and now he would lose his life. Yet neither of those things were why Bruce made this easy for Bast.

The wolf wanted him to get the job done and leave for a very specific reason. A reason that broke Bast's usually freezing cold heart.

"Come on," Bast pushed, jumping from one foot to the other. "I skipped the gym today. I need the exercise."

The wolfman raised one dark, bushy eyebrow at him. With his caramel skin and onyx hair, he reminded Bast of Idillia a bit too much.

His chest ached at the memory of Stella's mom. It had been twenty years, and the wound still hadn't healed. Bast doubted it ever would.

"Is being snarky how you cope with what you do?" Bruce asked flat-out. "Is that your defense mechanism?"

Spinning his sword in circles, Bast shrugged. "Whatever gets the job done, right?"

"The leopard shifter who hired you is a cancer to Hollowcliff. A commissioner who murdered and stole from good people." Bruce's lips pursed in a bitter way. "You shouldn't be doing his bidding."

"I'm not. I stand with no one but the bounty. Those are the rules."

"It doesn't matter. If you do his dirty work, you're with him, pal."

Bast couldn't say why being called that stung. *Pal.*

Friend.

"Tagrad is a mighty nation, and Hollowcliff is its heart," Bruce continued. "A nightling of your skills should fight *for* it, not against it."

The words pierced Bast's flesh and bone, clinging to his chest like tar.

Fight for Hollowcliff.

"If I don't seal the bounty, I'll pay the price with my life." Bast's tone rang awfully similar to an apology. Spinning in a circle, he ran his free hand through his hair. "The people who ordered your bounty asked that you suffer, but I can make you sleep before doing the deed. You won't feel a thing." Lifting his hand, tentacles of night bloomed from his palm.

Bruce's fists closed, but instead of fighting, he swallowed and nodded. "Will you get rid of my body?"

"Yes, as is customary." No body meant less questions, less evidence, which was why most assassins got rid of their kills.

"That's kind of you," Bruce admitted before taking a dejected breath. "Be quick, then."

It was evident the wolfman wanted Bast out of there stat. If the detective realized Bast knew about Michael, he would morph into a wolf and put up the fight of his life.

Stupid of him, really, to assume a trained assassin would've missed the existence of his son.

Bast's magic swam forward and wrapped around the wolfman's wrists and ankles. After a moment, Bruce wobbled on his feet, his eyes closing and opening slower and slower each time.

Almost there...

Just as he was about to fall, a young boy rushed out from a kitchen closet on the right. "Papa! Papa!"

Sobbing, he wrapped his arms around his father's legs.

Bast wanted to deal with Bruce's son later, mostly because he hadn't yet gathered the courage to end such a young life. He'd seen the kid from a distance, but now that Michael was standing there, crying his eyes out the same way Stella did when Idillia died...

Fuck.

Bast's breath caught midway in his lungs, his throat knotting, and his hands shaking. He clenched his muscles to stop it, but it was no use.

Halle fuchst ach! An assassin with a trembling hand. That was a first.

"Michael!" Bruce grumbled, despair taking over him.

Glaring at Bast, he began the shift, his fingers growing into claws as gray fur bloomed on his skin.

It wasn't enough. Bast pushed his magic forward, and soon Bruce's shift retreated.

The detective fell to one knee, the kid still clinging to him.

"P-please," he managed. "I beg of you."

"I didn't want to take this bounty. I've never killed a child, but an assassin doesn't choose," Bast admitted quietly, an apology in his tone.

"Don't," Bruce begged as he crouched on the wooden floor. "Please…" His eyes rolled to the back of his skull and he slumped forward, his body thumping against the floor.

Bast would regret this, it was the only certainty he had.

Still inside the apartment, he waited for sleeping beauty to wake up. It was taking him too long, so Bast poked Bruce's face and chest.

"Papa says you shouldn't wake a sleeping wolfman," Michael remarked from Bast's back, his chubby fingers digging onto Bast's shoulders as he tried to push himself up.

"Yet, we must." With one hand, he pushed the puppy upward. Michael promptly wrapped his chubby arms around Bast's neck. "You good?"

He felt the little one nodding from behind. "I climbed the mountain!"

A chuckle twittered in Bast's chest. "You certainly did, pal."

When Bast turned forward, Bruce was glaring at him with a mix of fear and confusion. "What on the heavens?"

"I'm here papa," Michael assured from behind Bast's back, giggling in the same carefree way Stella used to when she was his age. "We're safe!"

Raising his shoulders and his brow, Bast sighed. "So... we have a problem."

CHAPTER 8

Still in the past...

IT FIRST STARTED as an itch a few days after Bast left Bruce and Michael, an unending scratch in his blood that intensified with each passing hour.

Torture had been a part of his training. He could withstand the highest of pains, had remained strong while other fae lost their minds, but the burn of a broken bounty went beyond everything Bast knew.

It was as if his night consumed itself underneath his skin, corroding his flesh and bones at a slow pace. No, this wasn't torture.

It was one of Danu's hells.

Bast bellowed. He cried. His throat hurt because screaming was all he'd done for the past... hours? Days? Weeks?

Hard to say.

Writhing on the bed, he roared in agony, but what came

out was a weak, cracked sound that hurt his pride. His chipped nails caught on the sheets as his fingers dug into the mattress, which was drenched with his sweat—and maybe some pee.

He begged an unknown force to end it all, but his pleas remained unanswered.

Cruel shig, whomever they were.

Stella came rushing from the kitchen with a wet cloth and a bowl of liquid that smelled awfully like aloe vera and chamomile. As if that could save him.

"Bast, please," she begged, tears in her eyes as she wiped the cloth over his damp forehead. "Tell me what to do. Everything my magic heals, the bind to the bounty destroys!"

"You can't... save me, little sister." He attempted a smile but winced in pain.

This was the price Bast paid for failing to kill his target; the price that would cost him his life. And strangely, he was fine with it.

"I'll call for help," Stella assured.

Pointless. Only Master Raes could lift the magic that tied Bast to the bounty, and he'd never do that, no matter how strongly the old Sidhe favored him.

A heavy, blissful pull of exhaustion dragged Bast into the start of slumber, but he couldn't sleep yet. He had to ask Stella to stay with him during his final hours, beg her to avoid his mentor at all costs, but he couldn't keep awake anymore.

He could barely speak.

"Stella," he slurred.

Bast was too weak to scream, too frail to cry or think. Everything went dark as he plummeted into a void inside himself.

Stella...

"You fool." Master Raes' voice echoed through the darkness suddenly, and Bast forced his eyes open once, twice, only to succeed on the third time. "You didn't kill the target," his mentor added, glaring down at him with absolute fury.

Bast swallowed, his throat feeling coated in sandpaper and broken cords. He couldn't remember the last time he'd drank any water. "I… had to draw a line."

"Assassins do not draw lines, youngling," he countered with a tone as dry as Bast's throat. "Do you regret it?"

That was Bast's chance, his salvation.

He wouldn't take it.

Even crushed by a mountain of pain, he grinned. "I regret nothing."

"Where is he, Sebastian? Where's his son?" Raising an eyebrow, Master Raes crossed his arms. "I must finish the job to free you from the magical bind."

"You'll never find them." He tried to take a deep breath, but choked on his spit instead. The violent cough took a while to subside. "I didn't dishonor the League, Master. I would never. The client believes we killed them both." Bast writhed when another wave of blinding pain impaled him from head to toe.

Halle, breathing, no, simply existing hurt.

"Bast, please," Stella whined in the back, tears tracking down her cheeks. "You'll die."

"I'm fine with that." He forced a reassuring smile, but failed spectacularly. "I saw you in that little boy, Baby Sis. I couldn't do it."

Grumbling a curse, Master Raes stretched one hand to Stella. A foggy tentacle of magic shot at her, wrapping around her neck. His sister's eyes widened as she clawed at her throat, her feet lifting from the ground.

Panic set deep in Bast's chest. "Master? Let her go."

The old fae scowled at him. "Don't forget who I am, *Yattusei*." He turned to Stella, and a certain pity overtook his features. "I always admired your mother, halfling. Your life was never fair, neither was your brother's, but I will *not* tolerate insubordination."

Bast forced himself up. His flesh hurt, his bones pounded, and he was in so much pain he might've pissed himself again, but it didn't matter.

"I'll face my destiny." He opened his arms, his head feeling horribly light. "Just leave my sister out of this. Hurt her, and I'll kill you before crossing Danu's veil, I swear it."

Stupid really, to make such a threat when he couldn't even stand. His vision blurred, the room fading in and out.

Shit.

Bast took a deep breath, his stomach twisting. He'd throw up any minute now, and then he would faint. Surely, he wouldn't return after that.

Shaking his head, Master Raes finally opened his hand and the magic instantly retreated into his skin, allowing Stella's feet to touch the ground.

Relief washed over Bast as his sister took in deep breaths. He could plummet into his endless night now.

"He can't go on for much longer," Stella told Master Raes, her voice hoarse. "Even after Bast was disowned, you had no issues with him marrying your own daughter. You must care for my brother enough to see this path is destroying him." Her voice seemed to come from a great distance.

"Sebastian is the son I never had, yes," Master Raes countered quietly. "This is why you both still live."

Another wave of exhaustion slammed into Bast with the fury of a tsunami, until he couldn't feel his legs anymore. No, he couldn't fall asleep. He couldn't abandon Stella there, alone with Master Raes... but darkness dragged him under anyway.

"Bast?" Stella's voice echoed faintly through oblivion. "Wake up."

His eyelids were as heavy as boulders, but he slowly forced them open to see his sister's blurry form. Smiling at him, she caressed his forehead. "You were having a dream."

Daylight stung his eyes. His entire body ached, but at least he could breathe right again. Granted, his lungs hurt, but he didn't feel oncoming vomit every time he inhaled or exhaled.

"Was I?"

She nodded. "You were mumbling about Hollowcliff and fighting for something good."

Damn you, Bruce.

"Sounds like a load of crap," he grumbled before slamming a hand on his pounding forehead, the crippling pain only then hitting him again.

Fuchst ach, dying might have been better than this.

"It was beautiful," she shrugged. "Master Raes lifted the bounty, by the way."

Bast gaped at her. He didn't know why he was so surprised, considering he was, well, *alive*.

He'd never thought of himself as a lucky creature, and yet, there was no other way to describe what had happened.

Sheer fucking luck.

Forcing himself to sit up, his bare feet touched the cold marbled floor. "Sorry if I scared you, little sister." He nudged Stella's shoulder with his.

"You really did." A moment passed while she held his gaze. "Bast, I'm going to the continent."

"No." He shook his head and winced, still suffering from the pounding inside his skull. "We've talked about this."

"We did, and I'm going. It's what my mom wanted."

"Yes, but Father won't let you, remember?"

"I don't care what that *baku* does. Besides, if you come with me, he won't do a thing." She took both his hands, her blue eyes shining with hope. "Don't you see? Master Raes has never lifted a bounty in his entire life. As long as you're no threat to him or Karthana, he'll never go after you, which means the League won't take the bounties *'Father'* offers for our heads."

He chortled. The fact they'd been spared by Master Raes was a giant miracle. Bast really shouldn't push his newly found luck.

"If that were true, which it isn't," he clarified, "Father will hire other bounty hunters."

"You can take them," she countered with absolute certainty. The complete faith she had in him warmed his heart. "The king will eventually get bored, you'll see, and then we'll start a new life in Hollowcliff!"

"Baby Sis…"

"You gave away your childhood, your very soul, to protect me." Stella watched their intertwined hands. "You killed, and you killed, and you killed… I think you've had enough."

He blew air through his lips. "That's nonsense."

"You enjoy killing?"

He had a talent for it; a gift, but he didn't take joy in murdering someone. He'd simply become numb to the bloodshed after seeing it—well, *causing* it—for so long. Besides, Bast had never assumed leaving the League with his life, or Stella's, was possible. And yet, it might just be, thanks to his relationship with Master Raes. Thanks to the bond they shared, the one he'd never had with his own father.

Bast's chest lightened and ached at the same time.

"You're a good fae, Bast." Stella pushed her shoulder against his. "Enough with death, pain, and destruction. It's time to be free."

"It's not that easy," he muttered.

"We're going, period. We can be happy in Hollowcliff, and deep down, you know that, too."

He swallowed dry, his heart pounding in his chest. "What about Karthana?"

"Take her with us."

He couldn't. If he did, she might become a collateral of the Night King's wrath.

Sure, Bast could protect Stella, but could he protect Karthana at the same time? If something happened to her, Master Raes would kill Bast, but he'd kill Stella first and force him to watch.

So, no. Definitely not Karthana, which raised a new set of problems he would have to tackle. Problems that intensified his headache—was it bad he felt relieved for leaving her behind?

Looking down at his fingers intertwined with Stella's, Bast wondered if he could ever atone for his sins. Let his blood-soaked hands do some good.

Fight for Hollowcliff...

Forcing himself to stand, he balanced on shaky legs that proved surprisingly reliable.

Master Raes would hate him for leaving, and so would Karthana. If his mentor didn't end Bast right on the spot, he would never forgive him, and that was the best-case scenario.

Leaving Leon and his mom, though... that would hurt Bast the most.

Freedom came with a heavy price.

Bast ran a hand through his hair as variables flashed in his mind. "This is crazy, and we'll probably get killed." Still, a smile creased his lips.

Freedom.

"All right. Fuck... " he said as if he were convincing himself to jump off a cliff.

Stella clapped her hands. "Yes! It's a clean slate, Bast. We can be anything we want!" She seemed to consider it twice.

"I'm positive I would make an excellent healer. I could even go to the Curative University!"

Healing fit his sister's gentle nature perfectly. Bast had no doubt Stella would excel at it.

As for him? He'd been an assassin his entire life. Doing something other than killing felt wrong, yet, so right at the same time.

"I think..." he started, unable to predict where this might lead him. "I think I want to go after bad people."

Like Bruce did.

Pursing her lips, his sister frowned at him. "So you'll be an assassin with morals?"

"Not exactly. Bruce didn't kill others to find justice. I suppose that's what I want to do," he mused.

Her jaw dropped, a certain disbelief in her manner. "Are you saying what I think you're saying?"

"I am." Bast smiled as his entire life, oddly, and suddenly, made sense. "Stella, I want to become a detective."

CHAPTER 9

THE NIGHT COURT'S castle took up the entire upper half of the middle mountain, twirling along the rock's façade, and blending perfectly with the starry sky—not to mention the island itself. A white marbled titan with teardrop-shaped roofs and open arches throughout its body, it faced the continent like a lighthouse, or a watch tower.

Hard to say which.

"Whoa," Mera whispered to herself as she followed Bast into the palace.

Forget about the fancy mansions and penthouses from Tir Na Nog. This place was nothing short of spectacular. It somehow reminded her of a giant white dragon snaking around the mountain, defending its nest.

Weaving through ample marbled halls and corridors, they ended up following a spiral, marbled staircase without walls, just thin white columns for support.

The pathway traced the mountain's stone façade, and the view from that high up was amazing. White faerie lights shone softly down below, spreading across Lunor Insul and toward the dark ocean, while neon birds cut through the night. In the distance, beyond the line of water, city lights shaped the coast of Tir Na Nog.

Not that Mera had any time to appreciate the landscape. Her partner was already pulling her toward the throne room; an enormous round construction with a domed ceiling, located at the very peak of the mountain.

"Bast, you're here as a Hollowcliff detective," she reminded him when the stairs ended before a great, ample hall with a wooden double-door that had to be at least ten feet tall. "You'll need to act the part, even with your brothers."

He frowned at her as if she'd said the most obvious thing in the world. "Of course, kitten."

"Good. I'm glad we're on the same page."

He pushed the door open, which was a remarkable feat considering how heavy it looked. Strolling inside, Bast kept his arms wide open.

"Missed me, *malachais?*"

Mera slammed a hand on her forehead.

Great. Just... great.

The throne room was open on all sides through giant archways that showed an incredible 360-degree view of the ocean—and the island itself. Wind should be blasting everywhere from this high up, so there had to be some sort of magic shielding the inside.

In the center of the enormous dome, a navy circle had been engraved on the white marble floor with the word *"Impernokto"* at the bottom.

Three Sidhe stood around the circle. The first, Mera recognized at once; Seraphina Dhay, Bast's mother—and the reason why he winced in regret the moment he realized she was there.

"Sorry, Mom," he muttered as they stepped closer to the group.

Giving him a sad smile, his mother merely nodded.

Still in mourning, Seraphina wore a raven black dress that covered her from neck to ankle, and a dark veil that shadowed her face. Her pink eyes gleamed from behind the see-through fabric.

Turning to Mera, she bowed her head slightly. "The weather is lovely today. It will rain flowers, you'll see."

Mera repeated the gesture, sorrow knotting her throat. "I think it might."

Bast gave her a grateful nod.

The queen's hands shook slightly. It must be hard for a mother to be standing there, not knowing what would happen next, even if her mind wasn't fully... present.

Would her kids kill each other? Argue? Fight? Miraculously behave themselves?

Mera had no idea, either.

"We apologize for the short notice," Bast told the other two nightlings. "But time is of the essence."

The biggest fae in the space—a remarkable feat considering Bast was the tallest male Mera knew—gaped at her partner with glistening pink eyes identical to Seraphina's. He was on the verge of saying something, but the words didn't come out.

The other fae, who was the spitting image of Benedict, stepped forward. This must be Theodore, the monk—and Ben's twin brother.

The two might share the same face, but even at first sight they seemed so different. Unlike Ben's cropped hair, Theodore's graphite threads were tied in a long braid that reached his knees. Instead of a fancy suit, he wore a humble white robe with a golden rope tied around his waist.

"We're family, Sebastian." he offered kindly. "There's no need to apologize."

Placing both hands on his chest, Theodore bowed to

them. This was the way Danu's followers greeted others, so Mera mimicked the gesture.

"Thank you both for your collaboration," she offered.

Heck, she might become a better diplomat than Charles Grey, though considering how the vamp behaved, that couldn't be incredibly hard.

"It's good to see you, Theo." Bast bowed to him as well. "I'm hoping Big Brother didn't tell Corvus and Benedict about this meeting?" He nodded to the big fae, but didn't make eye contact with him.

So that was Leon, the older brother.

His skin was a shade lighter than Bast's, his muscles bulged and evident underneath the white shirt and perfectly tailored navy pants he wore. He had a silver belt wrapped around his waist with the crest of the Night Court engraved on the buckle—a half-moon crossed with a curved dagger.

Leon shared Bast's high cheekbones, straight nose and moonlight hair, only his tresses cascaded behind his back in long curls, highlighting his straight and regal posture.

Apparently, being stupidly handsome was a family trait.

"You're back after years, Bast," he finally spoke. "Of course I told them you called for a meeting. We're family, brother." Scratching the back of his neck, he scoffed. "Punctuality, however, has never been one of those *shigs'* strengths."

"You're a fool," Bast spat, not bearing to look his brother in the eye. "You do know Corvus put a bounty on my head, right?"

"I heard about it yesterday. Surely his intentions were good. Corvus has a different way of feeling, but that doesn't make it any less real."

Finally, their gazes connected, but Bast scowled at him. "How can you be this naïve? You're supposed to become the Night King!"

Leon swallowed, his eyes brimming with tears. "I suppose I'm a fool indeed, especially for hoping this reunion would be fruitful." Shaking off his sadness as if it was dust he'd gathered over time, he turned to Mera. "It's a pleasure to meet you, Detective, despite the circumstances. I'm Leon."

He spoke with the poise and kindness of a great king, which he'd soon become as the oldest son.

Hollowcliff granted the Night Court a world of power and trust, so Leon would become a ruler almost like in the old days, when fae courts were basically different countries —as long as he abided by Tagradian law.

Since Charles Grey was there to "control" his practices, Leon would be free to do whatever he wanted, which was a good thing according to Bast, who'd assured her his brother was the best of all Dhays, and the most sensible Sidhe in Hollowcliff.

Still, Bast couldn't face him. Couldn't be kind to him, either.

She bowed her head at Leon. "Mera Maurea, and the pleasure is mine. Also, do forgive my partner for being an ass. I believe deep inside, he is happy to see you."

The future king's eyes lit up. "Forgiving him is one of my specialties, Detective."

"Of course I'm happy to see my brother," Bast grumbled, his arms crossed. "I'm just pissed he told Corvus about our meeting today."

"You are? I mean, happy to see me?" Leon asked, genuine shock grazing his features.

Approaching Bast, he stood right in front of him, forcing his little brother to face him. They stared at each other for a while, until Bast gave a rolling shrug of assent. Grinning, Leon trapped him in a big hug that lifted Bast off the ground.

"You're breaking my back," Bast grunted, but Leon didn't let go.

"I've missed you, brother."

Bast huffed in annoyance, but eventually let go of his walls and hugged him back. "I've missed you too, *baku*."

A giddy sensation invaded Mera's chest as she watched the two, one the queen seemed to share. Seraphina Dhay also had a smile on her lips, but her attention quickly drifted to the outside, toward the unending sea.

"If only we could all get along the way they do," Theodore confessed as he approached Mera's side. With a despondent sigh, he pointed to an empty space toward their left. "They're coming."

As if on cue, two clouds of night and stars swallowed the air above that spot, and a pair of faeries blinked into existence before the clouds dissipated.

Mera recognized Benedict immediately. He wore the usual fancy black suit, but this time, he held a glass of wine in his hand.

"Don't let Ben fool you," Bast's previous words rang in her mind. *"He's nothing but a philanderer and borderline alcoholic."*

"You shouldn't drink so much," Theodore chided.

"Where's the fun in being sober, brother?" He winked at Mera in a playful hello. "I see you've already met the detective."

The fae next to Ben watched Mera with a wicked grin on his fiercely beautiful face, and a prickly sensation crawled up her spine. His skin was bark-colored, contrasting perfectly with his bright yellow eyes, while his short, spiked hair was the color of the moon, a similar shade to Bast's and Leon's.

Corvus had a dangerous kind of beauty, the type that dragged people under before they realized it. A beauty similar to Bast's—though her partner would hate her for comparing him to that brother.

"Ah, you must be Karthana's replacement," he said in a

perfect English as he eyed Mera up and down. "I'm unimpressed."

Offering him her hand instead of bowing, just to spite him, she countered in fluent Faeish. "*Aes gafrin eres tu, Corvus et baku.*"

'I guess you're Corvus, the asshole.' Or idiot, depending on the intonation.

Shaking her hand, Corvus' eyes widened with excitement. "Perhaps you're not as underwhelming as I assumed."

"Perhaps."

Their contact didn't last long, however. Bast shoved his brother away from her, standing between them with his shoulders hunched and his fists balled. "Don't go near her, you *malachai.*"

Corvus wiped his shoulders as if his brother's touch had tainted the fabric of his black suit. It was the mirror image of Benedict's, except he carried a silver necklace with a pendant shaped like a half moon, which stood out discretely against the silken black fabric.

"You needn't worry. She's not my type, brother dearest." He narrowed his feral eyes at Mera. "I don't fancy humans in my bed."

"Forgive me for worrying," Bast countered casually, his manner shifting from angry to careless way too quickly. "Can you blame me, though? You seem to enjoy taking my leftovers."

Wait, what?!

Since when was Mera his leftover?

Corvus lost his playfulness, his fists balling. "For the sake of Mom, I'll pretend you didn't just demean *my* betrothed. *Our* friend."

"For *your* sake, Corvus," he growled, "you better fucking behave, you deceiving *shig!*"

Bast's magic thrummed from his core, slamming against Mera's own, his relentless night pushing to get out.

Crap.

Things were escalating quickly. Mera had to put a stop to this before her partner charged at his own brother. Stepping closer to Bast from behind, she laid a hand on his shoulder. "Remember why we're here."

Bast turned to her, and in his blue eyes, Mera saw him centering his thoughts. As if he'd found something in her, something that gave him balance.

He took a deep breath, followed by another.

"You're right, Detective Maurea." Clapping his hands together once, he surveyed his brothers. "I need access to Father's quarters, and I've come to ask permission from Leon to do so. Before you ask, this is official Hollowcliff business. I can't disclose any information at this time."

Raising one silver eyebrow, Corvus scoffed. "Are you serious?"

"Of course I approve, Bast." Leon nodded courteously, ignoring Corvus' remark. "Though I can't fathom what you think you might find in there. Father went peacefully in his sleep."

"It's standard procedure," Mera lied.

She didn't want to startle the Dhays, especially since she and Bast didn't have proof of murder.

Yet.

"Very well." Leon showed them a set of stairs to the right which went down the mountain's façade—a path similar to the one they'd taken to get here—before leading the way.

Bast ordered the rest of his brothers to stay with their mother. Theodore nodded, Benedict rolled his eyes, and Corvus grumbled a curse under his breath. Mera could swear he'd grunted *"This is stupid,"* but she couldn't be sure.

She and Bast followed Leon down the stairs, until they

reached a small hall with a white-painted door. Taking a set of keys from his pocket, Leon opened it, and as the lock clicked, a miniature firework popped in the air.

"The room has been locked since father's death, as it is our custom," the future king explained before Mera could ask. "It should only be unlocked once the new king is crowned."

"The lock is enchanted to alert the priests of Danu if the room opens before time," Bast added as they entered the space. "They won't like it, but I'm certain Theo can smooth things out."

The moon cast a soft glow across the king's bedroom, highlighting the dust that set atop the furniture. Running a finger over the armoire, Mera drew a line across the thin specks.

Having this place locked the moment the king died had been a ginormous stroke of luck. They had a nearly immaculate, potential, murder scene to survey. Yet, nothing seemed out of the ordinary, nothing really jumped at her... until Mera's attention fell on a white box on the night stand near the king's bed.

Her heart skipped a beat. "Bast. Look!"

His gaze followed hers to the half-open box of chocolates. "Danu in the fucking prairies. Could it be that easy?"

Could the murderer have been that careless?

Hurriedly, Mera pulled out the black device that resembled an epi-pen from her pocket, and removed the cap. Going to Lunor Insul to solve a crime meant getting a ton of gadgets from the CSI team back in Clifftown, all thanks to Ruth. Including the handy device that could analyze substances for poison.

Sure, magic could be useful, but science? It had its perks.

She pushed the needle at the end gently into one of the bonbons.

Three blinks and a beep. Green light.

No poison.

"Surely this is futile?" Leon asked from behind. "If I recall correctly, mom ate some of those, and she's fine."

If that was true, he had a seriously valid point.

Mera tested the next one to make sure, but it was also clean. Sighing, she scratched the back of her neck. "A dead end. Great."

"Not yet." Bast narrowed his eyes at the box. "Try the cherry ones. They were Father's favorites."

With a nod, she pressed the device's needle into the cherry bonbon. Three blinks and a bleep.

Red light.

CHAPTER 10

IF HER PARTNER had followed procedure, he would have bagged the box and left with Mera. Bast did bag it safely, but asked Leon to winnow him back to the precinct in Lunor Insul instead.

The future Night King nodded, and a circle of darkness and twinkling stars immediately split the air beside him in two. He and Bast entered it casually, as if walking through a door.

"Hey," Mera shouted, but before she could join them, the portal—only way to describe it, really—collapsed onto itself.

Jerks.

A few moments passed until the circle of void opened behind her, and out stepped Bast with his brother, minus the evidence.

"Where did you put it?" Mera begrudgingly asked her partner.

"Somewhere *safe.*"

Mera knew him enough to get the message. *Safe.* Quite literally.

He had placed the box inside the precinct's safe, but he must have used his magic to hide that from Leon somehow.

"Well, thanks for bringing me along, *partner*," she grumbled.

"In Bast's defense, all humans puke when winnowing for the first time." Leon intervened. "Profusely, if I might add."

Well, Mera wasn't human, but she wouldn't correct him on that.

"Shall we?" Shrugging, her partner went out the door and headed back to the throne room.

She and Leon exchanged a confused glance before following after him.

Once they arrived, Bast surveyed his brothers with a cruel smirk, his eyes glinting with mischief.

"What is it, Sebastian?" Corvus asked, impatience coating his tone.

"Oh, nothing much," he countered. "It's just that one of you bastards killed Father, to which I'd say good riddance, but," he raised his index finger, "I'm a detective, and that means it's my job to bring the culprit to justice."

Grabbing his arm, Mera yanked him aside. "What are you doing? We shouldn't accuse anyone at this point. We can't prove the killer is one of your brothers."

"But it's obvious, isn't it?" He frowned, his manner awfully calm considering... well, everything. "The killer knew exactly what kind of chocolate my father liked. Also, they spared my mom."

His logic was kind of solid.

A killer without any connection to his mother would've poisoned every chocolate to guarantee the job was done. Then again, a servant who loved his mistress but not his master could have done the same.

Bast once mentioned the Night Queen used to have a fire in her, but it had left her eons ago, along with her sanity. *"Father broke her in a way,"* he'd explained. Which would constitute one hell of a motive for murder, *if* Seraphina herself hadn't asked them to investigate the king's death.

Charles Grey, for example, made a much better suspect, but so did everyone with access to the castle. Narrowing the pool of suspects down to Bast's four brothers was careless at best, and stupid at worst.

"Is it plausible? Yes," Mera snapped quietly, "but that doesn't mean we can accuse them of murder, you idiot. Not this early in the game."

"Wait," Benedict asked. "Father didn't die of natural causes?"

"He was poisoned," Leon stated as he stepped forward. "Which means the detectives will have our full cooperation. However," he addressed Bast, "I believe *our* family is innocent. You'd do well to keep your investigation impartial, *Detective.*"

Mera found an unrelenting strength under his tone, the might of a protective big brother, or maybe, of a king in the making.

"Innocent before proven guilty, right?" With a shrug, Bast turned to the rest of his brothers. "So, which one of you was it? My money is on the obvious choice." He tilted his head toward Corvus.

Nostrils flaring, his brother closed his fists. "How dare you, *baku?*"

"Easy, you two." Theodore nodded to their mother, who stood on the verge of tears.

Seraphina had suspected her husband was murdered. It's why she'd come to Tir Na Nog to ask Bast for help, but she certainly hadn't imagined that one of her children might have done it.

Groaning inwardly, Mera rubbed her forehead, her other

hand resting on her waist. Bast was royally fucking with this investigation.

With his family, too.

"I wished my whole life that you boys would get along." A sob escaped the Night Queen's lips, and she promptly took a white tissue from her dress' pocket. "Yet, the light does not shine where there's shadow. The song of demise caught up to your father, and it will catch up to all of us."

Song of demise?

Odd thing to say, but Bast's mother didn't always make sense.

Seraphina's gaze abruptly shifted to the floor as if she'd lost herself in thought, her impending cries dying in her throat.

Walking to her side, Leon took her hand. It looked small and frail against his. "We'll get along, Mom. We promise," he assured soothingly as he stroked her back.

She kept staring at the marbled floor, failing to acknowledge his presence.

"Detective Maurea," Leon called, "Will you watch these buffoons while I walk our mother back to her quarters? Also, please tell Sebastian that if he insists on mistrusting his own blood, then he must suspect *me* as well."

"Certainly," she agreed.

One of them had to keep a professional façade, and that sure as hell wouldn't be Bast.

"Your father ruined you," Seraphina mumbled as Leon led her forward, her gaze lost and dazed. Her head suddenly snapped up at Mera, pointing to something at the back of the room.

Only now did Mera notice the dais at the far end of the vast space. An ivory throne, shaped like a thousand pointy bones, stood atop the platform, its red velvet cushion carrying a silver crown atop it.

Spiky and uneven, it seemed like the crown had been made out of thorns. It couldn't be comfortable to wear, but Mera supposed it had been crafted this way to show the strength and resilience required of the Night ruler.

Yeah, faeries could be unnecessarily cruel like that.

There was something else, though. The material... it didn't resemble the kind of silver found on land. It was way too smooth, too shiny. Mera had seen a crown like this only once.

On top of Mother's head.

Sea silver was rare, however, and never to be gifted to landriders. No waterbreaker in their right mind would've done it, even before the great war.

That crown had probably been enchanted by faerie magic to look that ethereal. It was the only logical explanation.

"The crown ruined my husband." Seraphina's voice broke as she sniffed back tears. "It will also ruin my children."

"I won't let that happen," Mera assured rather abruptly, only to regret it a moment later. Keeping Corvus and Bast out of each other's throats might be damn near impossible.

With a broken smile, Seraphina bowed her head to her in thanks.

"Come on, Mom," Leon whispered, gently leading his mother past a door.

Once they were gone, Corvus turned to Bast. "How dare you accuse me? You've always been such an insolent *shig*, Sebastian."

"Oh, *I'm* the *shig*? That's precious!" He scoffed. "You came up with an elaborate scheme to kill me!"

"No, no." He shook his index finger left to right, his yellow eyes shining wickedly. "That was a bonus. I simply wanted your presence at my wedding. If you survived, that is."

Okay, so Corvus *was* kind of an asshole, she would give that to Bast.

"I find it awfully convenient that Father died around the same time you put a bounty on my head," her partner snapped. "Don't you think?"

"A remarkable coincidence, though I'm not alone in the list of sons who hated him." Stepping closer, Corvus set his hands behind his back. "None of us liked the guy, especially you and Leon."

"Fuck you," Bast snarled as darkness filled his irises. "Why on all of Danu's prairies did you want me at your wedding?"

Feigning shock, Corvus slammed a hand on his chest. "You're my brother, Sebastian. I simply wanted you there during one of the most important days of my life."

"Bullshit."

"A big, smelly one at that." With a chuckle, he raised his shoulders. "Fine, you caught me. I wanted to rub my happiness on your miserable face, you *suket*."

Mera wasn't sure if *suket* meant fucker or cunt. Actually, it might mean both.

Stepping closer to Corvus, Bast sneered. "That's the brother I know."

"Indeed." He scowled at her partner with a certain hurt. "All that aside, do you truly believe I'd kill Father? What would I gain from it?"

Not exactly a denial.

Bast's beady, pitch-black irises reflected Corvus. For the first time since they'd gotten here, Mera feared the darkness inside her partner might take over him.

"You had nothing to gain from Idillia's death, either," he remarked with a dangerous stillness, the kind that hid an ocean of pain underneath.

"Oh, please. As if you've never killed innocent people, Sebastian."

Bast stepped back, like his brother had slapped him in the face. Quickly recomposing, he poked Corvus' chest, pushing him backwards. "Your bride, or should I say *my* bride? She's quite upset you used her in your little scheme. I doubt there will be a wedding after all."

"Detective Dhay, that's quite enough," Mera warned, knowing he'd gone too far. Still, both Dhays ignored her, much to her annoyance.

Corvus' lips formed a line, his fists balling. "I helped Karthy forget who you are, *malachai*. She'll forgive me for what I did. She wanted you there for our wedding, too."

"I believe that." Bast smiled eagerly. "Maybe she was having second thoughts."

Stepping forward, Theodore raised his hands. "Brothers, please. Leon's coronation will happen soon. We should take this time to reconcile and rejoice under the blessings of Danu."

"Shut up, Theo!" Corvus and Bast yelled in unison.

The three began arguing while Benedict simply watched, downing his wine with an expression of utter boredom in his face. Finding Mera's attention, he raised his glass at her.

Before she could wonder why he'd done that, a servant holding a silver tray with a glass of red wine came from behind, slightly bowing at her.

"Excuse me, madam detective," said the servant, a banshee with completely white irises, green skin, and shark teeth. Her cerulean hair was tied in a low pony, matching her uniform —a silky navy shirt and pants that looked strikingly fancy. "Prince Benedict wants to say thank you for putting up with this madness." Blushing, she stared at her own feet. "His words, madam, not mine."

Drinking on the job felt wrong, but a bit of alcohol might help Mera get through this hell of a day with her sanity in check. She narrowed her eyes at the three Sidhe ahead, who kept behaving like children.

Idiots.

Accepting the glass, she thanked the servant, and raised it at Benedict. The velvety liquid sailed smoothly down her throat as she took the first sip.

Hmm, it tasted rich and sweet.

Was wine supposed to be sweet?

She couldn't remember, but damn, it tasted amazing. Mera downed two full gulps, and made a note to ask Benedict the brand of the wine.

"I don't give a fuck about you or Karthana, Corvus!" Bast yelled, drawing her attention. "Marry her for all I care, but admit to hating me your whole life! Admit to wanting me dead!"

Corvus raised his shoulders. "That's far from a secret, isn't it?"

Mera giggled quietly, which didn't seem entirely appropriate. Hell, this wine worked fast.

"Can't you both get along?" Benedict complained loudly. "All this arguing is awfully tedious."

Corvus craned his neck at Bast. "It truly is, don't you think, brother? How about we play a game instead?" Turning to Mera, he motioned for her to approach. "Come to me, *nobatchi.*"

The word had a loving cling to it. Mera guessed it must mean something close to sweetheart, but if that dickface thought he could talk to her like that and she would waltz toward him, he was seriously mistaken—her legs were already moving.

Her grip on the wine glass loosened, and it shattered into a million pieces as it hit the floor. The red liquid spluttered against the white marble.

"Oh, I'm sorry," she said, her tone soft and breezy. Not at all like her own.

"You can clean that later, *nobatchi*. Just come to me."

She smiled, happy that Corvus wasn't mad at her for breaking the glass.

It made no sense.

The tingling of foreign magic spread inside her body, coursing through her veins, and Mera fought it as hard as she could, yet the spell had begun taking over her movements— her thoughts, too. Her muddled brain set her feet firmly on the floor, but she kept walking.

A goofy grin marred her face and she couldn't pull it back. Mera yelled, but no sound came out of her lips.

Poseidon in the trenches, what was happening?

Soon, she forgot why she fought against herself. She only wanted to reach Corvus and do as he said.

No, no, no!

Bast glared at her, frozen like a statue. "Corvus, you didn't," he croaked.

Ah, yes. Through her haze, Mera recalled why she'd been trying to scream.

The prick had enchanted her.

CHAPTER 11

THE WINE...

It must've been enchanted to muddle her mind. Faerie food and drinks could make humans, plus the occasional supernatural, more compliant and suggestible—not to mention utterly ridiculous.

Mera's head drifted between the dread of awareness and the joy of utter bliss, a sensation both wonderful and terrifying.

"Sarking baku!" Bast yelled as he tried to fetch Mera by her hand, but tentacles of night had already wrapped around his wrists and ankles, holding him in place. They'd bloomed from the marbled floor, vibrating in tune with the magic that swirled in Corvus' core, but there was something else... a second layer of power which reinforced the first, and it came from Benedict.

Two against one.

Bast could shout and fight as much as he wanted. He wouldn't be able to move.

Even bewildered and raging, her partner was beautiful.

An easy smile curled Mera's lips, even though she knew she had no reason to be smiling.

"What does *sarking* mean?" she asked.

Bast gaped at her, utter horror in his eyes as he struggled against his binds. "Kitten, snap out of it. Don't fear the consequences," he urged meaningfully. "Free yourself."

Snap out of what? She'd never felt so fine in her life.

Although she tried, Mera couldn't quite grasp the meaning behind his words. Like they spoke the same language, and yet, not at all. "Free myself?"

I'm trying, her own voice grumbled from somewhere deep inside her, the sound muffled as if coming from a great distance.

Mera should've known better than to accept an offer from a fae household; the sensible half of her understood that, the half that flickered in and out of existence. But the other half, the dominant one, felt so good.

Too good.

Did the source of her joy really matter? Happiness had been such a rarity in Mera's life. She should grab this chance with all her might.

Actually, she already had.

"Sarking means 'fucking', *chichi*," Corvus explained as he gave her his hand. "But it can also mean godsdamned. It's all on the intonation, you see."

Only Bast called her *chichi*, which meant kitten. Having someone else say it felt... wrong.

She took his hand nonetheless.

"Let go of her, *malachai!*" Bast roared.

Ignoring his command, Corvus bowed his head and smelled the curve of Mera's neck. "Ah, Sebastian. I take back what I said. Your human is exquisite." He eyed her up and down in a sleazy manner that made Mera's conscious half want to cover herself, and the aloof one proudly show off. "She's got a raw and wild beauty, doesn't she?" At this he turned to Benedict, who simply sipped his wine and shrugged.

That distant voice in her head grumbled, *I'll make this bastard pay. I'll make them both pay.*

Pay for what?

A dazed happiness rushed over Mera, spreading through every crevice of her body. Not a single worry weighed in on her shoulders. She couldn't remember the last time she'd felt so carefree.

"Corvus, you will stop this at once," Theodore demanded as he stomped forward, but Benedict grabbed his wrist and pulled him back as if he was made of air and twigs.

Theo glared at his twin, who merely shook his head in a warning. It was enough for Danu's little follower to step back and lower his head.

The monk is weak, the raging voice inside Mera growled.

Leaning closer to her, Corvus rolled a russet lock of her hair around his fingers. "Why don't we put some makeup on that hard face of yours? Maybe a day in a spa, a nice dress, and who knows? You might just be worthy of a Night Prince."

"I might?" Silly hope bloomed in Mera's chest.

"Of course, dear."

Fuck this! Fuck this very much!

Narrowing his eyes at her, Corvus scratched his chin. "Hmm, I see a bit of awareness in you. Tell me, could you possibly be awake in there?" He knocked on her forehead as if it was a door.

That distant voice was so dim Mera could barely hear it. *Fuuuuuuuuuuck yooooooouuuu!*

"Aware?" she asked, a certain confusion taking over her. "I don't understand."

"Corvus, stop right now," Bast warned, his jaw set as he kept thrashing against his binds.

His brother ignored the threat, his focus solely on Mera. "Of course you don't understand, *chichi*. What do you say, Ben?" Corvus turned to his brother. "I'm taken, but maybe we could wed her to you. Have her drink a cup of wine every day for decades on end."

Curling his lips in disgust, Benedict winced. "Not my cup of tea, brother."

"Oh, human?"

"No." He casually moved his glass in a circle, watching the red liquid dance. "Female."

"Ah yes, but it would be a marriage of convenience, you see. We'd have our own spy in the human borough. The light courts do it all the time."

Yeah, inter-borough spy games weren't exactly old news. Even Clifftown, the human borough, had ways of monitoring the others in Hollowcliff, but if caught, those breaking the law went to jail for a long time.

Mera's awareness surged closer to the surface, yet not enough to free her from the wine's enchantment. Bile swirled in her gut, but she couldn't quite grasp why she felt so bad. She was so happy...

She might throw up soon, though. If she did, would she let it out or swallow it back, maybe choke on it?

It depended on what Corvus told her to do.

"*Rae-henai!*" Bast growled. "You will pay for this with your life, I swear it!"

"Oh, do you? If I told your partner to eat my shit," he walked closer to Bast, "she would. Wouldn't you, darling?"

Mera nodded with a moronic grin, when all she wanted was to scream. Another wave of foolish happiness slammed against her, dragging her thrashing consciousness underneath it.

"And if I wanted to fuck her in front of you, brother, I could do that, too." He turned to Mera. "What do you say, *sweetie pie?*" he added in English.

A strange giddiness took over her, but a terror unlike any other pricked at her lungs.

"I would enjoy that," she numbingly answered.

How about I cut off your dick instead, asshole?

Bast writhed against Corvus' and Benedict's magical binds, his teeth grinding, his canines sharper than a lion's. His bun undid itself, curtaining his face in moonlight-silver hair that brushed atop his beady black eyes. "I will end you before that, *suket!*"

Corvus eyed Bast with complete contempt. "Detective Maurea, will you ask my brother to stop being an idiot? Also, do remove your shirt."

She smiled at Bast. "Please stop being an idiot." Taking off her jacket, Mera began pulling up her shirt.

No, no, no!

Thank Poseidon she was wearing a bra.

With one easy toss, her white shirt pooled on the marbled floor, next to her black leather jacket.

Bast stopped struggling and went incredibly still. "Kitten, you have to fight this."

"She can't." Corvus clicked his tongue. "What a shame, *chichi.* You're wearing a bra. Remove that as well, yes?"

Tears pricked her eyes. No matter how hard Mera pushed her hands down, they went up, toward her bra straps. The part of her that guided her movements and feelings couldn't be happier, though—she was having a blast!

The other part of her wanted to put a knife into Corvus' chest.

"Stop!" Bast roared, his voice breaking midway as his chest heaved with panic. "I'll do anything you want. Just free her."

Corvus raised his hand and Mera stopped moving. Strolling toward her, he draped one arm over her naked shoulders.

"Anything?" He smacked a kiss on her cheek and Mera felt sick, but that stupid smile didn't leave her face. "What kind of anything? Perhaps apologize for accusing me of trying to harm my own kin?"

"Yes, I'll apologize." A snap of darkness flashed between him and Corvus, meaning that the promise was sealed. "Please," Bast's voice failed. "You don't understand. She's my—"

"Enough!" Leon's voice boomed from behind. Instantly, a crack of darkness swam through the air, releasing Bast from his night binds. "What is going on here?"

Mera clapped her hands as her partner rushed to her. "Yay!"

"Are you all right?" he asked, but before she could tell him she never felt better in her life, Bast was already checking her face, then the rest of her body as if she'd been physically hurt.

"I'm fine." Leaning forward, she licked his neck. "You taste good..."

Bast froze, his Adam's apple going up and down as he watched her. Shaking his head, he grabbed her shirt and jacket from the floor. Mera barely noticed he was putting them back on her.

Thank you, the faint voice in her head whispered.

Stomping into the throne room, Leon slapped Corvus on his face so hard, he spun twice and nearly fell. "How dare you?" he raged. "Need I remind you that Detective Maurea is here representing Hollowcliff? That you could and *should* go to jail for threatening her, or any female, in such an abhorrent manner?"

"Brother," Benedict interrupted. "It was all in good fun. Corvus would never—"

"You have a sick sense of fun." His lips formed a line, his disappointment almost a physical blade. "I expected more of you, Ben."

Tears glinted in Benedict's eyes. He opened his mouth to speak, but swallowed back his words instead, wiping the corner of his eyelids with the palm of his hand.

"Defend your precious little brother, Leon, like you always have!" Corvus pointed at Bast, a bitter scowl marring his features. "He accused me of murder! He insulted Karthana! I've killed people for less!"

"Oh, poor Karthana," Mera mumbled to Bast. "Why is she offended? She's such a nice fae…"

He hugged Mera tighter against him. "Never mind."

Leaning her head on his chest, she rejoiced in the warmth of his embrace.

Hmm, nice...

"Why are you such a *shig* to Bast?" Leon's tone wavered with a deep sadness. "Do you hate him because he stole the title of little brother from you when he was born? You *humiliated* an innocent woman just to spite him," he added with disgust.

Corvus gaped at him, as if Leon had just stabbed him in his chest. "I… I-it was never that simple. Bast started it!"

"Kneel!" the future Night King bellowed, his voice thundering across the open hall.

Corvus fell harshly on his knees. He winced in pain, but kept his teeth gritted, holding the scream that clearly pushed out in his throat.

"He's hurt," Mera noted, that familiar aloofness still holding her under. She went to help Corvus, but Bast wrapped one arm around her waist, stopping her from taking a step forward. Leaning back against his strong chest, she forgot what she'd been about to do.

Ah... much better.

"Beg for their forgiveness!" Leon pointed at Bast and Mera.

Corvus shook against the power of the future king's demand—a ridiculously strong form of glamour. He screamed in anger, but he could only fight for so long.

The asshole bowed on the floor abruptly, as if an invisible force had crashed upon him. His forehead thumped against the white marble.

"Please forgive my insolence," he growled.

With her mind still fuzzy and spinning, Mera blinked at Leon, then at Corvus. "I want to go..." She pushed her face against Bast's chest.

"Understood," he agreed soothingly, ignoring his brother's plea. He took her in his arms, lifting her off her feet.

Mera's eyes fell closed as she heard the flapping of wings, and then a soft breeze lulled her to sleep.

She must've drifted off for a quick moment, but when she came to, Bast was already landing before the precinct. The orange of sunset bathed the landscape, seeping to the space around them.

He took her up the stairs to the apartment on the second floor, then opened the door.

Giggling, Mera nuzzled his neck as they went inside the living room. "Hmm, what are we about to do, Detective?"

"You need rest," he said softly, pushing the door to her room open with his foot. "That magic must've been freakishly strong to render an *akritana* powerless."

Gently, he laid her in bed, then helped her out of her jacket. Yet, Mera wasn't sleepy, not anymore. The happiness she'd experienced still buzzed inside her; still took over her thoughts and actions.

She wanted, *needed*, to share it with Bast.

In one swift move, she pulled him onto the mattress and straddled him, wrapping her arms around his shoulders.

Bending her head down, she nudged the tip of his nose with hers. "Be happy with me."

Deep down, Mera sensed she didn't have the reigns of her own body, not entirely, but unlike before, the faint presence inside her didn't object to what she was doing.

Bast gaped at her, his nostrils flared. "Mera, you don't know what—"

She pressed her lips to his.

At first, he kept his jaw locked, but she wasn't one to give up easily. Eventually, his body relaxed and his mouth caved to hers. Bast's hands grabbed the back of her neck as he deepened their kisses, their tongues fighting a war of their own, their breaths intertwined.

"I'm not strong enough," he grumbled as he nibbled her lower lip, his rock-hard erection growing underneath his pants, right between Mera's thighs. "We have to stop."

The hell she would.

Mera rocked her hips back and forth as they kissed, rubbing the bead between her thighs against his bulging length.

"You'll come in your pants, Sebastian Dhay," she whispered in his ear, giggling wickedly.

"Fuck, Mera..." He kissed her hard and long. "It's too good."

Fire pooled inside her while she kept rubbing, and a moan escaped her lips. It was their motions, the scorching burn of his delirious kisses, and his deft hands digging against her flesh.

Mera would explode soon.

Very soon.

"Oh, Bast," she moaned, feeling herself climbing higher and higher.

He bit the tip of her shoulder as she kept moving over

him, his fangs sinking in her flesh just enough to increase her pleasure. "We can't," he grumbled. "Shouldn't…"

In that moment, exhaustion weighed down on Mera at once, her flesh and bone suddenly as heavy as stone.

What's happening?

She fell sideways, her body completely limp, but Bast took her in his arms right on time. Laying her back on the bed, he kissed her forehead.

Only then did Mera realize that tentacles of night and stars had wrapped around her ankles, sucking any energy she had left.

The bastard was forcing her to sleep.

"But you want this," she protested drowsily. The bliss of oblivion crashed down on her, and Mera's eyes closed. She couldn't open them again. "I want this, too…"

A bitter sadness rang in his tone. "You don't know what you want, kitten."

CHAPTER 12

THE SMELL of pancakes and freshly brewed coffee wafted through the closed bedroom door, waking up Mera. Her belly grumbled in response.

She expected a major headache as a result from the enchanted wine, but so far, she felt fine.

Well, not exactly fine. A deep groan escaped her when memories from last night rushed back to the surface.

Poseidon in the trenches, she'd not only stripped in front of the royal family, but also dry-humped Bast.

Mera glared at the bedroom's sky-blue ceiling, shame freezing her from head to toe. Could she sink into this bed? Hide from the rest of the world?

Hell, she'd made a total fool of herself, especially with her partner. Thankfully, Bast kept a cool head and stopped her before... yeah. Both her hands slammed over her face, a prickly sensation thrashing in her chest.

'He doesn't want us,' her siren whimpered.

That didn't, *shouldn't*, matter. He'd done the right thing, even if a part of her hated his self-control.

Sure, Mera should have known better than to drink

enchanted wine, but her lack of judgement didn't excuse what Corvus and Benedict had done. The evil dickwarts could have asked anything of her, and she would have gladly complied. Mera had never felt more terrified in her life, not even when she'd battled her own mother.

No, that wasn't entirely right.

She felt the same dread and powerlessness back at the Summer King's penthouse. Images of thugs punching and kicking Bast nonstop flashed in her mind. Dark blood poured over the left side of his face as Mera watched. All she could do was watch.

Tensing, she shook the memory away just as Bast's steps thumped outside, along with the clattering of cutlery and plates. He must be preparing breakfast, which was nice, but how could Mera face him without exploding in shame?

Fact: Enchanted wine or not, she'd wanted to bang Bast yesterday. Fiercely. And he was the one who'd kept his restraint, which was a first in their relationship.

Well, there was no avoiding her partner, not until they finished their assignment.

Gruffly getting out of bed, she stepped into the living room. Sunlight drenched the space in a warm morning glow, and for a moment, Mera wondered if she might be dreaming.

Bast had his shirt rolled up to his elbows, as he always did, but she couldn't say why it caught her attention this time. In any case, showcasing strong forearms like that should be illegal. Mera had no clue how she'd been able to concentrate on their cases this far.

Poseidon in the trenches, what was happening to her?

'Ha! Who's the horny one now?' her siren jeered.

Bast's bun was higher than usual and yet just as messy. The silver threads of his hair framed the sides of his face, and Mera gulped when a familiar fire pooled between her thighs.

"Morning," he greeted with a charming grin, dragging a chair back in a clear cue for her to sit.

"Morning," she countered quietly, avoiding eye contact as she dropped on her seat. A cup of hot coffee waited for her, and she took in its delicious scent before tasting the first sip.

Ah, bliss. Her muscles relaxed just a little.

From the open kitchen, Bast brought a plate with a stack of pancakes and set it between them. He sat on the chair across from her, then poured them fresh orange juice.

"Did you sleep well?" he asked with a smirk stamped in his ridiculously perfect face.

A furious blush rose to Mera's cheeks, so she focused on her coffee. "Look… I'm really sorry about yesterday."

Frowning, he placed a pair of pancakes on her plate. "Don't you dare apologize for what those *sukets* made you do."

"No, not about that. I meant about what *I* did to you… afterwards."

"Ah, *that.*" He poured syrup over his pancakes before handing her the small porcelain jug. "So, you're saying you *wanted* to do what we were going to do?"

"No! I mean, I did, but I didn't have control." She chided herself. "What I want to say is that it was wrong of me to 'attack' you. Thank you, for doing the right thing."

"Oh, kitten, don't thank me. I almost…" He shrugged off what he was about to say, then licked his lips in a wicked manner. Like a wolf about to feast. "I'm certain we'll get other chances."

Other chances?

Poseidon in the trenches, they were partners! Chances were out of the question, and yet, Mera wanted to jump Bast right then, and shove that bulging part of his inside her.

Down, girl!

Taking a deep breath, she bit her bottom lip. Mera

couldn't blame her siren this time. Then again, they were one and the same, so did it matter?

"I'm sorry for what happened back at the castle. I felt the power thrumming in my veins, the darkness pulling me into its infinite pathways... but it wasn't enough to break free of Ben and Corvus' magic."

"Bast, it wasn't your fault."

He chewed a piece of his pancake and shrugged, obviously ignoring what she'd said. "If it's any consolation, I went back after you fell asleep. Ben had already left, but Corvus was still there, so I took the opportunity to teach him a lesson. With my fists."

"That's technically police brutality."

"Is it? I'd call it a family feud. Brothers fight all the time, don't they?"

She rolled her eyes. "How very faerie of you."

It might not be right, but Mera was glad he'd avenged her, at least a little. Sure, it was a petty sentiment, but that didn't make it any less true.

She took a bite of her pancake, followed by another, and when she realized, she'd finished both stacks.

Heck, she must've been starving.

"Your brothers are assholes, I'll give you that." Taking a long gulp of her orange juice, Mera set the glass back on the table. "However, we need to focus on our investigation. Once we arrest your father's murderer, we can worry about Corvus."

"Maybe we'll kill two birds with one stone."

"Bast..."

"Corvus is behind this." His mouth contorted into a downward curve. "I can feel it in my gut."

With a sigh, Mera scratched the back of her neck. Yes, Bast was biased. Yes, she couldn't trust his judgement, but every good detective knew that a gut feeling shouldn't be ignored.

"All right, then." She wiped her lips with a napkin. "Let's prove it."

～

Bast sat hunched over the precinct's table as he dusted the left side of the chocolate box for fingerprints. The magnifying glasses strapped to a headband around his forehead made him resemble a mad scientist from old movies.

Mera focused on the open computer on her lap and stared at the screen. A circle swirled in the center while the system scanned the first batch of fingerprints.

"How's it going?" Bast asked from the table, his focus locked on the box.

The program still said, "*Image processing.*"

"Running." She sighed. "It takes time."

Lifting his head, he frowned at her, and Mera had to hold a giggle. His eyes looked gigantic through the magnifying lenses, making him resemble a cute turtle.

"You're incredibly calm about the enchanted wine episode," he said, "especially considering what Corvus did to you. Are you certain you're fine?"

Despite the dark subject, Mera couldn't hold her laughter. Bast looked both ridiculous and adorable.

Rolling his enormous turtle eyes, he lifted the glasses. "I'm serious."

"Sure, I'm angry." She cleared her throat. "But my partner once told me he was a detective first, and a bastard with a grudge second."

Raising an intrigued eyebrow, he gave her a cocky grin. "Your partner is a wise fae."

"He has his moments. Between you and me, he's a bit full

of himself." She winked at him playfully. "Besides, you already punched Corvus, so…"

"Ten times before Leon stepped in."

"Seriously?" She waved her hand dismissively. "Consider my honor defended, *ser* Dhay."

"I can't wait to put him behind iron bars." Crossing his arms, Bast stared ahead. "My reckoning with that *shig* has been a long time coming."

"We're detectives," Mera reminded him as she clicked on the screen. "We don't do reckoning."

"When it comes to Corvus and I, that's the only way it will end," he stated with absolute certainty, his gaze lost. "With violence, blood, and one victor."

"I'll pretend you didn't mention murdering someone, *Detective*," she countered, "Only because I recognize an empty threat when I hear it." Though in all truth, Bast's threat had been far from empty.

"Mera, Corvus is an asshole and a killer."

"So are you."

He cocked his head left, a flash of anger rushing behind his eyes, yet it quickly faded when he seemed to consider it twice.

"Fair point," he admitted.

The program kept searching the prints through the Tagradian database. Mera had ensured the system would ignore the matches on Bast's mother and father, so she hoped to get at least a partial from the murderer.

She checked the screen for a while, idly wondering if she should tell Bast what had been on her mind.

Screw it.

"To be fair, you're not completely innocent," she blurted. "You shouldn't have lost your mind and provoked Corvus in the first place. You're here as a detective, remember?"

He glared at her, his jaw hanging open. "Oh, sure!" He threw his arms up. "Blame this on me."

"I'm not saying it's your fault. Not at all, but you called Karthana *your* left over. You said Corvus was her second choice, and you accused him of murder without any proof. That wasn't proper detective behavior, was it?"

Looking out the window, he clicked his tongue. "We'll interview the palace's staff the day after tomorrow. Do you have your questions ready?"

Changing the subject must have been a lot easier for him than admitting he might've been wrong.

"I have plenty," she assured. "We're not getting out of there without answers."

Bast turned to her, studying Mera with a certain admiration, his gaze lost and focused at the same time. "You're the strongest Tagradian I've ever met, and one fine detective." A soft smile creased his lips. "What would I do without you?"

She turned to the screen before a violent blush conquered her cheeks. Changing the subject might be a good idea, since all she wanted was to kiss Bast senseless. "How was it growing up in the palace?"

He removed the headband with the goggles, ruffling threads of disheveled hair that made him look way too appealing.

Running a hand through his locks, he shrugged. "Good and bad."

"Great answer, bud."

He chuckled. "There were good things. My mom, for one. Father might have been a cruel prick, but Mom was kind, and she always watched out for us." A veil of sadness fell over his face. "When her mind started to drift, Leon took the job."

"He did?"

Bast nodded, a sweet smile blooming on his lips. "Big Brother blew on my wounds when I was a kid, and he taught me how to wield a sword. I love lemon pie, so Leon wouldn't have his dessert after dinner, only to hand it to me when Father wasn't looking." Bast leaned his elbows on the table. "He's the glue that keeps us together. He tries, at least."

'Mental note,' her siren whispered, *'bake Bast a lemon pie. Also, learn how to bake.'*

"That's a huge responsibility," Mera said.

"It is, but Leon never complained." He seemed lost in his memories for a moment. "So, yes. Mom, Leon. Stella. They were the good. Master Raes…" Raising his brow, he blew air through his lips. "I guess both good and bad. He found a darkness in me and set it free, which I later realized was bad. But he took me in as his own, and that was good."

"What about Karthana?"

"Complicated." He shrugged. "Good, because she was my friend and my first… well, *first*. Bad because she wanted something I couldn't give."

"Love?"

"That, too."

"And Corvus?"

"Most children feared the Boogey-banshee when I was young. I feared Corvus, and how easily he could take things from me, though I never let it show; never told a soul." His lips turned into a line as a world of pain marred his expression. "That bastard is bad, Mera. Bad to the fucking bone."

The fingerprints turned out to be a dead end.

From the batch, Mera had gotten a foreign partial that could belong to the murderer, but it wasn't enough to identify them.

So close…

After that, Bast decided to pay a visit to Charles Grey, since the vamp kept profiles on the palace's employees.

If any of the nightlings they would interrogate tomorrow had a history of violence, or a criminal record, maybe they could've killed the Night King. Sure, it was a long shot, but Mera and Bast grasped at straws, so it was worth investigating.

She decided to stay behind to call Ruth and update her and Asherath on their findings, especially since the Night King's death had officially become a murder investigation.

Once she got off the phone with them, and having no profiles to analyze yet, Mera decided to go through the case again.

From what they could gather, the box of chocolates had arrived in the mailroom. The package? Lost.

Not good. Not good at all.

The Night King then received the gift, shared the bonbons with his wife, and all was fine and dandy until he dropped dead two days later from a heart attack. If Seraphina Dhay hadn't asked Bast and Mera for help, the king's death would've remained ruled as natural causes.

This meant the killer was calculating, smart.

Careful.

The kind who was hard to catch.

Rubbing her forehead, Mera let out an exhausted sigh, when three knocks came from the door.

Weird. Bast had been gone for thirty minutes. He couldn't be back already.

Could he?

Her hand hovered over her gun as she stepped toward the door, more out of instinct than anything else.

She yanked the door open, and when she saw who stood there, she pulled out the weapon, swiftly aiming at his head.

Clicking the safety off, she placed her finger on the trigger. "Give me one reason not to shoot."

Corvus raised his hands in surrender. "Bast will never forgive you for stealing the satisfaction of killing me from him."

CHAPTER 13

Somewhere in the past...

IT HAD BEEN seven years since Bast and Stella arrived in Tir Na Nog, and five since he'd become a Hollowcliff detective.

All respect for the victims aside, he loved the rush of a new case. Analyzing the circumstances and motives, catching the clues that led to a culprit, then seeing the bad guy's raging glare from behind iron bars. It all made Bast's blood pump faster.

It was also why he smiled to himself as he headed toward the murder scene, which wasn't entirely appropriate, but he didn't really care.

In the past, he'd been an extraordinary assassin, yet much to his own surprise, he'd become an even better detective. Stella had also adapted incredibly well, as Bast knew she would.

It had taken a lot of negotiating with Master Raes, and at least half of Bast's wealth—mercenaries would always be mercenaries after all—to buy their freedom from Lunor Insul, but in the end, everything worked out for them.

A tiny drop hit Bast's head, and he looked up to the overcast sky that blocked any shred of moonlight. His good spirits immediately vanished.

Bast hated nights like this.

Once he reached the small apartment building, he spread his wings and flew up to the fourth floor, which also happened to be the last, soon landing on a large balcony that doubled as a landing pad.

Two patrol officers waited for him inside, a banshee and a Sidhe wearing indigo suits, the standard uniform of their department.

How the killer had entered the place was clear—he'd smashed right through the balcony's glass doors. A profusion of tiny shards peppered the mahogany flooring.

Bast stepped into the living room, the glass crunching underneath his shoes, while he observed the scene.

The victim, a male who looked to be in his thirties, was lying on the floor a little too neatly. Almost as if he'd been asleep, except the killer had gouged his eyes out—the gaping holes cried dried blood.

He wore a fitted, pleated suit that screamed Brickstreet, the money district from Evanora, the witches' borough. According to the file, the dead warlock, a Tom Blackwater, had been to Tir Na Nog on "business" as a "consultant".

Translation: he was there doing illegal shit with the light courts.

"I'm glad you're here, Detective Dhay," said one of the officers, a spring Sidhe with yellow hair and skin as dark as Bast's. "The hotel manager called it in. He's in the lobby if you want to question him."

"And let you tamper any further with my crime scene, Willowby?" he grumbled. "I'm not stupid."

The officer gasped in shock. "Excuse me! I would never tamper with evidence!"

Unless Willowby's friends from the light courts asked for a favor, that was.

Bast and his Captain knew the bastard was corrupt to his core, but they didn't have any evidence, and even if they did, being a detective in Tir Na Nog meant playing a dangerous game of chess.

Better the devil you know than the one you don't.

Most boroughs were fairly clean, though, which broke Bast's heart. Even Lycannie had gone through a major cleanup recently, thanks to Bruce's nephew, and some help from Bast himself.

When he gave the corrupt commissioner an "incentive" to talk—the same commissioner who'd ordered the hit on Bruce—*halle*, the *suket* blabbed. He admitted to all his crimes, which meant Bruce and his son could finally return home. All in a good day's work.

Doing the same in Tir Na Nog, however, was a different story.

Not only were the light courts careful, and a lot more powerful than a corrupt commissioner, they were also *everywhere*.

"Argue with me, Willowby," Bast dared, his tone freezing cold, "and you know your fate."

So, Bast wasn't exactly Mr. By-the-book.

Over the years, his partners had been either incompetent morons or corrupt fuckers. The morons he'd ignored, until they asked for a reassignment, while the corrupt ones suffered mind-breaking injuries on the job. Horrid "accidents" that forced them to give up on the police force altogether.

Willowby gulped, because he knew Bast was behind it all, and yet, he couldn't prove it. No one could.

Oh, the irony.

In Bast's defense, he did the government a favor. Tir Na Nog was at war with itself, and the light courts were winning. One less asshole on their side, one less headache for him and his captain.

Besides, he always gave them a choice. Either they jumped the ship or Bast threw them off.

Hardly unfair, was it?

"What do you think happened?" the banshee next to Willowby asked. Funny how she hadn't bothered defending her partner's honor.

"I could tell you, but I don't want Will's bosses finding out." Willowby opened his mouth in indignation, but Bast raised a finger. "I swear to Danu, I'll rip your wings and throw you off the balcony."

"Let's check the other rooms, Lizinet," the *malachai* told his partner with a huff. "Detective Dhay clearly needs space." With that, they left.

Finally.

Bast narrowed his eyes at the body. No signs of a struggle, which was odd, considering the killer had smashed through the balcony's glassed doors.

He must've been fast. Remarkably so.

Crouching near the victim, Bast analyzed the clean cut across his neck. It was fresher than the eye wounds, which meant he'd died *after* his eyes were removed. Next, he found a minuscule perforation in the base of the victim's neck; something only a needle could've done.

A paralyzing dart.

That was why the warlock showed no signs of struggle.

Bast had murdered plenty, and he'd seen horrible things, but paralyzing someone so they'd be fully awake and helpless as their eyes were scooped out, demanded a high level of cruelty.

Taking a cloth from his pocket, he wrapped it around his palm and laid a hand over the victim's forehead.

Still warm.

Bast jumped to his feet and turned to the dark corridor that led to the living room.

The silence. He should have paid attention to the silence.

"Willowby?" he called, hoping the idiot would answer.

He didn't.

Bast's night thrummed inside him. He might not see his enemy, but he knew he wasn't alone.

"Your friends are dead," the deep tone came from the darkness of the corridor. "I hope that's fine with you."

A rush of red, blinding anger flushed Bast's head, not because Willowby was dead—good riddance—but because the banshee, Lizinet, seemed to have been an honest fae, and those were a rarity nowadays. Yet, Bast could barely register her loss, because *he* was here.

"*Sarking shig,*" Bast growled, his fangs growing sharper.

Corvus stepped into the living room, revealing himself. With the League's dark uniform, he blended perfectly with the night, though his white hair and yellow eyes gave him away.

The bastard hadn't changed a bit. Still as tall as Bast, his eyes feral and calculating. Still a fucking prick.

"I should've recognized your work," Bast grumbled, his hands fisting.

Corvus took it as a compliment. "I do make cruelty an art, don't I?" He shrugged nonchalantly. "The people who ordered the bounty asked for his eyes. So I gave them his eyes."

"Did you have to keep him alive through it all?"

"He was a corrupt warlock, Bast. I assumed punishing the guilty was your thing now?"

Yes, but not in that way... and yet, if the evil was too great, shouldn't it be silenced?

Shaking his head, he dismissed the thought. Bast didn't need to kill bad guys to stop them, even if sometimes he wished he could.

He pulled cuffs from his pocket. "Corvus Dhay, you're under arrest." A bitter sensation invaded his tongue because he was a hypocrite. A giant, fucking hypocrite. Yet Corvus had murdered two cops, a line he'd come close to crossing, but never did. Sure, Bast wasn't a saint, but his brother... he listened to the demons in their blood; the demons Bast knew all too well. "You have the right to remain—"

With a loud laugh, he pointed to Bast's fitted gray pants, vest, and white shirt. "I'm sorry, I can't take you seriously when you dress like that."

"It's my uniform, *malachai.*"

"It's ridiculous!" He strolled toward the balcony, his hands behind his back. "I'm leaving the League, by the way. I'll open a club back at the island with Benedict. I would invite you to the opening, but let's be honest, your mopey ass would ruin the mood."

"You're under arrest," Bast pushed.

Corvus spun on his heels. "You know I'm not turning myself in."

An eager grin cut through Bast's lips. He threw away the cuffs, and they clinked against the hard-wooden floor. "I was hoping you'd say that."

Jolting forward, he nailed one punch on Corvus' face, then one jab at his stomach, nearly sending his brother toppling over the balcony. The fast *baku* dodged Bast's last attack, and cartwheeled back into the apartment.

Corvus stopped in the middle of the living room, near the body. His yellow eyes glinted in the darkness. "Killing you will make my day, *brother.*"

"Likewise!" Bast ran toward him, but Corvus charged and kicked him on his stomach, flinging him against a wall.

All breath fled Bast's lungs as his back slammed against the concrete, his skull cracking on the harsh surface. If only he'd raised a magical shield in time... Maybe he'd lost his touch.

Maybe Corvus was too fast.

"Leon asked me to check in on you." The *malachai* panted through gritted teeth. "You abandoned us, and Big Brother still cares about you the most." His tone overflowed with bitterness. "How fair is that?"

"Maybe Leon likes me because I'm not a fucking monster," Bast grumbled as he forced himself atop both feet. Wobbling, he managed to stand upright, which he counted as a victory.

"We're all monsters," Corvus argued. "You're just his favorite beast."

"Fuck you."

Bast willed his darkness forward, and a wave of night and stars rushed toward Corvus, making the entire apartment tremble, yet the *shig* swerved at the last minute. Bast's darkness hit him on the shoulder before slamming into the center wall, blasting into the corridor.

When the magic retreated, a huge chunk of the wall and the hall were gone. On the distant left, where the first bedroom should've been, a gaping hole showcased city lights and faerie buildings outside.

Wincing, Corvus glared at the wound on his shoulder. The skin on the spot looked darkened and purpling. "Why did the night bless you? Why were you granted this power while the rest of us... Why?" He bellowed. "You! An undeserving, ungrateful prick!"

Bast didn't answer, mostly because he had no clue either.

At least, he'd somewhat recovered from Corvus' attacks.

A deep, horrid howl burst from Bast's throat as he charged forward, all the pent-up anger he had for his brother shaping into sound. Bast nailed three punches on his face before the asshole jumped away.

Wiping blood off his nose, Corvus stared at his tainted fingers. "I hate you, Bast. You were given everything, and you threw it away. You left us for..." his lips curled as he motioned to his uniform, "... *this*. You were destined for greatness, but you settle for the mediocre."

"I'm happy. Not that you ever cared," he countered, still a little dizzy. Bile swirled in his stomach.

Fuck, he was in worse shape than he'd thought.

"I'm ashamed to call you family." Corvus gnarled.

It stung, though Bast would never admit it aloud. Concentrating his magic in one final blow, Bast's darkness bloomed around him, enveloping his body in an aura of night and stars.

Corvus clicked his tongue. "You've always hated me, but after I murdered Idillia—"

"Don't you dare speak her name," he growled.

"I did that for *you!*" Wrath, pure, burning wrath took over Corvus' face. "You ingrate little shit!"

"No, you did that to prove a point!" Bast was so angry he could barely see straight. Tears stung his eyes, but he'd never give that *suket* the satisfaction of seeing him cry. "You wanted to show me you could always take Stella from me. You said it yourself; you turn cruelty into an art! *Rae-henai, wu malachai!*"

Gaping at him, Corvus swallowed as if he'd eaten something sour. "I guess you see me better than I see myself, little brother."

Bast pushed his magic forward, but Corvus' darkness enveloped his own body, his power shaped like a fae-sized bullet. He jolted toward Bast and pierced his magic the way an arrow pierces flesh.

Bast would've raised his own shield, but Corvus was already on him, punching his face twice, increasing the ringing in Bast's ears and the dizziness in his head.

His vision blurred as hollow thumps smashed against his cheekbones, over and over again.

Raise... the... shield...

He was too weak.

Bast barely realized he'd fallen with his back on the floor, while Corvus straddled him and kept punching.

He tasted blood. It flooded his mouth, going down his throat. Choking on it, he coughed, but Corvus didn't give him time to breathe between his attacks.

What a way to go. Suffocating in his own blood, murdered by his own brother.

"You don't deserve the night!" Corvus yelled as he punched and punched. "You never deserved Karthy either!"

True. Very true.

With his last strength, Bast pulled an impulse of darkness that burst from his core and flung Corvus away, giving himself a last-minute lifeline.

Stars shone from the corner of his eyes, but Bast couldn't tell if they belonged to his magic or if he was losing his mind. Coughing and wheezing, he crouched over as air burned down his lungs.

"You," he spat dark blood on the floor, "You're dead to me, Corvus."

Near the balcony there was enough light that Bast could see tears tracking down his brother's cheeks.

Incredible, really. He didn't know the asshole was capable of crying.

"I don't give a shit, Sebastian." With that, Corvus leaped from the balcony and into the night sky.

CHAPTER 14

Corvus flashed Mera a charming grin. Bold of him to do that while she pointed a gun at his head.

"May I come in?" he asked.

His teeth matched the color of his white hair. His yellow eyes had the cunning and wilderness of a feral cat; eyes identical to Bast's, except for the color.

"You should go before I shove a bullet into your brain," she warned, every muscle in her body tensing.

Corvus rolled his eyes in a very Bast-like manner. In fact, they had the same height, the same defined muscles. The same aura that oozed wickedness.

"I promise I'll behave, Detective." He put a hand to his chest.

Yeah, right.

Today, Corvus wore a white suit with a black shirt that fit his lean frame perfectly. Sure, he was an asshole, but an asshole who resembled a model in a magazine. If only he were as ugly outside as he was on the inside…

Life wasn't famous for being fair.

His silver necklace and half-moon pendant stood out

from the silken darkness of his shirt. "It was a gift," he nudged the pendant, noticing where her focus had drifted. "From Mom."

Corvus Dhay might be compelling and dangerous, but Mera wouldn't be fooled by this cunning dickface.

Not again.

Stubbornness, however, seemed to be a Dhay family trait. She knew the asshole wouldn't budge, so she stepped back and showed him inside while keeping her aim. "Be my guest, you *shig*."

He didn't seem offended at all. Strolling into the space, he casually pointed to the gun. "Won't you lower that? I come in peace."

"Does it make you uncomfortable?"

He shrugged. "It's bad manners."

"I'll keep it where it is, thanks."

Cocking his head to the right, Corvus watched her with puzzled golden eyes. "I suppose I deserve that."

Supposed? That dickwart *supposed?*

Something in Mera snapped. Jaw clenching, her finger shook on the trigger. "You deserve much worse for what you did to me."

"Yes, I do."

The confession knocked her off-guard.

Corvus turned to the leather sofa on the right—the precinct's "waiting room"—and dropped on the cushioned seat. "I came here to apologize. The darkness in my family tends to take over sometimes. It's a gift and a curse. *Se infini nokto drin wun hart.*"

"The infinite night inside your heart?"

"Indeed. Bast told you about it, no?"

He hadn't, and thanks to the confusion in her face, Corvus noticed.

"Oh, he truly should have." Clicking his tongue, he shook his head. "Have you seen Bast bleed?"

"I have."

Her partner's blood was slightly darker than normal, a deep wine red that neared black, but Mera had assumed this was a general nightling trait.

"Nightblood, as we call it, is exclusive to the royal house. It makes us more powerful than the average Sidhe, but it doesn't come without a price. Nothing ever does," Corvus went on, completely ignoring the fact that she kept aiming her gun at his head. "Thanks to our blood's affinity with magic, it often drives us to madness. It releases our wildest, rawest nature. As you've seen, Leon and Theo suppress it a lot better than Bast, Ben, and I."

Nightblood.

So Bast wasn't only battling his demons. He was battling his genetic code, too.

"That's why you forced me to undress myself?" she asked. "Because deep down, you're mad?"

"Aren't we all? At least a little bit?" he winked at her. "Besides, 'forcing' is such a strong term. I didn't force you to do anything, I simply asked politely."

Closing one eye, she aimed at the center of his forehead. "You need to do better than that."

"Fine! Danu in the damned prairies..." he grumbled before putting a hand on his chest and bowing his chin. "I'm sorry you were caught in the crossfire. I'd only meant to hurt Bast, not you. Then again, you were a fantastic way to achieve my goal."

"Do you enjoy doing that?" she asked.

"What?"

"Hurting Bast."

Maybe Mera was losing her mind, but she spotted agony

and pain behind his feral golden eyes. However, it vanished as fast as it came.

"We each appease the darkness inside us in our own way," he went on, utterly dismissing her question. "Bast gives in to his demons when he's bringing culprits to justice. Jailing them is usually enough, but he did mass-murder all those fae from the Summer Court. That, Detective, was entirely *Yattusei*."

Mera gasped. "It never went on public record. How did you know?"

"I recognized my brother's work." He shrugged. "Leon and Theo rise above the nightblood's influence, Ben lets go when he's partying, and as for me... most battles I lose. Spectacularly. But it's a price I'm willing to pay to keep a straight head. You don't want to see me without my wits, I assure you." Corvus waved his hand carelessly. "In any case, I would've never let you show yourself to my brothers."

"Liar."

He raised his shoulders carelessly, then laid one arm over the couch top. "Have you heard about the mad queen?"

At first, Mera thought he was referring to Mother, but how could he have known about Queen Ariella? Her blood froze at the mere memory of that bitch, yet with a deep breath, Mera assured herself she was safe.

The queen had been dead for over a decade. She couldn't hurt Mera.

Not anymore.

"The mad queen was our ancestor," he added, watching her with curiosity. "And also the reason why the light courts banished nightlings to this island millennia ago."

Ah. Different mad queen, then.

"Her reign was of ruthless bloodthirst and pain," he continued. "Great-great-whatever-grandma became a figure so despised, that her existence was stricken from most books." He winced as if in pain. "I hate to say this, but the light courts were the heroes back then, Detective."

Light courts and heroes in the same sentence felt wrong. So wrong.

"Mad queens." Snickering, Mera shook her head. "They pop up like daisies."

"No, they don't." His brow furrowed in confusion. "There have been plenty of mad kings, but only one mad queen. None topped Nissa, however. No king was so fierce, so calculating, so efficient in their cruelty." His gaze seemed lost for a while, as if he couldn't decide if he feared or admired his ancestor. "Nissa had a unique sort of night inside her; a night not much different than Bast's. It turned her into a mighty conqueror. In those days, half of the continent belonged to her."

Mera knew that nightlings had been exiled to Lunor Insul after a ruthless war with the light courts, back at the epoch of great magical realms when Tagrad didn't exist. Back when humans occupied the bottom of the power chain. Yet, she'd had no idea why until now—the literature on the subject had been severely lacking.

She kept her gun aimed at him, refusing to lower her guard. "Are you here to give me a history lesson?"

"Not intentionally. I'm simply trying to express what a royal taken by nightblood is capable of. Members of my family aren't born mad, but we do have to fight our tendencies. If we're not careful, madness can grow in us slowly, undetectably, until it's too late to get any help."

"That sounds like a bad excuse," Mera countered. "Shouldn't the magic's influence have dimmed over time? If it's in your blood, I mean," she asked, genuine curiosity taking over. "Unless you married each other to keep the genetic pool intact?"

Poseidon in the trenches, could Seraphina Dhay be related to

133

her dead husband?

"We did it in the beginning; brothers marrying sisters and all that." Corvus' lips curled in disgust. "However, we soon realized nightblood doesn't work that way. It's more like a virus that's contracted when we put a nightling in a female's belly. Usually, the mother doesn't catch it, but it's not unheard of. We suspect that's why Mom…" He trailed off.

So, if Mera ever had babies with Bast, she could… why the hell was she thinking about this?

"It's convenient that you decided to drop by when your brother isn't here," she noted.

"If he were here, we would've gotten into a fight, as we always do. Hardly productive, isn't it?"

He did have a point.

"We both know you didn't come here to apologize." She wiggled her gun at him. "Also, you were perfectly aware of what you were doing to me back at the palace, which means you're not mad, just an asshole. So, be done with it."

"I see why Bast likes you." Grinning, he licked his lips. For a split second, Mera found in his expression that hint of madness he'd mentioned, but it disappeared as quickly as it came. "I'm here to give you what humans call a 'heads-up'. I believe Bast is right. Nightblood might have cursed one of my brothers, thus driving him to kill Father."

"One of your brothers? Don't forget you're our number one suspect."

He shrugged, his fingers tapping on the sofa's padding.

Mera rubbed the bridge of her nose, hating that she couldn't decipher his true intentions. "You and Bast are eager to pit the murder against one of your own. Why?"

Hunching over his knees, Corvus gave her a sad smirk. "We fear what nightblood can do, and rightly so."

"Your fear is clouding your judgement," she pointed out to him. Baffling, really, that they couldn't see that for themselves. "Besides, the Night King's death rings like retribution, not madness."

Oh, crap. That's why Corvus told her the story of the mad queen.

That sneaky bastard!

If one of his brothers had murdered their father—which wasn't written in stone yet, at least to Mera—they could plead insanity. He was covering his family's ass!

"You asshole," Mera muttered. "By the way, did Karthana leave you already?" That just to spite him. Just for fun.

Who said someone needed nightblood to be wicked?

His eyes shone with delight mixed with a certain sense of pride. "She hasn't, but Karthy understands the hardships of nightblood, so she will forgive me eventually. My intentions were noble, Detective."

"They usually are. That's the thing about intentions." Against her better judgement, Mera placed her gun back in its holster. She might be losing it, lowering her guard in front of a proven psycho, but it felt like the right thing to do. "You, on the other hand, are anything but noble."

"True." He stood and headed for the door. "Do tell Bast I believe he's right, and that we should work together to solve our… *common issue*."

A laugh burst from her lips. "Pigs will fly before he agrees to that."

Corvus frowned as if she'd meant that literally. "It could be arranged."

Damn faeries.

"You killed Stella's mother to spare Bast, didn't you?" Mera asked as he turned the handle.

He gaped at her, shock clear in his pretty features. "I'm surprised my brother shared that *episode* with you. He must trust you a great deal, Detective. But I wouldn't say I—"

"If you hadn't killed her, she would have taken Stella

away, and that would have destroyed Bast. It doesn't excuse what you did, though, and I wish I could bring you to justice," she said point-blank. Yet, the case was cold, and Corvus didn't seem inclined to admit to murder in front of a jury.

"I assumed detectives had exceptional people-reading skills." He chortled with contempt. "Yours are terrible."

Maybe.

Maybe not.

"If what you said is true," she went on, "then you and Bast are battling the same demons. Thing is, he has a way better moral filter than you do." Mera studied him intently; the bewildered stare in his feline eyes, his flared nostrils, his pursed lips. "I wonder if you're jealous of that, or if you want to protect it, somehow. Maybe deep down, in your own twisted way, you care about those you love."

He narrowed his eyes at her, anger swirling in his yellow irises. "Make no mistake, Detective. I hate my brother, and hurting him is my favorite past time."

"Yeah, he hates you too." She let out a weary sigh. "Yet, you keep trying to reach out to him for all the wrong reasons, and perhaps, the only right one." She let the words linger in the air, the way the first winter snow fell to land.

A muscle ticked in his jaw.

"You're a *sarking* fool." Corvus pulled the door open so harshly, he nearly snapped the hinges out of place. "If Bast refuses my offer, I'll still find the culprit before you do. Thing is, I'll help him escape."

"*If* he's related to you, right?" she corrected. "Don't worry. Whatever you do, your insanity plea will never stick. Besides, you're still our main suspect."

"I suppose there's that as well." Corvus gave her a sideways grin filled with bitterness. "Perhaps I *am* the murderer, Detective, and you just let me walk away."

CHAPTER 15

BAST STOOD in the living room, his body a statue as he watched the night outside through the window.

Gentle faerie lights outlined his form, and a few even ventured inside the space, drenching the living room in a silver twilight. Mera couldn't help but feel like she was immersed in a dreamscape.

Sitting on the sofa, she stated the obvious. "You're angry."

"No," he countered without turning to her, his tone eerily controlled. "I'm perfectly fine."

Yeah, right.

She might never understand the complexity of her partner's layers, but of this she was certain: Bast was furious, and not because his visit to Charles Grey had been a total waste of time.

Corvus. It was always about Corvus.

Mera got up from the sofa and went to him, pulling Bast slightly back so he would face her. Her partner kept his arms crossed, his anger awfully contained. His eyes, though... they were freezing cold.

Nightblood, the thought came to mind.

Yattusei.

Mera placed her palm on his chest, ignoring the grim sensation that nestled in her gut. "Your brother didn't hurt me."

"He could have."

"Then I would have defended myself."

"Like you defended yourself at the palace?" he snapped back without a hint of emotion, his tone a sharp blade that cut her to pieces.

"I was caught off guard, you *baku*. Your endless fighting with Corvus was driving me insane." Mera rubbed her forehead. Getting into an argument with him was counterproductive, even if she reeeeally wanted to. "Bast, you're a great faerie and an amazing detective, but until you face the truth about your brother, you'll never move on from this mess."

Raising one dark eyebrow at her, he leaned his head slightly forward. "Tell me this *truth* I'm failing to see, then."

With a deep breath, she gathered all her courage. "You and Corvus might be more similar than you'll ever admit."

The way he glared at her, with pain and fury mixed together... it broke her heart, but Mera wouldn't apologize for speaking the truth.

"I'll ignore what you just said." Spinning on his heels, Bast ran a hand through his hair. "You were in grave danger, Mera. How can't you see that?"

"You mean because of Corvus or the nightblood?"

"Both!"

She shrugged. "Blood is blood in the dance of the macabre."

"It's not that. Get this in your head: you can't trust him."

"I can't trust you either." Hurt invaded his face, so she quickly added, "When it comes to your brothers, that is."

Bast scowled at her, but Mera found a hint of agreement in his face. As if he saw her point, though he'd never admit to it. Either that, or Corvus was right—her people-reading skills sucked.

"What are you trying to imply?" he challenged.

Shit, he was forcing her to say it.

"This whole situation is extremely personal for you." Mera's throat squeezed itself, but she couldn't back down now. "Let me take the reins on this case, partner."

He stared at her with undecipherable blue eyes, that nonchalant frost back on his perfect face. "You think you know me so well, *Detective*."

She laid a hand on his shoulder, physically trying to reach for Bast because her words clearly couldn't. "It's difficult keeping a clear head when there's bad blood in the family. I learned this from experience."

He stepped closer, his presence looming over her, and if Mera didn't know better, she would have been afraid.

No, *terrified*.

Dipping his head, he leaned into her ear. "I'm sure you do, *akritana*. After all, something horrible must've happened to force you into the continent, where your kind is killed on the spot *if* they survive passing through the protection zone. Which they never do. Tell me, how did you do it? What's so special about you, Mera Maurea, if that's your real name?"

An ice dagger to the heart had to feel better than that. Tears gathered in her eyes, but she refused to let them out.

His reaction proved her point, though.

"Bast, you're too close to this," she repeated quietly, sniffing back her unshed tears. "It's stirring *something* inside you. Push me away all you want, but you're still my partner, and I *will* look after you."

Blinking, Bast shook his head and stepped back, his eyes wide with shock. "Kitten, I'm sorry. I..."

Her palm lifted, stopping him. "I don't care. We're here to

do our job, so keep that damn darkness, nightblood, or whatever it is, in check. I'm going to my room."

She turned to leave, but he grabbed her wrist and pulled her to him, slamming Mera against his chest. Bast cupped her cheeks before she could pull away, and then she didn't want to leave him anymore.

Poseidon in the trenches, his lips were incredibly close. If she stood on the tips of her toes…

"I'm sorry." He rested his forehead on hers. "I'm so very sorry. And you're right, I can't see this case clearly. I'm fucking grateful I have you by my side, kitten, you have to believe me."

They stood like that for a while, in silence. Just the two of them, until Mera took a deep breath and gently put her hands atop his wrists. "My last name used to be Wavestorm."

His jaw dropped. "As in from the royal line?"

She nodded.

"Who could've guessed it?" He brushed her bottom lip gently with his thumb, his focus razor-sharp upon her mouth. "We're both stray royals."

Mera never thought of it that way, but yeah. They were.

"I'll try to keep my temper under control, partner." He kissed the top of her head, then let her go.

'What?' her siren whined. *'Come back!'*

Not the time, Mera told that horny bastard, even if she also ached for his touch. *Not a good idea, either.*

"Let's get some rest." Turning around, Bast went to his room. "We have a big day tomorrow."

It started with a crown and it belonged to her mommy.

Mera observed the piece, which rested atop Queen Ariella's head. The crown had a gentle glow to it, like that of the moon reflecting on the ocean's surface during perfectly clear nights.

"Watch it all you want, merling," the queen said without glancing down at Mera, her russet curls floating lazily around her. "It will never be yours."

Mera frowned. She didn't want that silly crown. Sure, it was pretty, but it seemed heavy and spiky.

'That's not Mother's crown,' a distant voice reminded her. 'It used to be filled with beads and adornments, but it was never thorn-shaped.'

Where had Mera seen that crown, then?

Watching her tiny, chubby hands, she giggled. She didn't know why, she just did. Mera turned to Mommy, who towered over her, and hoped she would also laugh, but Mommy never did.

Ever.

Mother. Mera had to call her Mother. The queen got upset when she called her Mommy.

They were floating atop the sandy ocean floor, amongst a crowd of waterbreakers who stared ahead. Mera could barely see what was happening because her arms and legs weren't strong enough to propel her up for long, and she hadn't mastered waterbreaking like the older kids yet.

Turning to her Mommy, Mera noticed she looked annoyed.

No, she looked angry.

A freezing cold tip-toed down Mera's spine. Nothing good happened when Mommy was angry.

"Here you go, little one." Uncle Barrimond grabbed Mera from behind, and lifted her so she could watch.

Ahead, under an arch of colorful corals, a priest floated behind two waterbreakers.

The first was Professor Currenter. He looked dapper in his white bodysuit and golden corals. His faded-yellow hair was held in the usual tight bun behind his head.

Mister Maelstrom, one of the staff from school, dressed the

same way—only his corals were silver. Taking the professor's hand, he smiled sweetly.

Mera clapped her little palms in excitement, which was pointless, but it'd come more out of instinct than anything else. Professor Currenter clapped when he was happy, and he'd shown her how to do it. He claimed it was a remnant of his time on the surface, back when waterbreakers had their own place on land—he called it a 'borough'.

"I claim you, Harold Currenter," Mister Maelstrom pronounced loudly, "I claim you through the seven seas. I claim you under the forever sky, and the endless blue."

Professor Currenter caressed his cheek. "I claim you, Yuri Maelstrom. I claim you through the shallows and the deeps. I claim you under the tides, and the currents, and the storms."

Mera didn't know happiness herself, doubted she would ever feel it, but she'd seen it in others. Professor Currenter and Mister Maelstrom were so, so happy...

She wished Mommy—Mother—could be that joyful one day. That she could treat Mera with the same kindness Professor Currenter did, but when she turned to the queen, she nearly screamed.

Instead of her mother, a rotting corpse glared at her.

Mera could see the tendons through the gap on her left cheek, and the dark inside the empty socket where her right eye should've been. Three of her ribs showed behind her tattered bodysuit and flesh, and half of her right arm was nothing but bones.

The queen smiled wickedly at Mera, enough that she could see all her teeth and parts of her jaw. She snatched Mera's puffy cheeks with her right hand, her bones icy against her skin.

"Regneerik is coming, merling." Her cracked and hissing voice didn't belong to living things. The queen grinned wider, stretching the skin left on her face. "You're not ready."

Mera's heart beat faster as horror crawled down her spine. She was about to scream when someone beat her to it.

The bellows came from a distance. Mother disappeared, along with Professor Currenter and the rest of the waterbreakers around them.

Only the screams and the ocean remained.

Mera frowned, trying to recognize the sound.

That voice... she knew who it belonged to...

Bast!

CHAPTER 16

WITH A GASP, she jolted awake. Her brain hadn't fully caught up, but Mera was already jumping off the bed.

She'd been dreaming before, but she couldn't remember about what... something with corals and corpses.

It didn't matter. Bast was in danger.

"Corvus!" he yelled from inside his room. "Don't!"

Mera's heart thrashed in her chest as she rushed through the living room. Poseidon in the trenches, if Corvus hurt Bast, she would explode that bastard from the inside out without a second thought. Let him have a taste of the macabre.

"Bast!" She slammed the door open to find him writhing on the mattress.

He was utterly alone.

"I'll fucking kill you!" Bast kicked his blanket away, showcasing a strong naked chest peppered with glowing blue dust and sweat. As if his body was the night sky reflected in a pond.

'Why is he wearing black boxers?' the siren grumbled in disappointment.

"Stella, don't watch!" he cried.

Rushing to him, Mera climbed on the bed and put a hand over his forehead. "Shh, it's okay."

Bast shook his head left and right, his fingers digging deep into the mattress.

"It's okay." Her waterbreaker glamour flowed into her words, diving into his skin. "You're safe."

"I killed them," he mumbled as his breathing slowly steadied. "I killed them all." Eventually, his body stilled, and he exhaled deeply. "Death and darkness."

He stayed still, quiet for a while, his sweat clammy against her palm, but Mera didn't move. She didn't want to wake him. Instead, she studied the glowing specks across the bridge of his nose, the perfect curve of his lips.

Fixing a strand of damp silver hair off his face, she smiled. "I'm here, partner."

With her voice, Bast blinked awake slowly, until he was staring at Mera with puzzled blue eyes which matched the glow on his skin.

"Kitten?"

"You were having a nightmare." She caressed his cheek before realizing how inappropriate it was. Pulling her hand back, she cleared her throat. "You okay?"

His gaze locked on hers, like heavy chains that wouldn't release her. "I don't think I am." An easy grin spread on his face. "I might need some company tonight."

She slapped his very naked, very sweaty, chest. "Smartass."

She attempted to stand from the bed, but he held her wrist.

"Stay? Just for a while?" Scooting over to the left, he patted the empty space beside him.

That was a bad, bad idea, but Mera was already lying on her back and staring at the ceiling, scared shitless of what they might do—and at the same time, hoping madly that it would happen.

Her siren fanned herself, and she couldn't hold still.

'This is it,' she cheered. *'This is the moment we've been waiting for!'*

Leaning on his elbow, Bast observed Mera, his eyes curious and kind. There were no walls between them as they looked at each other.

"Tell me about Mera Wavestorm," he asked carefully.

Turning back to the ceiling, she swallowed dry. Mera was expecting a world of things, but not that. Then again, Bast had told her everything about Stella and his brothers. What Corvus had done, the countless lives Bast himself had taken in the League's name... He'd even told her how Theo, the monk, used to read him stories late at night, and how once, Bast and Ben pranked their Father so badly, that they got sent to the dungeons for a week.

He told her things that build a picture of his past; things that mattered.

Repaying the favor was only fair.

"My mother abused me constantly," she began, not knowing exactly where that would lead. "The things she forced me to do; the things she did to me, to her own people... at one point, I snapped." Mera turned to him as a familiar sorrow and regret knotted in her throat, but she swallowed them back. Over the years, she'd become an expert at it. "Like you, I was too young when I had my first kill."

Bast nodded, but didn't say a thing.

"I speared a trident into my own mother, then fled Atlantea with her body," Mera went on. "I assumed the magic inside the forbidden zone would've ended me. I was only thirteen, and ready to die, Bast."

A pair of tears escaped her eyes, but he wiped them with his thumb.

Against Mera's better judgement—and Ruth's advice to trust no one—she continued.

She told him about Professor Currenter and Belinda Tiderider. About the horrors Mother had inflicted upon her own people. Mera told him she'd been banished from Atlantea, and that she'd gone on a suicide mission to bury the queen in shame. How Ruth had found her, dazed and lost while walking on a beach.

The Cap had given Mera her last name and a new life.

Mera told him how Ruth protected her, even when the law said she should've shot Mera in the head. It was why Mera joined the force when she'd come of age, actually.

Sure, she wanted to protect and serve, but she also wanted to make the woman who'd saved her, who'd given her life back, proud.

In silence, Bast listened to all of it.

When Mera was done, she nervously cleared her throat. "That's it, basically." Taking a deep breath, she faced the ceiling again, not bearing to look directly at him anymore. "I never told my story to anyone other than Ruth."

"Thank you." He caressed her cheek. "I never imagined we had so much in common. You used to be a princess, and you also knew hate and pain at a young age." He played with a strand of her hair, his blue eyes fixed on it with a certain wonder. "Don't you find it remarkable we were assigned to each other?"

Now that she thought of it, yes.

"It was a huge coincidence," she admitted.

Dropping his head on the pillow, he watched her lazily. "Theo says that when we're born, Danu ties a golden string around our little fingers. It connects us to who we're destined to be with."

Panic suddenly took over her, but she masked it with nonchalance. "Your point, Detective?"

'We know his point,' her siren whispered.

Chuckling low in his chest, Bast blinked slowly, his tone drawling with sleep. "I'm certain my golden string leads to you."

He scooted closer, then turned Mera on her side, spooning her.

"W-what the hell—"

Nuzzling the curve of her neck, he kissed her bare shoulder. "Stay?"

Mera's heart might have beaten out of her sternum. She swallowed dry as a cold sweat broke on her skin, until finally, she gathered enough courage to speak. "It's not appropriate for me to stay, Bast. We're partners."

Yet, he was already breathing heavily behind her, his arm limp around her waist.

Damn it.

She should go.

'We don't want to wake him, do we?' her siren whispered.

For once, that asshole was right. Besides, Bast seemed so peaceful, his body so warm against hers... maybe she should stay in case he had another nightmare.

Sleep slowly washed over Mera, and soon her muscles relaxed.

She couldn't tell exactly when she'd drifted into a peaceful slumber, but she did dream of golden strings.

CHAPTER 17

Mera had hoped questioning the palace's servants would have led them somewhere, but the first day of interrogations was a total bust.

The faeries working in the mailroom claimed the chocolate box had disappeared before they could deliver it to the king. They also said they hadn't seen anyone suspicious sneaking around the palace, not at the time of the murder or recently. Which meant either the killer was stealthy, or a familiar face.

Her partner might be right. Maybe one of his brothers had done it.

Bast and Mera had spent an entire day asking the servants the same set of questions—*How long have you been working here? Did you see anything suspicious around the day of the murder? Anyone with a white box?*

She'd expected at least a small clue, but the case was getting colder than the artic.

Today, they'd began the last batch of interrogations. Their first witness, the cook, didn't shed any light into the murder, same as the rest of the servants. Their second witness, a

Rheina Warlow, was a trembling, elderly fae who gaped at Bast as if he was death itself.

Rheina had pale, wrinkled skin and dark hair—an uncommon look for a nightling, but not incredibly rare. Mera asked her several questions, but Rheina barely unclenched her jaw to answer. Instead, she kept staring at Bast with utter terror, her hands quivering.

Her partner leaned closer to Mera's ear. "She's never been my biggest fan. I'm only getting in your way, partner, so it's time to grab those reins you talked about." He tapped his legs and stood. "Meet me at the gardens when you're done."

With that, he left.

The elderly fae exhaled in relief once the door clicked shut.

"I apologize," Rheina said in a raspy tone. "But I was there when he decapitated the assassin sent for the wolf girl. *Yattusei* was a youngling, and he murdered a grown fae like it was nothing. Nothing, I tell you." Rheina's milky eyes glistened. "I was relieved when the king disowned him, and he had to move away. That child scares me."

"Detective Dhay was protecting his sister. It's what his father should've done, instead of ordering her death." Mera kept her tone poised and calm, hoping it would hide her annoyance.

Huffing, the old fae raised her chin. "The wolf is not his sister. She's a dirty bastard who should be resting under the earth."

Mera wanted to slap Rheina in her cold, merciless face, but that would count as police brutality *and* elderly abuse in one strike.

"You have no reason to fear Detective Dhay," she assured with remarkable poise.

"If you believe that, it's already too late for you." Rheina pointed at the door. "He has the mad queen's curse. I'm sure of it."

"That's quite enough," Mera snapped.

This bitter, wrinkled fae hated and feared Bast just for protecting his little sister. Mera wanted to tell Rheina to fuck off, but she had a job to do. Biting back her tongue, she turned to the questionnaire in her notebook. "Did you see anyone carrying a white box around the palace near the time of the king's death?"

"No," Rheina answered point-blank.

Mera's gut-feeling blared with red warning signs.

Something was off.

"Are you sure?" Leaning forward, she pushed her siren's glamour into her tone. "Try a little harder for me, will you?"

Rheina immediately frowned, which highlighted the wrinkles in her pale face. Her head went red, veins bulging under her skin as she fought against herself. After a long while, her lips trembled, certainly because she tried to keep the answer from her.

"Go on," Mera pushed, adding a final spark of glamour to the command. "I can see you are conflicted."

A lie, but also a perfect excuse to hide Mera's glamour.

"Well, now that you mention it..." the old fae swallowed, sweat beading atop her puckered lips. "I might have seen Theodore Dhay with a white box, heading toward the throne room." She inhaled deeply, a certain relief washing over her. "I thought it might have been an offering from Danu. I suppose I was wrong."

Rushing out of the room, Mera headed to the gardens to find Bast leaning over the marbled railing of the palace's outer porch.

He watched the vast garden ahead, with its exotic flowers of a thousand colors and sizes that decorated the lush green. Birds chirped in the distance as a soft wind played with the free threads of Bast's loose bun.

He looked... peaceful.

Mera's chest shrunk to a dot. How could she tell him he was right? That the murderer was indeed one of his brothers, just not the brother he'd hoped?

Stepping beside him, she leaned her elbows on the rails. "What's up, partner?"

"Nothing much... I just wish Leon had used our mind link to warn me Father had died. Maybe if he had, this case wouldn't be getting so cold."

"I guess he wanted to protect you. He has a severe case of older brother syndrome, doesn't he?"

Bast chuckled. "He really does. Or maybe, he assumed I wouldn't care about Father's death."

"Do you? Care, I mean?"

He seemed to consider it for a split second. "Not really, no."

"Then Leon knows you better than you think."

"He always has." Bast observed the gardens in silence, until eventually, he let out a weary sigh. "The past days have been a monumental waste of time. At least we have a nice view." He nodded to beyond the gardens, toward the rest of Lunor Insul, the ocean, and the continent in the far distance.

She put a hand atop his, her heart breaking. "It's pretty wonderful."

Mera's job had many unpleasantries, but telling Bast about Theodore, the brother who read him stories late at night when he was young, the brother who was a freaking monk... well, it might top them all.

Studying her hand, Bast intertwined his fingers with hers. "I never thanked you, did I?"

"For what?"

"Sticking around."

Guilt weighted on her, but before she could tell him the truth, he continued. "I'm aware you asked your Cap to reassign you after... "

... the bloodbath at the Summer King's penthouse.

Mera blinked. "How did you—"

"Before we left for Lunor Insul, Ruth told me that if you asked her to be reassigned again, she would grab a pair of scissors and cut my manhood into a thousand tiny pieces. She said *'that ought to teach me'.*"

Mera flushed furiously, her cheeks burning. Clearing her throat, she let out a nervous laugh. "You know she would do it, right?"

"Absolutely." He chuckled. "I assured her we weren't involved romantically, though we technically shared a sex dream." He winked at Mera, never letting go of her hand. "I don't think your Captain bought it."

"Yeah. Ruth's smart like that."

They stayed that way for a while, their hands intertwined, their gazes locked. Mera then studied his fingers, wondering how she could give him the news.

Poseidon in the trenches, why was this so hard?

"I'm glad you're still my partner," she stated quietly.

"Do all partners sleep with each other, though?"

She swallowed wrong and coughed, her throat scratching and her eyes watering. "We didn't!" she countered through the violent fit.

"Don't get me wrong, kitten. I enjoyed sleeping with you the other night." He nudged her shoulder with his while she coughed like a motherfucker and her cheeks caught on freaking fire. "I wish we could have an encore, actually."

Patting her own chest, Mera tried to recompose, her coughs slowly waning. "Okay, technically we slept together."

She thought twice about it. "But we didn't *sleep-sleep* together."

He frowned at her with amusement. "That's what I meant, though I'm not against what went through your mind just now."

Sneaky, damn faerie.

"You snore, *malachai*," Mera snapped.

Bast's busty laughs danced around her, a carefree sound that brought a smile to her face. Raising one eyebrow, he leaned closer. "Newsflash, you snore too, kitten."

"Fine, but no more about golden strings and sleeping in the same bed." Her siren raged in complaint, but Mera ignored her. "We have enough on our plate. Besides, we're partners."

He shrugged nonchalantly. "Can't make any promises."

Slapping his shoulder playfully, she carved his beaming smile in her memory. Mera might not see it again for a while.

"Bast, I have to tell you something." There wasn't a good way to do it, nor a right time, so she went ahead. She had to. "One of the servants saw Theodore carrying a white box to the throne room."

Bast's nostrils flared and he let go of her hand. "Not possible. It was Corvus."

"Bast—"

"No!" He slammed his palm over the marbled railing, his canines growing sharper. "This is not... it can't be. Agh!" Stepping back, he slammed both hands on his head, bending over. "*Fuchst ach!*" he bellowed in pain.

"Bast!" Mera didn't know what to say or do. Despair squeezed her lungs, stealing her breath. "What's going on?"

"It's Leon! Aaagh!"

Bast screamed until suddenly he snapped his spine straight, his chest heaving up and down. His wide eyes turned into pitch-black orbs. "Leon is in pain."

CHAPTER 18

THEY BURST into the throne room to find Leon and Benedict at the far end, near the dais with the ivory throne. The two brothers stood over something lying on the floor.

Bast sighed in relief, his attention locked on his older brother.

"Leon is all right," he muttered to himself as the pitch-black in his eyes vanished. "He's all right."

Their harsh steps tapped against the vast marbled hall as they hurried toward the dais. Yet, as she and Bast approached, Mera realized that Leon and Benedict were standing near a body.

A pool of wine-colored blood that neared black spread underneath the victim, drenching Leon and Benedict's shoes; so much blood in fact, that it became clear this was a murder scene.

The dead fae wore a long white robe, with a golden string wrapped around his waist. The same robe from Danu's followers.

"No!" Bast boosted toward the body, his voice cracking into a thousand pieces. "Theo!"

Mera tried to follow him, but he was remarkably fast.

Leon promptly turned and caught her partner midway, swinging Bast away before he could reach the monk's body.

"Let me go!" Bast yelled, pushing against his older brother, and stretching his hand toward the victim.

Leon was stronger, and he wouldn't let him pass, even if tears streamed down his cheeks, and his bulky arms trembled.

It was odd seeing such a big and strong fae so vulnerable, yet Leon wasn't just a brother to them.

He was their surrogate father.

"He's gone," Leon croaked. "He's with Danu now."

A world of sorrow crashed into Mera's chest as she witnessed the scene ahead, but she had to focus. She had to bring Theodore's murderer to justice, if only to make them pay for causing Bast so much pain.

Benedict stood near his twin's body, watching the dead monk in complete shock. As if half of him was there and the other half wasn't, a behavior awfully similar to his mother's.

Thankfully, Seraphina Dhay wasn't there.

Mera's heart tightened as she gave out the first order. "Leon, Benedict. Step away from the body."

At that moment, they were her main suspects.

Leon quickly obliged, dragging a thrashing and screaming Bast with him, but Benedict simply stood there, watching his brother. Getting a reaction from him might be an impossible task.

"We didn't do it," Leon assured, sniffing back his tears as he held down Bast.

"That might be true, but I still need to investigate." Stepping closer, Mera repeated her order to Benedict, but he didn't react.

Well, she had to go ahead and hope he wouldn't be a

threat. The fact Benedict resembled more a coma patient than a potential murderer certainly helped put her at ease.

The victim's dark-gray hair and white robe were sticky with his own blood. Theodore stared lifelessly at the ceiling, his mouth slightly open as if he'd passed between one breath and another.

"*Halle!*" Finally pushing himself away from Leon, Bast spun in a circle. His hands shook, and his lips trembled as if he was holding down the ugliest of cries. "*Halle fuchst ach!*"

He rushed toward Mera, but she raised her hand, stopping him in his tracks. "Stay with your brother."

Bast blinked, as if coming to himself. Taking a series of steadying breaths, he lowered his shoulders. "I'm fine. I can do my job."

"Sit this one out, partner. That's an order."

"Bast, please..." Leon cried. "I tried to protect my family. I... I failed." His voice broke as he burst into ugly sobs. "Forgive me."

Bast gave Mera one last lingering glance before going to his big brother. She couldn't tell if he was pissed or grateful. Probably pissed.

Well, tough luck.

Her mouth opened to ask Benedict to move away one last time, but she decided it was pointless. So Mera kneeled close to the body with him standing beside her.

He didn't move, didn't speak. He simply stared.

Theodore's massive bleeding had been caused by a sharp cut across his carotid artery. Mera had seen enough death to know that Theodore's had been merciful. People who survived these types of wounds, as few as there were, reported it being akin to falling asleep.

Whoever had done this cared for the monk. Which didn't look good for Leon and Benedict, her prime suspects.

At all.

Mera focused on what she knew. Rheina Warlow had seen Theodore taking the chocolate box to the throne room. And now he was dead.

Scenario number one: He was both a monk and a murderer, which constructed one of the most mind-boggling profiles in her career, but Mera couldn't discard it. If Theo was indeed the Night King's killer, then someone must've found out and decided to take justice in their own hands.

Scenario number two, the more likely one: Theodore had carried the box without being aware of its contents. When Bast and Mera proved the chocolates had been poisoned, the monk realized that whoever gave him the box was the murderer. And instead of informing Bast and Mera, he decided to talk to the killer first.

A mistake that cost him his life.

Rubbing her forehead, she sighed. Mera hated to admit it, but Bast and Corvus were right.

Someone in the royal family might be responsible for this killing spree.

To cross out scenario number one, she would have to ask Rheina if she'd told anyone else about seeing Theodore. Not probable, since the old fae had tried to cover for him before, but Mera had to be sure.

Removing a handkerchief from her pocket, she covered her palm before closing Theodore's eyes. After that, she touched his forehead.

Still warm.

"Kitten," Bast called out.

His gaze held a world of grief and anger, but he didn't shed a tear for his brother. Neither did Benedict, but to his own credit, he couldn't do much in his state. Her partner pointed to the monk's left hand. "He is... *was* clutching something."

Mera opened Theodore's palm. His fingers revealed a silver necklace with a pendant shaped like a half-moon. Gingerly grabbing it with the handkerchief, Mera raised it higher.

Poseidon in the trenches...

Bast's fists balled, his nostrils flaring. "I fucking knew it!"

Leon shook his head in denial, but he couldn't argue with what the evidence showed. No one could.

Corvus had been there.

The CSI team arrived a few hours after Mera's call. Since they were Sidhe, they'd flown from Tir Na Nog to Lunor Insul upon her request.

The faeries documented every inch of the crime scene, tagged the body for analysis in the continent, then checked Benedict and Leon for traces of blood and DNA, which they were cleared of. Sure, they'd stepped on Theodore's night-blood, but so had Mera when she'd analyzed his wound—reaching for the body without leaving a mark on the floor had been impossible.

Too much blood.

Slashing Theodore's carotid without getting a spray of dark red on them would have been impossible, which meant the two Dhays weren't her main suspects anymore. Not a big surprise, considering Theodore had died holding Corvus' pendant.

Their testimonies didn't shed any light into the murder, however.

Leon had felt something was off with his brother through their mind link, but when he arrived, Theodore was already dead.

This was when Bast felt his older brother's pain.

Benedict, on the other hand, simply knew the monk was in danger. *"Twin bond or bad omen, Detective. Call it what you will,"* he'd stated once he'd managed to recompose. But like Leon, Ben had arrived too late.

To make things worse, there was no sign of a murder weapon anywhere.

Giving out a wary sigh, Mera noticed one of the fae on the CSI team staring at her. She wondered if she had something on her face, when the Sidhe approached—autumn court by the burning red hair, same as Captain Asherath's.

"Thank you for your service," he offered, bowing his head. "What you and detective Dhay did in Tir Na Nog was extraordinary." Looking back at his team, he smiled. "The light courts are abiding to the law now, most of the time at least. I can finally trust my colleagues, because our precinct is clean. You've helped change our borough in a way we never thought possible."

"Thank you," she said, feeling awfully undeserving. Leaning forward, Mera focused on his name tag. "Redford, right? Detective Dhay spoke highly of you when we were working the Summer King's murder. You were the only one he trusted in analysis back in the old days."

Old days that weren't so old at all.

He nodded, surprise and delight beaming behind his brown irises.

"It's not all on us, though," she went on. "If it weren't for good fae willing to fight for Hollowcliff and Tagrad, fae like you, cleaning Tir Na Nog would have been impossible."

"You're too kind, Detective Maurea." A certain grief flashed past his eyes. "Tell Sebastian I'm truly sorry for what's happening with his family, but if there's anyone who can crack this case, it's the both of you." His chest puffed with pride. "Hollowcliff's finest."

Someone called for Redford at the back of the room, and he excused himself.

His team bagged Theodore with care and a world of respect; a gesture that Mera truly appreciated. She was certain Bast would too, but he was long gone by then—when she'd asked if he wanted to stay, he told her he had a murderer to catch.

Meanwhile, Benedict had shut himself in his room, and Leon was preparing to deliver the news to their mother.

"We will return the body in time for the burying rituals," one of the fae in Redford's team assured before bowing to Mera. He then left her alone with the stretcher and Theodore's body for one last moment before their departure.

Unzipping the top of the leather bag, she studied Theodore's face. He looked peaceful, except for the dried stains of nightblood peppering his cheeks.

If only he could tell her who'd ended his life...

"I'll do my best to get you justice," she promised.

Zipping the body bag shut again, Mera placed her hand atop his head. Faeries had verses they spoke when honoring their dead; she'd learned them back in school. Bast's trick to unleash her Faeish might have brought back the words, somehow.

"May you rejoice in Danu's prairies and feast on her blessings," Mera muttered. "May the beloved you leave behind never forget you. Until the day we meet again."

That was all she could give him for now. Justice would follow later, even if it was the last thing she did.

Once Redford's team was ready, they left with the monk. Mera watched them go, a prickling sensation stabbing her chest.

If she had arrested Corvus when he'd visited her at the precinct, Theodore might still be alive.

~

Bast paced around the precinct by the time she returned at night.

Dropping on the old couch, Mera rubbed her forehead. "Redford says hello."

"Hmm," he grumbled mindlessly. "Corvus is on the run. I've searched for him everywhere."

Her gut told her they were missing something. That the answer wasn't as easy as Bast—and logic—wanted it to be.

"Doesn't it feel a bit too... odd?" she prodded, not knowing exactly what might be odd about it.

"Not if you know Corvus," he countered through clenched teeth.

There was no arguing with her partner, at least for now, which was perfectly understandable. So Mera changed the subject. "I glamoured Rheina once more before coming here. She didn't tell anyone else about seeing Theodore with the box."

"Of course. Corvus killed my father, and when Theo confronted him, the *malachai* ended him in cold blood." Shaking his head, he crossed his arms. "I should have slit his throat when he poisoned you with enchanted wine. None of this would have happened if I'd just..." he stopped himself.

If he'd just what?

Let the nightblood take over? Murdered his own brother?

He couldn't really mean that.

She studied Bast and the monumental loss burdening his eyes; a loss he kept tightly locked within his thousand walls.

"When I killed my mother, I sobbed." Mera wearily stood, going to him. "My brain refused to mourn her, but my heart did, even if she didn't deserve it. It sounds stupid, but a part of me wished we'd had a second chance. That if I'd seen past her rage and hate, things would have been different."

Bast frowned at her with annoyance. He must have guessed her point.

"I'm mourning Theodore in my own way. The thing is, I didn't know him enough. He went to the monastery when I was young, and he did visit us, but after I went to the mainland, we never saw or contacted each other again. Same with Ben..." His voice faded.

"You *knew* him," she countered. "The problem is that you'll never get the chance to know him more."

"We're not the same, Mera. The monk is dead. No use in crying over it, is there?"

Oh, Bast was calling her by her name. He only did that when he was horny or furious.

"That's awfully cold," she noted.

"It's life."

Stepping closer, she hugged him, pressing her forehead against his chest. Mera wished she could take all his pain and fling it far, far away... "I'm really sorry, Bast. Theodore seemed to be good and kind. I'm sorry you never got to say goodbye."

She could feel him swallowing dry, his muscles clenched, his heart beating fiercely. His hands hovered in the air as if he couldn't decide if he should hug her back or push her away.

"I knew Theo," he admitted quietly. "He read me stories late at night, and prayed to Danu for my safety."

Mera kept hugging him.

"I'm fine, kitten," his voice cracked, and he cleared his throat. "Thanks for being here. You can let go now."

She didn't.

Sighing in defeat, he wrapped his arms around her, his fingers clawing at her skin. "The last thing I told him was to shut up." His back heaved with repressed grief. "Theo was the kindest of us, and I snapped at him. He didn't deserve it, Mera."

"It's okay. I'm here, partner."

Bast buried his face at the curve of her neck, and for the first time since they'd met, Sebastian Dhay allowed himself to cry.

CHAPTER 19

LEON'S CORONATION, which had been scheduled for the night after Theodore's death, was postponed for five days. The future king declared a period of mourning, only to be lifted when he rose to the throne.

Back in the mainland, Redford worked quickly. He sent back Theodore's body within forty-eight hours, which was remarkable to say the least.

The burial happened on the same day the monk returned to Lunor Insul, on a clearing near the top of the tallest mountain, not far from the palace. His family set Theodore atop a wooden pyre, filling his resting bed with white flowers that matched his burial robe.

It was a small, and quiet ceremony that broke Mera's heart.

With a torch, Leon stepped forward and set the pyre on fire, his eyes glistening with tears. As flames engulfed the monk, he cried, Seraphina sobbed, Benedict... he merely stared, as if he couldn't believe his brother was dead. And Bast? He carried the weight of it all on his shoulders, utterly in silence.

They weren't alone in their sorrow, however. The entire island mourned the royal family's loss.

On the western side, tourists crammed flowers underneath a wooden statue carved with the Night Court's crest. On the eastern side, nightlings paid their respects by lighting thousands of rice-paper lanterns on the first night after Theodore's burial.

The lanterns drifted into the sky, floating past the faerie lights, until they mingled with the stars. A symbolic gesture, Bast explained as Mera stared in awe, that was meant to represent all the souls guiding Theodore into Danu's realms.

They'd remained in silence until the last lantern disappeared into the dark, and even then, Bast kept staring into the sky with his hands in his pockets and a mask on his face. A mask that hid his monumental sorrow.

Meanwhile, Corvus had disappeared into thin air.

On the second day of mourning, Mera stared at her laptop, waiting impatiently for Redford's e-mail with the results of the body's analysis, which according to him, were on the way.

Maybe the coroner's report would shed some light into Theodore's last moments; maybe it would help them bring his killer to justice.

The wifi connection in Lunor Insul was dreadful, however. Rolling her eyes, Mera slouched over the table.

Why couldn't faeries fully embrace technology?

Sighing, she watched the looping circle, until finally, a ping. She eagerly clicked the e-mail open and went through the report.

"Hmm, odd," she mumbled.

Bast, who studied the same files from across the table, didn't respond at first.

The precinct had a laptop, miracle of miracles, and he knew how to run the basics, which didn't come as a surprise, since filing reports in the system was a requirement for every Hollowcliff detective, fae or not. Still, it felt odd seeing him handle technology. It always did.

After reading through the file in silence, he took a sip from a glass of water next to him. "You need to be more precise, kitten."

She opened her mouth to speak, but thought twice. Corvus' fingerprints had been found around the victim's neck, stamped in Theodore's nightblood. By the hands' positioning and the amount of pressure exerted, the coroner deducted Corvus had tried to choke the monk.

Telling this to Bast didn't feel right.

Choking a fae with a slashed throat was not just overkill but a cruel thing to do. Not to mention that both killer and victim were his freaking brothers.

Well, Bast had access to the exact same report, so Mera couldn't hide that from him. He'd insisted he was fine, and that working the case would help him get through it, but right then, he must have regretted it.

Closing her laptop, she set it aside. "Your father was poisoned, but Theodore was brutally killed. Two vastly different methods, don't you agree?"

"Corvus is resourceful," he retorted without paying her any attention, his focus on the screen before him. "Stop making excuses for the *shig*."

"I'm not," she lied. "It just seems strange. You have to admit that."

"Nothing is odd when it comes to my brother," he countered drily. "Oh, by the way..." He threw the water from the glass on her chest.

Sure, Mera could have bent the liquid midair, and avoided the mess, but how could she have predicted her prick of a partner would do that out of nowhere?

Her white shirt got soaked.

Forcing a poised tone that masked her rage, she raised one eyebrow. "Sebastian, why the hell did you do that?"

"I was wondering if you could shower without giving away your secret." He laughed with mischief. "I wanted to see if you'd turn into an *akritana*."

Mera tugged at the sticky, wet fabric. "I only turn into a waterbreaker if I'm immersed in sea water, *malachai*."

"Is that so?" His focus lingered on her see-through shirt, particularly on her breasts. As if he wanted to unclip her bra with his stare alone.

Maybe checking if she would turn hadn't been his only motivation...

Bast licked his lips, but suddenly shook his head, as if ridding himself of something. Like impure thoughts, for example.

"Well, now I know." He went on to study the screen as if what he'd done to Mera had been no big deal.

Asshole!

She fumed, but as a detective, she couldn't kill Bast and get away with it.

In theory.

"Did the Sidhe guarding Karthana and Master Raes report any attempt of contact from Corvus?" she asked, though slapping Bast's pretty face felt way more appealing.

"They didn't, but I'd expected that. Corvus is smart. He wouldn't risk it," he said absentmindedly, scanning through the report. "The murder weapon was a curved blade."

"Does that help us?"

"Moon blades fit the description, and every assassin in the league has one. Maybe Master Raes can help." Closing the laptop, he stood. "I'll pay him and Karthana a visit."

Karthana? Why?

"I'll come with you." Mera jumped to her feet at once.

She hated the idea of leaving Bast alone with Karthana.

The fae clearly had feelings for him, even though she was betrothed to Corvus, and no matter how often Mera's partner played it down, he had feelings for *Karthy*, too.

Bast pivoted on his heels, standing in her way. "It's best if I talk to them alone, kitten."

Mera abhorred the sting of petty jealousy, but it pricked her chest nonetheless.

"Yeah, I bet you and Karthana will do a lot of *talking*," she huffed, crossing her arms.

He stepped closer, towering over her, and Mera wished she could pull that smug look from his face.

"I never took you for the jealous type," he said with a naughty grin.

"It's inappropriate, that's all. Then again, so is the fact you're working this case." *Dickwart*. "You do remember your precious *Karthy* is promised to Corvus, right?"

"That murderous prick is going to jail soon, so she's technically available." He licked his lips again as he ate Mera with his eyes, his focus lingering on her soaked breasts.

Warmth shot up her cheeks, and a funny tingling bloomed between her legs.

"Karthana isn't my first choice, of course," he continued. "But you said no funny business between us, so I'm... what do you say in English again? Ah, *branching out*."

"You would seriously sleep with your brother's betrothed?"

Shrugging, he shoved his hands in his pockets. "That would show him, wouldn't it? Besides, as long as she consented to it..."

"You're not that much of an asshole!" At least, Mera hoped he wasn't, though she might be wrong. "Karthana likes you more than you like her. Sleeping with her would be cruel."

"I obviously wouldn't do it. I'm not as cruel as Corvus."

All his humor vanished at once, a certain pain filling his blue gaze. "Though you're right to expect that of me. It's in my blood, after all."

"You're *better* than your blood. Better than Corvus."

"Am I?" he countered quietly, before stepping even closer. Lazily twirling a lock of her hair around his finger, he smiled. "Nightblood makes me want to do wholly inappropriate things sometimes..."

Not the nightblood's fault, buddy.

Of course he was teasing her, being the prick that he was. A hot, strong prick, who smelled of pinewood and smoke, and was standing way too close.

Blinking, Mera cleared her throat. "How about you concentrate on the case, and not your dick?"

"My dick, hmm... about that." Hooking one arm around her waist, Bast pulled her to him, slamming Mera against his chest and his rock-hard erection. "I thoroughly enjoy seeing what jealousy does to you, partner. You look sublime when you're outraged."

"Bast..."

His fierce, looming presence shallowed her breaths. The exchange was entirely wrong, but she didn't pull away.

She didn't want to.

"I *am* focused on the case," he assured her. "But do you understand how hard it is to do my job when you're around? All I want right now is to shove you against that wall and fuck you raw, but that's not how this works, is it?"

'Do it! Please!' her siren begged.

His lips looked so soft... Mera wanted to bite them.

"What do you mean by *'this'*?" she managed, her voice hoarse. *No.* Whatever he'd meant didn't matter. "W-we're partners," Mera said mostly to herself. "The case comes first."

"I need more," he growled, his canines growing sharper.

More? As in connecting the ends of a golden string?

Mera gulped, her nipples hardening under her bra. Even if she fought her most basic instincts, her body betrayed her.

"Couples aren't allowed to be paired as partners." She breathed sharply, the bridge between her legs soaking wet. "If our Captains find out, they'll reassign us."

It was one of the reasons why she'd never attempted anything with her former partner, Julian. Also, he was her best friend.

Shit!

She'd completely forgotten to call him. Julian would be monumentally pissed once they finished the case and she returned to Clifftown.

If she returned. After all, Bast was her partner now, and he was based in Tir Na Nog.

Mera's throat knotted at the possibility of staying in fae territory permanently. Clifftown was her home. She didn't want to abandon it; didn't want to abandon Jules, either.

"You don't understand," Bast whispered, kissing the curve of her jaw. "I'm *painfully* aware we can't be together, and still, you're my first thought in the morning, and my last thought at night." He brushed a lock of hair off her face with his free hand. "I can't have you because your heart is still in Clifftown, and those are the rules of this damn thing. You can't be mine, and I can't be yours halfway."

Was this about Jules?

Bast wasn't making any sense, but it felt like this was about her former partner… somehow?

Screw that. His lips were painfully close; too close. Mera opened her mouth and pressed herself against Bast, forgetting about Clifftown, her duties, and Julian himself.

"You're not making any sense," she breathed, letting the need in her core bloom to the surface. Brushing the light-silver hairs at the nape of his neck, she shrugged lightly. "I'm here, aren't I?"

A mischievous grin cut across his lips. "We could always fuck. As long as our Captains don't find out…"

"That's a terrible idea," Mera lied. Right then, it sounded like the best freaking idea he'd ever had.

"Is it so bad?" Leaning forward, Bast's lips brushed her ear. "Tell me to stop, then." The bastard nibbled her lips with a soft kiss.

Her breathing accelerated as the last shred of common sense left her. Mera should've stepped back and untangled from him. Instead, she leaned forward and kissed him back.

'Yes!' her siren cheered as his tongue invaded Mera's mouth.

She understood how wrong this was. How hooking up with him was the last thing Bast needed after the emotional turmoil he'd gone through recently, yet…

'Perhaps it's exactly what he needs,' her siren argued. *'Some well-deserved release.'*

Mera didn't care if that horny asshole had a point or not. Trapped between Bast's delirious kisses and his throbbing erection, she couldn't think of much else.

His fingers dug into the back of her head, desperately bringing her to him with an insatiable hunger.

Letting her instincts take over, Mera rubbed her nether parts against his crotch and clawed his perfect, hard bum. "You're mine, faerie" she claimed in between heavy kisses that left her breathless.

Bast gulped, his Adam's apple bobbing. "You'll drive me mad, *akritana*." Lifting her by her thighs, he sat her atop the table.

Mera's legs wrapped around his waist, slamming his massive bulge against her entrance. In between hungry, passionate kisses, she unbuttoned his vest, then his formal white shirt. Her leather jacket was already on the floor, her soaked white shirt thrown aside, showing Bast her lacy black bra.

He stopped and watched her for a moment, complete devotion beaming from his burning gaze. "I'm scared of how you make me feel."

That's all he managed to say before his mouth crashed back against her lips.

Expertly, he unbuttoned her pants and one hand plowed beneath the fabric, his finger rubbing against the pebble between her thighs.

"Bast!" Mera gasped, clinging to him.

A chuckle rumbled low in his chest. "You'll come in your pants, Detective."

The vindictive prick!

Bast's fingers were quick and deft, rubbing her effortlessly. Fire built inside Mera and she moaned loudly. "Oh, you *baku*…"

She could curse all she wanted. He wouldn't stop.

His hands… Poseidon in the trenches, his fucking hands!

With each stroke, Mera climbed higher and higher within herself, reaching for her aching release. It astounded her how much she ached for him; how fast she headed toward her climax.

Licking her neck, Bast slid two merciless fingers inside her, and pleasure rushed to her head and limbs. Mera was flying, soaring as her partner kept rubbing and fingering her.

Desire piled inside her, the throbbing delirium too violent for her to hold. "Don't stop!" she yelped, her breaths short and her mind spinning. "By the ancient gods, don't stop!"

He nuzzled her neck. "I have no intention of stopping, my love."

My love…

That was all it took.

Mera's vision went white as she let go and screamed his name, thrashing against him, again and again, each wave of pleasure a tsunami that dragged her under. Her quivering body slowly turned to jelly as her furious orgasms waned.

Fuck, they must've heard her on the freaking moon...

Removing his fingers, Bast showed them to her—they were soaked in her own oils. Sucking them as if savoring a mouth-watering nectar, he moaned, a feverish blush going up his cheeks. "You taste like paradise, Mera."

She stared at him; this fierce force of nature that crashed onto her constantly. Her partner. Her...

Love?

No, Mera couldn't think about that now. They were tangled in good, old-fashioned fucking, nothing more.

Playing with the waist of his pants, she tugged it lower. "I need more, Detective."

"Then more you shall have." He kissed her violently, his tongue claiming her mouth as she unbuttoned his pants and freed *him*.

Her fingers eagerly wrapped around his massive shaft, and Poseidon in the trenches, it might hurt when he plunged into her, but oh, how she looked forward to that.

Mera stroked him gently, and Bast grunted into her mouth, his hands cupping her cheeks as he kissed her harder.

Three harsh knocks slammed on the door outside.

No, no, no!

"*Rae-henai!*" Bast barked at the entrance. "Come back later!"

The knocks became more insistent, until a muffled voice accompanied them. "Please! I need help!"

Grumbling a loud curse, Bast pulled away from Mera and fixed his pants. His hardness made it difficult for him to zip, but it was quickly waning with the interruption.

Mera sighed despondently, her core aching for that part of him inside her.

'Talk about terrible timing,' her siren huffed with frustration.

Bast took a recomposing breath as he finished buttoning his shirt and vest, then fixed his hair. Lifting one index finger at her, he stared at her sternly. "To be continued."

She didn't know how to feel about that.

With desire no longer clouding her judgement, Mera understood how close they'd come to making a monumental mistake. The weight of her recklessness crashed down on her as she put her shirt back on, and buttoned her pants.

In truth, she'd expected this from a loose cannon like Bast, but she should have known better. Ruth had taught her better.

Mera worked with him, for crying out loud! Sleeping together would only complicate things. A lot. She couldn't remember the last time she'd felt so embarrassed.

Bast headed for the door, yanking it open, and nearly breaking it off its hinges. "What?" he barked.

A banshee with red hair and brown skin dashed into the precinct the next second. She wore the palace servants' sleek navy attire, and she was panting while shaking profusely. Her fully white eyes held horror inside.

"Help," she croaked in between rushed breaths. "Please, detectives, attend to the palace at once!"

"What happened?" Mera asked.

This couldn't be good.

Fear and sorrow flashed across the banshee's face. "It's Prince Leon." She took a deep breath. "Someone tried to kill him."

CHAPTER 20

A few weeks ago...

THE EARLY MORNING sun ventured through the window, waking Bast. He inhaled deeply and stretched on the bed, only to realize this wasn't his mattress. Or his sheets. This wasn't his room or apartment, either.

A naked banshee with green skin moved sheepishly on his left, her head propped on his arm, while the Sidhe on his right—Spring Court by her blonde hair and pink skin—still dragged through her slumber.

Smiling lazily, he wondered if they'd mind if he woke them for another round. After all, his cock was more awake than Bast himself.

Before he could get to it, though, a small pressure poked the back of his skull. He immediately knew who was calling through their mind link.

Rae-henai...

Well, he could always pretend to be asleep.

Hmm, best not to. The last time he did that, Fallon found out—Danu knows how—and he put Bast on *sarking* desk duty for a whole month.

"What is it, Captain?" he asked aloud, waking his partners.

"I need you in the precinct," Fallon's voice rang in his mind. *"Now."*

"I'm kind of busy."

"I said now, Bast." Their mind link went quiet.

Odd. Fallon was rarely this curt or grave.

Shit must have hit the fan, an expression he'd just recently learned. Say what you will about humans, but they could be brilliant in their cursing.

Gruffly getting out of bed, he noticed the Sidhe and the banshee exchange a disappointed glance as he put on his clothes.

"Are you sure we don't have time?" They played with each other's hair. "We'll be quick, we promise."

Grinding his teeth, Bast swore to himself he would curse Fallon to the end of days. "Sorry, sweethearts," he grumbled as he buttoned his vest. "Duty calls."

Bast leaned on the wooden wall in Fallon's office, his arms crossed while he watched his captain.

He might look a lot younger than Bast with his spiky auburn hair, big green eyes, and a profusion of freckles, but the captain was a lot older, and smarter, than he seemed.

Bast had applied to the force the moment he and Stella arrived in Tir Na Nog. However, as a former assassin, his chances were non-existent, and he would have been lucky if the police didn't arrest him—hard without evidence, but still a risk.

Yet Fallon accepted his application immediately, which had to be one of those miracles humans raved about all the time.

"You up for a fight?" Fallon asked him during his first interview. "We have a world of cleaning up to do."

Bast didn't think twice before agreeing. Still, guilt weighed down on him. The police's background checks clearly sucked, and here was this fae, giving Bast a chance when it was the last thing he deserved.

"Sir, I must warn you, I used to be an assassi—"

"It's not on public record and you've never been arrested, so I don't care," Fallon countered without hesitating. "We all have shit in our past, but to do this job, I need someone who bends the law just enough to get things done. Someone who might have crossed the big lines, but wants to atone for that. Redemption is a mighty motivator, Sebastian Dhay." At that, he stared at Bast point blank. "So, tell me. Are you the fae I'm looking for?"

"Yes, sir!"

As the years passed, new memories replaced old ones, until the thought of Lunor Insul didn't bring Bast any pain.

Didn't bring him any joy, either.

It was a bittersweet sensation, especially when he remembered Leon, Karthana, and Master Raes, but it was never enough to call it regret.

Uncrossing his arms, he stepped closer to Fallon's desk. "No way."

The captain frowned at him, leaning back on his fancy leather chair. "You think you have a choice, *baku?*"

"Fallon, we have enough work in Tir Na Nog, and I'm a vital part of your plan here," Bast argued with a degree of respect, hoping that would give him extra points. His captain hated ass-kissing, but Bast was desperate enough to try it. "You're smarter than any fae in this borough. You know that assigning me to babysit a human detective is a waste of resources. Give her to someone else. Jada loves humans, especially the females."

"I need Jada elsewhere. Look, Bast, I can count on my fingers the number of fae I trust in this precinct." Fallon raised one red eyebrow at him, silently daring him to disagree.

He couldn't, of course.

"It's not every day that a light court king gets murdered," he continued. "On Clifftown, nonetheless."

"Some fae enjoy the pleasures of human flesh," Bast argued. "Nothing wrong with that."

"Absolutely, but the light courts deem sex with humans as shameful, and now one of their kings died in the arms of a woman, *in the human borough*." He pointed out, propping his elbows on the mahogany table. "Ever since the news broke, they've been agitated. The *shigs* are afraid. Make no mistake, Bast, this *is* our chance to nail them, especially if whoever killed Zev Ferris is from a light court."

"Fallon…"

He slapped the table. "This is our checkmate, I feel it in my bones. I'll trust no one other than you to deliver the blow. Understood?"

Bast groaned, his lips curling because he knew there was no point in arguing. He wouldn't make it easy, though. "Fine, but I want someone to winnow me there."

"Learn to do it yourself." His captain turned his attention to random papers scattered on his desk.

"I can't break the magic barrier that protects Clifftown. Also, I can't fucking winnow."

The captain stared at Bast from below his eyebrows, seeing right through to him. "Your magic, your night as you call it, is ridiculously powerful. You can do anything you set your mind to, if you focus."

"I was an assassin for *years*. If I'd been able to winnow, I'd have learned it a long time ago."

"Sometimes I swear to Danu it's like having a child," Fallon grumbled as he rubbed the bridge of his nose. "Fine. I'll get you winnowed into human territory, which is illegal by the way."

Bast winked at him as he went for the door. "Small sins, Captain. It's how we get things done in Tir Na Nog."

"You can't come in here!" the puffy human officer yelled the moment Bast entered the apartment.

With his bushy moustache and flushing pink skin beading with sweat, he seemed to be the type who had a talent for eating those *donuts* humans so loved. The sugar powdering his facial hair was evidence enough.

Rolling his eyes, Bast pushed himself forward. "I can do whatever I want."

Not true. He couldn't harm the idiot without causing an incident between the boroughs.

Bast went on for maybe three steps before the *baku* stepped on his way again.

"You can't take this case from us. A human was murdered in here."

Odd that he'd assumed Bast would take over the case instead of helping solve it. Then again, most crimes involving faeries in other boroughs were handed on a platter to Tir Na Nog, all thanks to fae bureaucrats in high places claiming cultural insensitivity—whatever that meant.

Never mind that they were corrupt as fuck, and on the light courts' payroll. Never mind that those same bureaucrats worked their way inside Bast's precinct to guide investigations in their favor. Those *sukets* forced Fallon's hand,

and his captain *hated* that, but his political power only went so far.

Yes, the other boroughs had every reason to hate the fae. Honestly, Bast wasn't a fan either, but he was there to do his job and this *malachai* blocked his way.

He pushed the human starkly, throwing him on the floor —diplomacy be damned.

"Danu in the fucking prairies," Bast grumbled as he approached the two figures with their backs to him; presumably the two detectives in charge of the crime scene. "Are all humans as stupid as your colleague?"

"I don't know," the female on his right turned to him. "Are all *pixies* assholes like you?"

As a former cold-blooded assassin, and a seasoned Hollowcliff detective, Bast never froze. *Ever.* Yet, he froze then.

Humans weren't an exotic choice for him—he'd laid with plenty before. This one however, looked simply exquisite. Different from everyone he knew in every single way, and he couldn't pinpoint why.

Mera Maurea, at least he hoped this was her, didn't have a perky nose or a high cheekbone. She didn't have a gentle face, either. Her lips weren't full like the faerie princesses from old stories, and her hair didn't flow smoothly like silk.

Still, she was jaw-dropping.

Her green eyes had an intensity that stole his breath away. As if they saw Bast for everything that he used to be, was, and everything he would become. Those piercing emeralds matched her straight nose and strong chin; her dark eyebrows, too.

Mera wasn't a gentle snowfall, or a sweet ray of sunshine. She was the hurricane that swept entire cities into the sky; the thunderstorm that preceded the end of days.

And her tits. *Halle.* The fucking tits...

She assessed him as much as he assessed her. By her shallow breathing and the slight opening of her perfect mouth, she clearly approved of what she saw.

A lazy grin spread on his lips. "Mera Maurea?"

Please say yes.

She nodded.

A weird, light sensation fluttered in his chest, but Bast had to focus. He was there to solve a case, not stare at the woman who hardened his *plaything* simply by existing; a strong reaction that could mean a world of things, specifically that she might be his...

No, Bast didn't believe in stupid folk tales.

Turning to the male on his left, he cleared his throat. "Julian Smith, I assume?"

The *baku* saluted him with a middle finger. "Yeah, and you are?"

Bast ignored the offense only because he was much more interested in Mera. "Sebastian Dhay." Shoving both hands on the pockets of his tailored pants, he locked his attention on her. "You can call me Bast. I'm here to investigate the murder of Zev Ferris, king of the Summer Court."

Her jaw dropped, her lips shaping an 'O'. Hmm, he wondered what he could stick into that tantalizing mouth of hers...

Focus on the case, Dhay, he chided himself.

"You're telling me that this guy," Mera pointed at the victim, "who's dressed like a leprechaun merchant, is a light court king? Are you serious?"

Bast gave her a dashing smile, hoping his usual charm would work. "Not everyone can dress well, sweetheart." He ogled her attire as if trying to prove his point.

Halle! Sweetheart? It felt... cheap. *Sarking jalls,* he couldn't take it back now.

Glaring at him, a furious blush rose to her lovely cheeks. "Sorry if I don't dress to your standards, *pixie*."

A loud laugh burst from Bast's lips. Mera was *terrible* with cursing. Theo surely had a filthier mouth, and that meant a lot considering his brother was a monk.

It'd been so long since they'd last spoke... Yet, Bast couldn't think about that now; couldn't delve on the past.

He had a case to solve.

"Your partner is most intriguing, isn't she?" he asked Julian.

The *shig* kept his arms crossed, not an inch of amusement on his face. "Respect the lady, or you and I will have a problem, understand?"

"*You* will have a problem, human," he assured with a grin. "I'll simply call it entertainment."

"The King of the Summer Court is dead and you're here alone?" Mera interrupted their exchange, looking past him. "Where's the cavalry?"

"Not bad, sweetheart." This time he did it because she looked cute when she was angry, but before Mera could scream at him, he raised his hands in surrender. "I meant no disrespect. I heard human women may either enjoy or hate the term, so I figured it was a fifty-fifty chance."

The glare those fierce green eyes shot him told Bast he better be careful. For the first time in his life, he feared what a human might do to him.

"I think you meant a world of disrespect." She stepped closer. "Call me sweetheart again, and I will bite off your fingers one by one, dickwart."

Dickwart?

Mm, creative. Bast would add the word to his vocabulary. Apparently, she wasn't as bad with cursing as he'd assumed.

"Is that a promise?" he asked wickedly.

Mera looked flabbergasted, her shocked expression incredibly titillating.

Fuck, how this human fascinated him…

"I'll be honest with you two," he went on, forcing himself to focus on the matter at hand. "We want discretion on this one. Your human captain traded that for minimum interference from our side. So here I am."

"Great," Mera retorted. "Try not to stand in our way, and—"

"No, no, you don't understand. I'm not here to assist you both. I'm here," he pointed at her, rejoicing in the revelation, "because I'm your new partner."

CHAPTER 21

LEON SAT DEEP in thought on a black padded chair, staring at the half-open window. A soft ocean breeze ventured inside his dark room, fluttering the black curtains and playing with loose strings of his wavy hair.

Bast's brother didn't acknowledge them when the servant Sidhe announced Mera and Bast had arrived. He still ignored them as they stepped closer.

"Leon," Mera began, pulling out a small pad from her jacket's pocket. "We came as soon as possible."

Sunlight peered through the small gap and softly graced the future king, highlighting his frame from the rest of his dark bedroom.

"Did you see the body?" he asked without turning to them.

She exchanged a worried glance with Bast. "Yes. We did."

The victim was called Vinci, a servant who'd eaten a poisoned pheasant meant for Leon.

Mera had seen gruesome in her line of work; was used to it by now, but even she hadn't been able to look at Vinci's body for long.

The corpse had swollen like a plum preparing to burst, his skin as purple as an amethyst. His eyes seemed ready to pop out of their sockets, and black veins coursed underneath his skin, like he was a vase about to crack. A stream of dried vomit clung to his jaw.

Bast explained that the poison was called *Nokto Yattu*, Night Death, and it suffocated the victim by swelling the walls of their throat. It also forced them to vomit, but since the way out was mostly blocked, bile stayed inside—and slipped into the victim's lungs. Which meant he'd drowned in his own puke.

"Vinci died protecting me." Leon's attention remained trapped on the half-open window. Birds chirped from a distance, the sky fiercely blue outside. "My family, my servants, they are dying." His lips trembled, his voice a whisper. "I can't protect them. How can I watch over an entire island?"

"You can't possibly blame yourself for this," Bast grumbled under his breath. "Stop trying to fix everything!"

Leon didn't seem to listen, or care. "Vinci insisted he should taste my food as a precaution, since Father had been poisoned. I rejected the idea, of course, but he was adamant."

"We've gotten the statements from the witnesses," Mera interrupted quietly, hoping to divert the course of the conversation. "Your mother's and the other servant's."

"How is she?" Leon asked absently. "It was a horrible thing to watch, Detective. The poison acted so quickly..."

"Mom's fine," Bast assured, stepping forward. "A little shaken, but she's seen worse."

Mera shuddered, wondering what could've been worse than that.

Ah, yes. Burying one of her sons.

Giving Bast a thankful glance, Leon returned his focus to the day outside. "Corvus didn't do this. He couldn't have."

"Wake up," her partner snapped. "He's not the fae you raised; none of us are. He killed Father and Theodore, and now he's coming after you, Big Brother."

"Why?" He pushed the chair back at once, and the wooden legs screeched against the marbled floor. Leon stood in the way of a bison about to attack, his nostrils flared and his fists balled. "Our family is twisted and wayward, I will not deny that, but why would our brother kill his own?"

"It's the crown," Bast muttered, and maybe Mera was wrong, but he seemed to shrink against Leon's looming presence. "Now more than ever, I'm positive that Corvus is after it."

"You think he would—"

"I *know* he would, especially if the nightblood has taken over. If we're all dead, he's the sole heir. A Night Prince losing his mind and trying to eliminate the competition isn't unheard of."

"Darren, the bloody. Rhelli, the rabid." Leon swallowed, his gaze lost on the floor. "Nissa, the mad queen."

"No way." Mera chortled. "Hollowcliff would never allow that."

"It's part of the treaty," Leon argued. "Tagrad doesn't care how a Night King is chosen, as long as they follow the rules of the agreement with the mainland. Also, as far as the Night Court goes, murdering each other is not particularly rare."

"Seriously?"

"Father and Grandfather were against it," Bast explained. "We've had a handful of peaceful centuries, but our history betrays us. Our blood, too."

Leon turned to Bast, his eyes glistening. "If the darkness caught up to Corvus, we must help him."

"Help is the last thing he deserves." Narrowing his eyes at his brother, Bast crossed his arms. "Why couldn't I feel you were in danger when the servant was poisoned? We set a mind link for a reason, Leon."

"I wasn't the one in danger." He raised his shoulders casually. "Besides, I didn't want to be an inconvenience. Sending Mardi to fetch you at the precinct was best."

"Unbelievable." Bast shook his head. "It's always everyone else before you. That has to change. You're about to be crowned as Night King, for Danu's sake! If you feel danger, you *will* contact me."

"Bast—"

"There's no arguing on this, Big Brother. Corvus doesn't know common sense or logic; he never did. And if nightblood has taken over him, then he's incredibly dangerous."

Mera didn't agree. For what she'd seen of Corvus, he was far from mad—simply a perfectly lucid prick.

"Fine. I'll warn you if I'm ever in danger again." Leon sighed in defeat. "What will you do to our brother once you catch him?"

Balling his fists, Bast gritted his teeth. "Guess."

Her partner was complicated, arrogant, and snarky, but deep down, decent and kind. Many shades of gray, but never dark. So, no, Bast would never kill his own brother.

Would he?

'His nickname is literally death bringer,' Mera's siren reminded her.

"You will not kill Corvus, if that's what you're implying, Detective Dhay," she warned pointedly.

"Why not? He's a threat to Hollowcliff, and a murderous—"

"Killing comes easily to you. It comes easily to Corvus, too. However, *you* are the Hollowcliff detective, *Yattusei*. Not him."

Shock mingled with hurt in Bast's sky-blue irises, but

Mera didn't care. Anything to snap him out of this... insanity.

Clearing her throat, she addressed Leon. "Our assumption, and bear in mind it's an *assumption*," she said specifically at Bast, "is that Corvus killed both your father and Theodore, and that he tried to kill you to get to the throne. Fact is, he's only tied to Theodore's murder. We can't condemn him for your father's death or the attempt on your life. Not yet."

She expected Bast to object.

He didn't.

Hope shone inside Leon's pink irises. "So he might be innocent, Detective Maurea?"

"We can't confirm that yet, but until we're certain, I want four of your best guards accompanying you at all times. Also, delay the coronation until we catch Corvus."

"Absolutely not. Delaying it might be exactly what he wants." Leon waved his hand in the air. "I'm a trained assassin as much as he is. Let Corvus come to me. Maybe I can knock some sense into his head."

Bast rubbed his face in exasperation. "Your soft heart will get you killed, *baku*."

Leon glared at him, as if Bast had just shoved a blade into his chest. "Forgive me for not wanting my brother dead, Sebastian."

Charles Grey once mentioned diplomacy was about compromising. He might be an addict vamp, but he had a point.

"Fine," Mera agreed. "The coronation will not be delayed, but you *will* have four of your best guards accompanying you. That's non-negotiable."

Leon turned back to the window, his hands held behind his back. "As you wish, Detective." His tone sounded colder, his posture stiffer.

Rushing steps clanked on the marble floor outside, until

coincidence of coincidences, Charles Grey burst into the bedroom.

His eyes were filled with red veins, his cropped auburn hair disheveled and messy, his lips cracked. The diplomat reeked of blood and booze. He watched them staring at him, then fixed the loose collar of his shirt. As if that could hide the fact Charles Grey was as high as a kite.

Bowing his head to Leon, he placed one hand on his own chest. "I came as fast as I could, my prince."

Mera narrowed her eyes at him. Charles Grey might not be tied to the murders, but she didn't discard him as a suspect, more out of a gut-feeling than anything else.

For now.

Leon's lips formed a thin line. "Where's Benedict?"

"Theodore's death hit him hard, my prince. He's been healing."

"If by healing you mean getting himself drunk out of his wits, and fornicating until his dick falls off, you better redefine the term." Leon stepped forward, every bit the bison about to charge. "You're dragging him down, Charles. You should know better than to mess with my family."

The vamp shrunk underneath the future king's bulky form, his lips quivering. "My prince, he's in mourning. It's understandable that—"

"You're a disgrace to the government you work for."

Not a lie, actually.

"Do your job as a diplomat, and assure the continent that the Night Court remains strong." Leon added, analyzing Charles from head to toe with utter disgust. "We've suffered direct hits, but with the detectives here to help, I have no doubt we'll prevail. Quote me on that, do you understand?"

Odd that Leon treated Charles an employee, not a diplomat who could report him to the continent at any time.

Addicts were easy to control, though, a fact the royal family clearly played to their advantage.

Charles' lips curved down as if he'd eaten something bitter. "Yes, my prince."

"Write it down or you might forget." Leon bent forward, scrutinizing every inch of the vamp.

The behavior didn't match Bast's older brother, but Mera supposed that a ruler, even a kind one, must have a strong hand. Besides, Leon could be overprotective when it came to his brothers, and Charles Grey wasn't a good influence to Benedict.

Well, to anyone, really.

A flash of bitterness passed by the vamp's eyes. "The crown changed your father. Don't let it change you, my prince."

Leon glared at him with a combination of disgust and hate. "I'm stronger and better than my father," he assured through clenched teeth. "Now, get out of my sight."

Charles bowed at the prince and started to walk away, but as he passed by Mera, his stare caught hers.

A secret swirled behind Charles' green irises; she couldn't tell how she knew, she simply did.

He hurriedly looked away, but he'd been busted. Mera made a note to pay him a visit later.

"If Benedict doesn't recompose, I'll hold you accountable, Charles. You don't want that to happen." Leon warned before the vamp reached the door. "The coronation will happen in two days and my family *will* be there." A muscle in his jaw ticked. "What remains of it, anyway."

"Yes, my prince." With a curt bow, the bloodsucker left.

"Leon…" Bast started.

"Is there anything else you wish to address, Detective?" he countered coldly; a mighty king not at all like Bast's older brother.

C.S. WILDE

Leon had obviously taken what Bast said about his good heart a bit too seriously.

"No," Bast muttered, straightening his spine. "Do make sure those guards are ready, and that they check your food."

"Will do."

Damn Night Princes and their pride...

"I can lend you my pin-pen." Mera pulled the device from her jacket's pocket. She'd brought it to the palace to confirm the poison that had killed Vinci—a necessity for filing a report later. "It already sent the results to my laptop, so I don't need it anymore. You can poke your food with this device and it will find traces of poison."

Leon's lips curled in disgust, as most fae's did when facing technology.

"Your guards can't check your food completely," she argued, "not unless they taste it."

"After Vinci? Out of the question," Leon snapped.

"I know. Look, it's either using this pin-pen, or getting poisoned and dying a horrible death. Your choice."

He watched her and the device dubiously, but eventually gave in.

"I must go to Master Raes," Bast stated the moment they landed before the precinct's door. "He has connections on the black market. If we find who sold the poison to Corvus, maybe we can trace his location."

Mera nodded, glad that her partner was returning to his usual self.

Hollowcliff's finest.

The air behind them suddenly rumbled, and a strange sensation settled in Mera's stomach. She had a bad feeling about this, whatever 'this' might be.

A circle of night and stars slashed through the empty space, as if a void was swallowing the air. In an eye blink, Corvus appeared before them.

He had dark circles under his eyes, his cheeks sunken in.

Pulling her gun, Mera aimed, but Bast was already pushing her behind him. As if she needed the freaking protection!

Assface.

"You've lost your fucking mind!" Bast growled, his night thrumming inside him, like a beast ready to pounce.

"Bark as much as you want, *malachai*." Corvus didn't show any emotion as he raised his wrists. "I'm here to turn myself in."

CHAPTER 22

Bᴀsᴛ ᴡᴏᴜʟᴅ ɢᴇᴛ a confession from Corvus today, even if it was the last thing he did.

Dragging a chair before the closed cell, he sat down and hunched over his knees, his fingers intertwined.

Silence swallowed the precinct, heavy and awkward, as he stared at Corvus.

The prick reclined on the cell's marbled bench, the back of his head leaning against the concrete wall. He peered at Bast with the same gravity, and that thing Mera once said about them being similar rushed to mind.

No. Kitten might be a great detective, but she'd missed the mark. Bast was nothing like this *sarking suket*.

Mera had left to Charles' house in order to question the vamp, mostly because she sensed he might be hiding something. A waste of time, really, since their culprit had surrendered, but at least this gave Bast the freedom to do whatever he wanted to Corvus.

Well, not exactly.

He'd promised Mera he wouldn't hurt the *baku*, assuring

her that he'd be fine, and that interrogating his brother alone might bring him closure—*halle*, even Bast didn't buy the bull-crap pouring out of his mouth.

Mera didn't either, of course. She was smarter than that.

As she headed for the door, she turned and stared at him dead in the eye. "I'd hate to be forced to arrest, or kill you, Bast. So don't make me."

With that, she left.

It was obviously a test, one he feared he might not pass. Well, it wasn't his fault if Mera had more faith in him than Bast himself, was it?

"The entire cell is coated in iron dust," he warned Corvus, clenching his teeth at the sight of the *shig*. "You won't be able to winnow or use your magic."

"I don't intend to. I gave myself in, *baku*. Remember?"

The prick had a point.

"Why did you kill Theo?" Bast pushed, reaching for a full-on confession.

Not a hint of emotion flashed on his brother's face. Corvus' stare weighed mountains on Bast's shoulders, his silence suffocating, yet Bast had expected nothing less of this cold-blooded psycho.

If he were to get a confession, he would need to be more resourceful.

"You slashed Theo's throat. You've always been a cruel bastard, but this…" He shook his head.

Nothing. Not a tick of a muscle.

Vicious malachai…

"Theo, for the little we saw of him, always tried bringing some sense into Ben's head," Bast went on, his chest heavy with sorrow. "His efforts were destroyed by the disease that you are, Corvus. So tell me! How did it feel to end your own brother's life?"

He kept watching Bast with canary irises that revealed nothing. With his sunken cheeks, and dark circles under his eyes, Corvus looked terrible. Like he hadn't slept or eaten in ages.

Good. Considering everything he'd done, he *should* feel miserable.

"I wish Theo hadn't gone to the monastery when we were young," Bast muttered, a knot tying in his throat as he leaned back on his chair. "I wish we had known him better."

"So do I."

The fucking audacity!

Bast raised his head, anger pulsing in his veins. "You don't get to say that," he spat.

Keeping his fists away from Corvus would be an impossible feat.

His brother's mouth set in a grim line. He didn't reply, merely kept watching Bast with that gut-wrenching stare that said a world of things he couldn't grasp.

Losing his patience, he slammed a foot on the floor. "Admit it, Corvus!"

He didn't, of course. No matter how loud Bast barked and growled, his brother wouldn't confess.

The prick was smart. Sneaky, too.

Cracking his knuckles, Bast stood from the chair. He walked in circles before the cell, as if he were the caged animal, not Corvus.

"You tried killing Leon. How dare you attack the one fae in this world who loves us as much as Mom does? Who was a better father to us than our own?"

A flash of hurt passed over Corvus' face, vanishing as quickly as it came. "I love our big brother. I'm grateful for what he did for us; what he gave up for our sake. I was there as he faced all his struggles, always by his side, while you were gone to watch over that *bastard* sister of yours. So, no, you don't get to lecture me about Leon."

Fire rushing up to his head, Bast stomped closer to the cell. He raised one finger at Corvus, his jaw clenched. "Don't you dare disrespect Stella again."

"I'll call that bastard whatever I want," he snapped with disgust, his tone a block of ice. "She took you from us."

"No. *You* drove me away!" Spinning in a circle, Bast ran a hand over his hair. "You all did when you didn't accept her! I had to become to Stella what Leon was to us. No one else would! She had no one, Corvus, all thanks to you!"

His brother's jaw hung slightly open.

Look at that; no comebacks. What a fucking miracle.

Bast's chest heaved up and down, his pent-up anger wearing him down as if he'd spent hours running.

They stared at each other for a long while, until Corvus cleared his throat and looked away. "I love Leon more than you'll ever know."

A truth for once.

"If you love him, why did you try to kill him?"

Crossing his arms, Corvus leaned the back of his head against the wall, his focus on the ceiling.

Guess talking time was over.

Exhaling loudly, Bast dropped back on his chair. "You'll never get the crown, you know."

"Too early to say that, little *Yattusei*." He winked at him before turning his attention back to the ceiling.

"You're behind bars, *baku*. You murdered Father, Theo, and you tried to kill Leon. You'll be in jail for a long time."

"I'm willing to do what's necessary for the greater good. If that puts me in jail, so be it."

"Was killing Theodore for the greater good?"

Corvus hunched forward, his hands intertwined. "I

suppose you'll take me to the continent soon. I'm sorry you'll miss Leon's coronation."

The *malachai* wouldn't admit to his crimes, no matter how hard Bast pushed.

"I won't miss our brother's ascendance to the throne. We'll head to the continent afterwards, and rest assured, brother, you'll spend the rest of your days behind iron bars."

Guilt washed over Bast, because some of Corvus' words had been true. Bast had hurt Leon when he left. The rest of his family, too. Perhaps he'd even hurt the asshole sitting before him.

"You're right," Bast admitted quietly. "I wasn't there for Big Brother, but I'll make up for it now that I'm back."

"Will you?"

Maybe Bast was imagining things but he found fear behind Corvus' yellow irises.

Odd... The prick feared nothing and no one.

"You'll be there for the coronation," Corvus repeated to himself, as if digesting what he'd said.

"Oh yes." Bast studied his own nails, feigning nonchalance. "Maybe I'll take Karthana as my date."

Wincing, Corvus waived a hand in the air. "Stop with this nonsense. Karthana might still have feelings for you, but you belong to the detective. This game of yours doesn't affect me anymore."

A chill ran down Bast's spine. "How do you know? About Mera and I?"

"It's quite obvious, isn't it? Even if she hasn't noticed it yet, even if a part of her is in denial, there's no running away." He tapped his chin with his index finger. "Actually, there is. She could always refuse you, couldn't she?" At that he smiled.

Sarking Suket...

"Your point?" Bast pushed, feigning a mask of nonchalance when he'd rather punch Corvus in his arrogant fucking face.

"I wish Karthy was to me what the detective is to you," he blurted. "I wanted it to be true so badly. So did she. In the beginning, we thought it was, but... we must face the facts. We're good, loyal friends, but we're not at the opposite ends of a golden string."

Did he want Bast to feel pity?

Tough-fucking luck.

"And still, you would marry her."

"Of course." Corvus tapped his foot nervously on the floor, which was a first. The *malachai* never let his emotions, or his state of mind, show. "Isn't marriage about being with your best friend? Building a life together? Karthana and I could do that perfectly well, but would it be fair to her? To us both?"

"You say that as if I care, Corvus."

Yet he did. Bast was glad Karthana would be free of this asshole. She deserved better than what his brother could give.

"Didn't expect you to care, Sebastian." Corvus' mouth contorted into a bitter line. "You never do."

Silence hung heavy between them for a long while. It weighed more with each passing second, but Bast didn't know how to break it, how to reach out to Corvus, even if an insane part of him *wanted* to do it.

What in all of Danu's hells?

"I saw the mad queen in a dream," Corvus stated quietly. "It was night time, and she was standing on a mountain's peak while thunder rumbled from above. The wind howled so loudly... Her white hair and black dress swooshed with fury, Bast." He lost himself in thought for a moment. "The lightning flashing in the distance highlighted five shadows standing before her, one for each of us. I think it began to rain... " He rubbed his face. "She turned to me and gave me the cruelest, red-lipped grin before she removed her crown... then set it on one of our heads."

Diversion tactics, nothing more.

"That doesn't mean anything. It was just a dream." Closing his arms, Bast leaned back in his chair, spreading his legs. "You want me to miss on Leon's most important moment. You always wanted to be Big Brother's favorite, and it killed you that I had the spot, even after I left." The glare Corvus shot him proved his point. "Funny. If you hadn't murdered Father, there wouldn't be a coronation, and I wouldn't have returned home. So I guess this is on you."

Variables ran behind Corvus' eyes, until he quickly glanced at the floor. "You should check on your partner."

Bast snorted. "Mera can take care of herself."

"Like she did when Ben gave her enchanted wine? Our brother is frail, and the nightblood is strong."

"Ben wouldn't hurt her," Bast assured both Corvus and himself. "He's not you, and now that you can't influence him, he'll be fine."

"Oh, please." Corvus blew air through his lips. "Are you that naïve, *Detective Dhay*? Ben does what he wants. Besides, he hasn't been keeping the best of companies lately, has he? I'm not the only bad influence in his life, brother dearest."

Charles Fucking Grey.

Their stares locked, their frivolous game of chicken nearing its end. Bast fully knew that Corvus was planting worms in his head, but the damage was done.

He couldn't leave it to chance, couldn't risk Mera being hurt in an unfair fight. If things went south, it would be a fae and a vamp against her.

Not that she couldn't defend herself, but if she revealed her *akritana* powers in front of Charles or Benedict...

Fuchst ach!

Bast jumped to his feet and raised one finger at him. "Stay put, *suket*."

He shouldn't worry about an escape. With the iron bars and cell coating, his brother couldn't go anywhere.

Still, Corvus let out a wolfish grin.

CHAPTER 23

CHARLES GREY LAID the tea set on the coffee table in his living room. "If you're here to see Ben, Detective Maurea, he's not receiving anyone. He needs space, you see."

Paintings of wild roses graced the spotless porcelain, a stark contrast to the rest of the vamp's messy apartment. Papers lay scattered on the floor, and dirty dishes piled up on the kitchen's sink.

Charles had set a cardboard panel over the hole on the door—the hole Bast had pierced with his magic. The window shutters were pulled down, drenching the space in an unsettling penumbra.

The vamp sat on the couch opposite to Mera. The seats reeked of something muggy and old, like the rest of the place.

"Twins," he went on, "even two as different as Theo and Ben, share a special bond."

"I understand." She nodded to the cups before them. "Polite of you, to offer me tea when you can't drink any."

"Oh, but I can." Grabbing his cup, he took a sip. "It simply doesn't sustain me. Rest assured, I can appreciate a good cup of tea, or a glass of wine." He winked at her.

Dickwart.

Mera looked around the apartment. The cups might seem clean, but given the lack of sanitation everywhere else, she decided best not to drink. Also, she didn't exactly trust Charles Grey, either because of his addiction or simply a gut-feeling.

"I'm not here to speak to Benedict," she explained. "I'm here to see you."

"Little old me?" Genuine surprise mixed with gratefulness behind his emerald eyes. With a grin, he spread his palm on his chest. "How can this disaster of a diplomat be of service to you?"

Well, at least he acknowledged he was a train wreck.

"You mentioned something about the crown to Leon," she pointed out carefully. "Can you tell me more about it?"

"Not really." He shrugged. "I meant to say power changes people."

"Do you believe Leon has changed?"

Shrugging, he shook his head. "Not particularly. He will, however. Every ruler does." He let out a long sigh. "The crown itself has a rather interesting story. It doesn't actually belong to the Night Court."

"It doesn't?" she asked, feigning interest. Maybe if she gave him room to talk, whatever he kept from her would come to the surface.

He leaned forward as if he was about to tell her a juicy secret. "Legend says, it was a gift from the sea fae."

Mera's blood chilled to absolute zero.

Sea fae. Sirens.

Waterbreakers.

"The crown is named Crown of Land and Sea. Mermaids gave it to the Night King millennia ago for safekeeping, until the day they call Regneerik." His eyes shone with excitement as he explained. "See, many historians believe Regneerik is about the end of the world, but some say it's about new beginnings. A fresh start. The Night Court, of course, buried the story. A king shouldn't wear a crown that isn't his own." He tapped his temple knowingly.

It felt odd hearing the lore and religious terms she'd grown up with, being repeated to her on land. Also, considering the bad blood between them, the fact landriders studied her kind was astounding.

"Is that so?" Mera asked, trying to hide the sheer terror that had taken over her.

"Indeed. On the day of Regneerik—what land fae call Argeddon—it is said that the promised one will rise to unite all kingdoms... or destroy them. The wording is a bit confusing on that part." His face scrunched up as he waved his hand. "Anyway, on that day, the crown will be given to the *Ahai-ni*, and he shall rule land and sea."

Ahai-ni. The promised one.

"Sounds far-fetched," she chortled with fake amusement.

"I'll admit the legend doesn't make much sense, especially since the creation of Tagrad already unified every kingdom into one... kind of."

"Mermaids are still banished," she muttered mostly to herself.

"Quite right." He raised his finger at her. "Which means the prophecy could technically be fulfilled. Either that, or the *Ahai-ni* will kill us all. Impossible to say, really."

Mera understood why Charles Grey had been hired as a diplomat in Lunor Insul. He clearly loved fae lore and history. Being here must have been a dream come true for him, at least in a distant past. Now, he was simply an addict without any control over his life, even if a shadow of the diplomat he used to be remained, buried under all of his mishaps.

Her heart thumped in her chest as Charles' version of

Regneerik whirled in her mind. She'd never heard of it before; never knew about a crown of land and sea. Air stopped midway in her lungs when Mera remembered how Madam Zukova had called her.

Queen of Waves and Dust.

Land and sea.

All nonsense, surely. The possibilities for interpretation were endless. Besides, Charles' stories were silly lore, nothing more.

"Are you all right, Detective?" he frowned at her with genuine concern. "You look awfully pale."

Swallowing dry, she nodded. "I'm fine. Just low blood pressure."

"Pity I can't help you with that." His eyes shone with malice as he finished his tea.

Well, better get her act together.

"What are you hiding, Charles?" Mera pushed, her patience wearing thin. They'd wasted enough time with silly old stories.

Before he could answer, the door to a back room opened and out came Benedict, covered in pajamas and a blanket.

The Night Prince dragged himself into the room, his gaze lost as if he were half-dead.

Standing up at once, Charles hurried towards him. "Dear, you should be resting."

Mera noticed the swollen bite marks on Benedicts' neck, the paleness of his skin. This wasn't someone in mourning, or depressed.

This was a fae on the verge of death.

It had been Charles' secret; what Mera's gut-feeling had warned her about.

The bloodsucker was killing Bast's brother.

Mera stood, her hand hovering over her gun. "I'll take

Benedict back to the palace, if you don't mind." She motioned for him to come closer. "Prince Dhay?"

He didn't react.

"Ben?"

He slowly blinked through his haze, only then realizing she was there. "Hello, Detective," he slurred, his forehead wrinkling as if he tried hard to focus. "When did you arrive?"

"Not long ago." She stretched her hand to him. "I'm heading out. Would you like to come with me?"

Deep down, some part of him must have known he would die if he didn't. Nodding slowly, he went to her.

"Sebastian doesn't deserve you," Ben mumbled, his blanket falling from his shoulders. He didn't seem to realize it as he stepped on the fabric, dragging one sluggish foot after the other. "I hurt you. The enchanted wine... I'm sorry."

"I forgive easily, it seems."

"Stop!" Charles growled, showcasing his fangs. "Detective, Ben should stay here."

"No, he shouldn't," Mera snapped. "I bet his nightblood tastes amazing, doesn't it?"

"I never gave it to him before," Ben assured with a hazed grin. "I thought he couldn't handle it, but Charles deserves it. He's such a good friend..."

Well, fuck. The vamp was hooked on what must feel like heroine on steroids.

"I'd never hurt Ben, but I need his blood!" Charles closed his fists, his irises becoming clear red.

She believed him. Addicts rarely meant to hurt others, but often did it anyway. "Charles," Mera warned. "Get it together."

"He couldn't hurt a fly." The aloof Night Prince kept trudging toward Mera. "He's a good one, our Charles."

A bit closer...

Barking a beastly sound, the vamp's fangs grew longer and sharper. "You're not taking Ben anywhere!"

Pulling out her gun, she aimed at his heart. "Hurry up, Benedict."

Back in Clifftown, Mera had handled her fair share of bloodthirsty vamps, hunting in human territory. They weren't much of a challenge—usually an iron bullet to the heart or head was enough to end or hinder them, depending on how old they were. Yet, she didn't want to do that to Charles Grey.

If anything, the vamp needed help, not a bullet.

Charles was about to pounce, when tentacles of night and stars wrapped around his wrists and ankles, pulling him to the floor. His chest and forehead smashed onto the marble. The bloodsucker writhed against the binds, but the tentacles were stronger.

The door slung open from behind Mera, revealing Bast against the light. Charles yelped as sun beams slammed against his face, giving him a reddish blush.

"Wondered if you might need backup, partner." Bast surveyed the scene for a moment, his eyes falling on his brother. A flash of concern passed in his blue gaze. "Is he all right?"

"He's safe now." She smiled at Benedict who nodded slowly, his attention on Charles Grey.

"My poor friend..." he mumbled before raising his head, as if he'd just remembered something. "Did you find Corvus yet?"

"Yes," Bast stepped inside, his night keeping Charles trapped on the floor. "He's back at the precinct."

Benedict blinked. "You *caught* him?"

"No, he turned himself in," Mera answered instead, still aiming her gun at Charles Grey as a precaution, but the vamp was limp and panting on the floor.

Bast's darkness drained him quickly, so he'd be out in a matter of seconds.

Benedict glared at them, utter horror flashing over his hazy stare. "Corvus surrendered himself... and you left him alone?"

He didn't need to complete the thought. Everyone knew Corvus never did something without a reason.

Gasping, Mera turned to Bast. "Tell Leon—"

"Already done," he assured. "Ben, Big Brother is coming for you, so stay put."

Charles Grey lost consciousness a moment later, so Mera shoved her gun in its holster, and jumped into Bast's arms.

"Don't leave me alone with him," Benedict muttered, a cry in his tone.

"Charles won't wake up for days, brother." Bast assured as his wings unfolded from behind his back. "Don't worry."

In one swoop, he took Mera through the open door, zinging into the sky.

It didn't take them long to land before the precinct. Hurrying inside, Mera hoped their fears had been unfounded. That Corvus would be waiting for them from behind bars, wearing that superior, irritating grin on his face.

But the bastard's cell was empty.

CHAPTER 24

IF OCEAN WATER could morph into silk, it would have been used to make Mera's sea-green dress. An insane comparison, surely, but it was the only way to describe the fabric of her nightgown. The sleeveless dress formed a "V" neckline that showed more cleavage than she was used to, falling down her waist with the grace of a gentle waterfall.

Twirling around, Mera watched herself in her bedroom's standing mirror.

The gown might be gorgeous, but it was seriously impractical. She'd had to attach her gun to a leather belt around her thigh, literally out of view and out of reach.

Bast should've known better when he'd dropped the black box on her bed without saying a word, then left to his room to get ready for Leon's coronation.

Well, Mera couldn't go in a T-shirt and jeans to the most important ball in Lunor Insul. Sure, she might be Hollowcliff authority, but Leon had insisted that tonight, she and Bast were his guests.

She appreciated the thought, but they were working a case. It had been three days since Corvus escaped, and still no sign of him. The chance he might show up during Leon's coronation was enormous, and yet, she and Bast had to appease the king-to-be.

Diplomacy, ugh.

So, here she was on a mission, resembling a freaking princess, and damn close to defenseless.

Great...

Fixing her hair in a loose bun that braided twice over her head, Mera couldn't help a satisfied grin. Ruth loved playing with her hair when Mera was younger, which meant that she had picked up a thing or two about grooming herself.

As she braided her locks, she admired the drop-shaped earrings that matched the color of her dress.

They must have cost a fortune. She had no idea how Bast had arranged for the clothes and jewelry that quickly, but it couldn't have been legal.

Once she was done, Mera made her way out of her room.

Bast stood in the living room, waiting for her. He wore a black suit with a silken onyx shirt. Silver embellishments decorated the hem and buttons of the suit, matching perfectly with his hair, which waved over the left side of his face down to his shoulders.

Her heart skipped a beat as she took in the sight of him. With his straight posture and fitted clothes, Bast looked absolutely regal.

'And hot as hell,' her siren added. *'Hmm, those bad boy vibes...'*

His stare burned through Mera while he slowly admired her, from the top of her head to the tip of her shoes. Smiling softly, he tilted his head left. "You look like a poem, kitten."

Bast had many talents, but he excelled at turning her knees to jelly.

"Thanks." She studied her shoes, sea-green to match the dress. "You have good taste, Detective."

His attention never unlocked from her. "I know."

Molten fire burned her cheeks. Clearing her throat, Mera patted her dress. "How did you get all this with a government salary? Did you rob a bank? I'd have to report you if you did…"

A busty laugh burst from his lips. "I might be a disowned prince, but I have some wealth. Besides, assassins are anything but underpaid." His shoulders rose and fell casually. "I had… investments."

"Investments? You lived in the slums of Tir Na Nog not long ago."

"I lived there *for a while*, yes. That house is one of my many properties, and a personal favorite, actually. It helped Stella and I when we arrived in the continent. Also, Father sent a new assassin every week. No one expects a prince to live in poverty, so I always had the element of surprise." He seemed to consider it twice. "I guess this proves money isn't everything."

"Spoken as someone who has loads of it." She crossed her arms. "Are you serious about this, or just screwing with me?"

"Screwing *with* you? Never. Screwing *you*?" He gave her a mischievous grin that reverberated between her thighs. "That's something to look forward to." Before Mera could blush any harder, he offered her his arm. "Shall we?"

Silver and white ribbons lavishly decorated the palace, glittering like precious jewels. They matched perfectly with the stars shining on the clear night outside, beyond the palace's open arches and ample halls.

Glistening faerie lights floated near the ceilings, casting the halls and stairways into daylight. They turned the castle into nothing short of a lighthouse which twirled around the tallest mountain.

Following the crowd into the throne room, Mera wondered if all this pomp and circumstance was how coronations went back in the day. Back when Tagrad was nothing but a dream, and faeries basically ruled the land.

The moon shone brightly above, as if the night itself blessed Leon's coronation. From this high up, it seemed like she could reach the silver orb by simply standing on the tip of her toes.

When she and Bast reached the throne room, Mera gasped. Night fae dressed in fancy gowns and suits crowded the space. Some dresses resembled stars falling from the sky, others the dawn and twilight. A couple of suits reminded her of a glass of wine, others dew drops atop a leaf in the morning, and some could only be described as wind gusts or waves crashing.

Mera wondered what kind of magic must've been imbedded in those fabrics. In her own dress, too.

She found Karthana and Raes standing on the far left, near one of the many arches that opened to the outside. Corvus' betrothed wore a long-sleeved purple gown with golden embellishments. Her plum-colored hair was clipped behind, draping down her bare back. Compared to everyone else's, Karthana's attire was simple and yet beautiful.

It fit her awfully well.

Her father stood beside her, wearing a navy suit that shifted to lighter gradients. Like fire burning, if fire were blue. Raes watched everything and everyone around the ballroom with piercing hawk-eyes.

Ah, he was also expecting a visit from Corvus. Maybe that was why Karthana had decided to come.

To see him again.

Raes' keen gaze found Bast and Mera amongst the crowd, and he nodded, a clear sign that he was watching for trouble.

Bast nodded back at him.

His daughter, however, didn't acknowledge their presence in any way. Considering they hoped to arrest Corvus, Mera couldn't exactly blame her.

Karthana had called off her engagement after Bast's brother became a fugitive, but she clearly still cared greatly about Corvus. It might not be betrothed love, but it was love nonetheless.

Soft, melodic tunes echoed throughout the throne room as servants with trays carrying finger food and drinks began milling about.

Mera had eaten before, of course. After drinking enchanted wine, she'd be damned if she ever accepted anything offered in a fae household again.

"I hope Corvus doesn't try something tonight." She nodded to the guards standing near every entrance of the space, and also at the base of the dais with the ivory throne. "Escaping would be impossible. This place is more guarded than Fort Mox."

"Maybe he doesn't want to escape," Bast countered as he surveyed the crowded hall. "But yes, Corvus would have to be stupid to try something tonight, and as much as I hate admitting it, stupidity isn't one of his traits." He seemed to consider it twice. "Doesn't mean he won't try, though."

"Well, it's about time we made a proper arrest. I'm not sure if Corvus is our guy, though," she muttered as she searched the crowd for anything that seemed strange.

"A proper arrest?" He arched one eyebrow. "Doesn't Charles Grey count?"

"He needs help, that's all." She shrugged. "A week behind bars should be good for him. Vampires are stronger than humans, and they recover faster too. His detox will be painful, yet quick."

And maybe, over time, Charles would return to his former self. Mera could only hope.

Bast shoved his hands in his pockets as they casually strolled across the ballroom. "You keep thinking Corvus is innocent. Why?"

"He turned himself in so we wouldn't attend the ceremony," she said mindlessly. "Sure, his pursuit of the throne makes sense, if he's ambitious enough. But something is missing."

"What if he has an accomplice?" Bast suggested. "Maybe Corvus would have his henchman do the dirty deed while we took him to the continent. It would be the perfect crime."

Mera's eyes narrowed at him. "You really believe your brother is the devil, don't you?"

"You would agree if you knew him."

The idea came to her the way lightning strikes, and she gripped Bast's arms tightly.

"Kitten?" He asked, his brow wrinkling. "What's wrong?"

"What if he's planning an attack on *all* fae here tonight?" she whispered, her blood chilling and a cold sweat breaking on her forehead.

It might be extreme, even for Corvus, but it wasn't impossible. If he was indeed infected by nightblood, if in fact he wanted to take over the throne... why not do it with a bang? Kill Leon plus his supporters in one go?

"That means Corvus would've tried to protect us by giving himself in." Bast chortled. "No, kitten. Not in a million years."

"But he could—"

"He couldn't." He caressed her hand gently, his gaze calming and assuring her. "Trust me. That's not his angle. Besides, Corvus isn't the type to perform mass attacks."

Trumpets sounded loudly, drawing everyone's attention to the dais at the end of the throne room.

Leon moved up the steps and away from the crowd. Loud clapping and the clamor of his people followed when he stopped on the dais, close to the ivory throne.

He looked simply magnificent. His long hair waved over the right side of his face, in a fashion similar to Bast's, except his wavy moonlight threads draped down to his waist. Leon's frock was made of a soft white fabric that reminded Mera of feathers, encrusted in glittering patterns. A belt wrapped around his waist, carrying the royal sword inside a beautifully engraved ivory sheathe.

Leon bowed to his subjects, something no light court king would ever do. It was also why nightlings loved their leaders more than the light fae loved theirs; why they'd followed mad kings and queens to the very end.

Their ruler loved them, and they loved him in return.

Maybe that had been why Hollowcliff allowed the Night Court to govern Lunor Insul almost freely. To avoid a civil war.

Not much different to what they'd done in Tir Na Nog, really, yet those days had ended, thanks to Bast and Mera.

The trumpets sounded again, and Benedict walked up the dais, wearing a gray suit that matched his hair.

He was in much better shape now. A few days of rest had worked wonders on him. Mera could barely spot the dark circles under his eyes.

His dark-gray hair was fixed neatly in a comb-over style, and he walked with a straight, nearly military posture as he carried a velvet pillow with the Crown of Land and Sea—if Charles Grey's story was to be believed.

Bast explained that according to tradition, a Night King could only be crowned by their own blood. Leon had asked

Bast to do it, but he was a disowned prince, and disowned princes couldn't crown anyone.

"Brother of Night," Benedict began, his voice booming around the throne room. "We're here today to pass the torch of leadership, the torch of strength, to you."

His tone and manner differed vastly from the party-animal who never took anything seriously; from the frail, dazed fae she'd seen back at Charles Grey's apartment; and from the numb brother who'd watched Theodore's body in complete shock.

'Save him,' her siren whispered.

Save him from what?

'Himself.'

Benedict continued. He spoke about how their father had begun his journey, and how Leon would continue it with grace, kindness, and a strong fist. He recounted childhood tales and Leon's adventures, telling the faeries in the room about his bravery, his heart, his nobility.

He told them how much he loved his brother, and how proud he was to call him family.

The story of a king.

Once Benedict was done, he stepped closer to Leon. "Kneel, brother."

Leon followed his command, utter joy and gratefulness beaming from his face.

Bending over, Benedict whispered something in his ear. Leon's grin vanished instantly, and as he glared at Ben, his brother set the crown atop his head.

The room burst with applause, the crowd cheering. "Long live the king!"

Trumpets boomed around them, filling Mera's ears.

Standing up, Leon turned away from Benedict and bowed once again to his people, this time not like a king, but an actor thanking the audience.

He didn't seem as confident as before. He wasn't smiling either.

"He's king now," Mera whispered, watching Leon and Benedict step down the dais. "Not much else Corvus can do."

"I guess not," Bast muttered with a confused frown. "Something doesn't feel right."

It absolutely didn't.

Suddenly, Raes grabbed Bast by the arm, startling Mera.

Where had he come from?

"I must speak with you, Sebastian. Now." He nodded at Mera absently, before pulling her partner into the crowd.

She attempted to follow them, but faeries had already closed in her path.

Great. Freaking great.

There she was, left alone in a room full of high-society fae… and possible accomplices to whatever Corvus was planning—*if* he had anything planned at all.

Nightlings welcomed human tourists, but not humans in general. Right now, Mera stood in nightling territory, inside an event reserved for the night fae. A sharp line cut through Lunor Insul, a clear distinction between what its inhabitants showed the world, and what they kept hidden away.

Mera was the only "human" there; on duty, granted, but still the only "human". Also, faeries would always be faeries.

If only they knew she was a siren… Well, they'd probably kill her on the spot.

Her eyes skipped the disdainful glances the room shot at her, to finally land on Benedict from across the room.

With a dismayed grin, he raised his wine glass to her. Mera couldn't tell what seemed weird about it, other than the fact it had happened before, back when he'd poisoned her with enchanted wine.

She peered at him, trying to figure out why her instincts tingled, why her gut-feeling sent her all sorts of warning signs, until she realized his eyes were glistening, and his hand was shaking.

Benedict was scared.

No, he was terrified.

Gone was the wittiness she'd witnessed moments ago; gone was his easy manner and proud posture. Either Ben was a remarkable actor, or he had another twin.

Crap.

If Mera had learned one thing as a detective, was that people did crazy things when they were afraid.

Ben must have noticed the worry on her face, because he turned away and hurried through the crowd.

Mera rushed to him, pushing high-nosed Sidhe out of her way. They glared at her with complete outrage, but she didn't give a rat's ass.

"Stop!" she yelled to Benedict, but either he couldn't hear her through the crowd, or he was officially on the run.

Mera dashed after him anyway.

CHAPTER 25

THE THRONE ROOM'S shiny ambience and loud music faded quickly, giving way to a complete darkness cracked by the moon and wayward faerie lights.

"Benedict!" Mera yelled, her voice echoing against the corridor's arched ceiling. "Stop!"

The bastard picked up the pace.

Mera's high heels clicked against the marbled floor as she rushed after him, the back of her shoes scraping against the skin and tendons behind her ankles.

Damn it!

What she wouldn't give to have her boots right now.

On she went, the loud clicking of her heels the only sound in the night while Benedict descended through the palace's outer stairways.

The path twirled around the mountain in a downwards spiral, sometimes showing them the island, sometimes the cliffside—and the steep fall to the rushing waves below them.

Benedict's form mingled with the night, only to reappear moments later a few steps ahead. He was winnowing between short-distances, which meant his magic must be too

219

weak to take him somewhere safe. He probably hadn't fully recovered from Charles' feast, and even if he had, winnowing demanded a great deal of energy.

"Ben, stop or I'll shoot!" she bellowed, knowing fully that she would have to halt and lift her dress to fetch her gun, which would cost her precious time.

Also, Mera wasn't looking forward to shooting Bast's brother.

Calling her bluff, Benedict didn't slow his pace.

Crap!

Mera's muscles ached, and fresh night air pricked her lungs. She had to catch him soon or she would lose his trail.

'We could always use the macabre,' her siren whispered.

Maybe, as a last minute resource. Yet if she did, Ben would find out her secret.

So, no. No macabre. Even if it meant losing his track.

Boosting forward, she moved as fast as she could, but when she nearly stumbled over her heels, Mera decided she'd had enough with them. Taking off the super expensive shoes, she flung them away into the ocean, hoping Bast wouldn't mind.

Mera went after Benedict bare footed, her chest and legs aching as she stretched herself to her limit.

Ben pivoted abruptly into an empty courtyard drenched in moonlight. Hurrying down the inner porch's stairs, he headed toward the grass, where he finally stopped and turned to face her.

Mera bent over the edge of the porch while catching her breath. "Why... the fuck... were... you running?"

His chest heaved up and down from the effort. "I didn't want company."

"No shit," Mera snapped between deep inhales, raising her head to study Benedict, the garden, and the vast ocean view beyond it.

Night covered the trees and flowers around him in a navy mantle, the darkness forming a perfect canvas for the neon patterns blooming on the foliage.

Mera blinked, realizing Benedict had stepped into a rainbow-garden that showcased thousands of different patterns across the darkness, breaking through the night. At the center of the space, the plants' colorful glow reflected on a small pond's pitch-black water.

The entire place looked outwardly, enough so that Mera lost a breath.

"Whoa..."

"Theo loved this place," Benedict muttered absently, and only then did Mera notice the purple specks of dust glittering atop his skin—a pattern all too similar to Bast's.

Captivated, she stepped into the garden, the grass prickling the bare soles of her feet.

Benedict stood in the middle, before a row of stone archways that led to the cliffside. The sound of waves breaking down below made for an eerie background noise.

"Are you okay?" Mera asked, genuine worry taking over her.

Fretting about a Sidhe, especially one such as Benedict, might be stupid, but she worried nonetheless.

He chortled without any amusement. "Haven't been all right for a while now, Detective."

Carefully, Mera stepped closer, trying not to startle him. "Why are we here, Ben?"

Studying his own shoes, he shoved both hands in his pockets in a very Bast-like manner. "I killed Theo, and my father."

What the...

Mera considered her options. She had to, even if she didn't fully believe him.

The cuffs were with Bast, so she couldn't arrest Benedict

yet. Should he choose to attack, though, she wouldn't be able to reach her gun fast enough, leaving the macabre as her only option.

She glanced at the water in the pond.

Yeah, she would have that, too.

Not that Benedict seemed eager to fight. In fact, his confession was awfully convenient, his timing too perfect. Wrapping himself in gift paper might have been less obvious.

"Nah," she replied. "I don't buy it."

He scowled at her. "Does it matter? I'm admitting my guilt."

"You're covering for someone."

Looking away, Benedict strolled in lazy circles. He propped both hands on his waist, raising his shoulders. "What good has the truth ever done to anyone?"

She didn't take the bait. "Why are you and Corvus so eager to take the blame for things you didn't do?"

"I'm guilty. I assumed detectives were more... pragmatic."

"Oh, we are." She tapped her temple. "It's why I don't buy your confession."

"Does it matter?" Ben studied the stone arches, the blowing wind fluttering his suit jacket. His gaze held loss and grief at the same time. "Please arrest me quietly. I'd hate to ruin my brother's coronation."

It hit her at once.

Ben loved his brothers, enough to go to jail for them. So did Corvus. It's why he'd given himself in, actually. To protect ...

A knot tied in her throat.

"It's Leon, isn't it?"

Benedict glared at her with sheer terror, his mouth half-open. He seemed to scrambled for words, but couldn't form any.

"Nonsense," he finally managed. "I admitted to—"

"He gave up his life, his independence, to watch over the rest of you," she stated, the pieces of the puzzle coming together as she carefully stepped closer to Ben. "Now, you're both doing the same for him."

Ben's jaw strained. "You don't understand. Leon isn't like father. He'll snap out of it, eventually."

Ah, there you go.

"If he's behind the murders, you must tell me right now," she pushed, her tone menacing, though Mera wasn't in any position to threaten him.

"It's not about *if*, Detective." He frowned at her as if she was the crazy one. "It's about why."

Leon had gotten the crown and more power than any faerie in Hollowcliff, all because his father was dead. So the first crime made sense. He had motive and opportunity, but why kill Theodore? Why frame Corvus? And most of all, why feign an attempt on his own life?

Leon loved his brothers, had given up a lot to raise them. Murdering the monk was out of character.

No, scratch that.

It was *insane*.

"The monster is dead," Ben muttered as he stepped closer to the pond, watching his reflection on the pitch-black surface. "Long live the monster."

"Nightblood," she realized. "It's taken over him."

"Maybe it's the crown." Benedict shrugged casually. "Mom always said that sanity is acknowledging this world is twisted. Insanity is believing we're in control."

Whatever reason for his actions, Mera couldn't let Leon walk free. "I have to arrest your brother."

"You can try." Pivoting on his heels, Ben faced her. His blue eyes gleamed fiercely against the darkness, the neon blue contrasting with the purple freckles crossing the bridge of his nose.

223

Mera stepped back.

The asshole stepped forward.

"Ben…" she warned.

"I would do anything for my brothers, but I don't want to hurt you, Detective." Once again, he showed her his wrists. "I beg you, arrest me."

Mera shook her head, her teeth grinding behind tight lips. She had to buy herself time, though for what, she didn't yet know.

"What did you tell Leon before setting the crown on his head?"

A soft smile grazed Benedict's lips. "I told him I'd go down for his crimes. That I hoped losing my freedom was worth it."

"I'm not arresting an innocent fae."

He tilted his head left, watching her as if she was daft. "You have no choice."

Literally.

It was either that or fighting Ben, which meant risking revealing her secret to him. Bad outcomes, no matter what.

Before Mera could make a decision, Benedict twitched and gasped, his sharp inhale nearly covering the squishy sound of metal cutting through his chest from behind.

Dark splatters of nightblood sprayed on her dress, but Mera barely realized it.

A blade. No, a sword.

Benedict had just been impaled by a sword.

Catching up to what had happened, she yelped and stepped back, shock reigning in over her academy's training.

Benedict glanced down at the blade poking out of his chest, the metal coated in his own blood. Shaking fiercely, he glanced up at Mera as a line of nightblood trickled down the edge of his mouth.

"Run," he croaked, before his body slid around the edge of the blade, and he fell face first on the grass.

Gulping, Mera faced the Sidhe standing behind Ben's limp form.

Leon's skin was coated in glowing-pink patterns, his cheeks drenched in tears. His sharp fangs grew bigger as his hair swirled against the wind, underneath the spiky crown atop his head. The sea silver shone softly, nearly mimicking moonlight.

He glared at his fallen brother with glistening, rosy irises that soon became pitch-black, all the wrath in the world burning inside him.

"*You* did this," he growled lowly, his focus shifting to Mera.

Poseidon in the trenches, he wasn't just any raging maniac, but Bast's big brother. She had to thread carefully— at least as much as she could.

"I'm not the one holding a bloodied sword, Leon," Mera countered pointedly. Maybe it could help him snap out of whatever had taken hold of him.

Absolute fury wrinkled his features, nearly turning him into a monster.

The mad king had arrived. And he was out for blood.

CHAPTER 26

STEPPING BACK, Mera glanced around, heart slamming against her chest.

She could, and *should*, run, but Leon was a powerful fae, who used to be an assassin for the League. If she tried to escape, the Night King would get to her before she reached the end of the courtyard.

Her options were the macabre and waterbending, but she wouldn't unleash her siren, not yet. Regardless of what he'd done, Leon was Bast's brother; not only that, but the one he loved the most. The only member of his family who Bast put on a pedestal, other than his mother.

Shit.

Gulping, Mera looked down at Benedict, who lied motionless near the edge of the pond. His arm was twisted onto his back, but his finger twitched slightly, even if the rest of him didn't move.

"We have to call a healer," she urged Leon. "Maybe we can save Ben."

The Night King glared at her, refusing to pay attention to

the body on the grass. "Trying to distract me is futile, Detective."

"He's alive, damn it!"

"Ben will join Theo in Danu's prairies soon enough. There's no salvation for him here." Leon's entire body quivered, his teeth clenching so hard Mera wondered if they would shatter. "No salvation for me, either."

A tingling sensation burned at the back of her head, as if someone was trying to push through the base of her skull.

"Let me in!" Bast's voice rang faintly inside her eardrums.

What a fantastic time to be losing it.

Taking a deep breath, she stepped backwards, distancing herself from Benedict. Mera might not be able to help him, but she'd make sure he would be safe until, *if,* someone got there.

Protecting a fae who neared his death might be pointless, but hope was an illogical thing.

Leon followed her slowly, the way a tiger did when on a hunt, silently challenging Mera to attack first.

"You're hurting your brothers," she stated, her voice shakier than intended. "You love them, Leon. What you're doing makes no sense."

Sniffing back his tears, he opened his arms, his sword still in hand. "I'm made of nothing but regret. Can't you see, Detective?"

The ashen taste of his magic set on her tongue. He was getting ready to use it.

Mera had to distract him for as long as she could… and then what?

She had no freaking clue.

"Why did you kill Theodore?" she blurted.

The madness in Leon's pitch-black eyes gave way to a world of sorrow. Lowering his arms, he glanced to his right, toward the dark pond and Benedict. "I asked Theo to give

Father the chocolate box. He knew I had killed the old prick the moment Bast told us the bonbons were poisoned."

"So he didn't report you," she stated.

Theodore should have come to them, not his older brother. If he had, he would still be alive.

"Of course he didn't. Theo was Night Court *and* my brother." Leon scoffed, his focus still on Benedict. "He begged me to turn myself in, said Danu would forgive my sins." His nostrils flared, his breathing accelerating. "Father's was *one* body atop a pile of corpses. Why should his death be any different from the hundreds haunting my past?" Leon waved his hand violently as he turned to Mera. "We used to be assassins! What about those deaths, Theodore? Should I pay for them? Should Bast and Corvus pay?"

Technically yes, but she wasn't about to open that can of worms right now.

"Theo told me we must do better," he spat, his face wrinkling with bitterness. "He said I'd given him no choice, and that he would go to Bast. What a time for him to grow a conscience!"

Shaking his head, Leon clicked his tongue.

"My little brother would be forced to arrest me. How was that kind, Theo? How was that right?" Knocking on his temple, he gave her a knowing grin. "The monk made no sense, you see, because the nightblood had taken over him. No one deserves to live in madness, Detective. Ending Theo's pain was a mercy."

"Was it?" Mera swallowed as panic set cold and deep in her chest.

Leon was so far gone… Maybe he'd been right.

Maybe he couldn't be saved.

"Years as an assassin taught me how to kill quickly and without leaving traces," he explained. "But Corvus meddled, as always. That *baku* winnowed into the throne room at the last minute. It's a gift of his darkness, you see. Bast's corrodes and destroys, mine shields like any other, and Corvus, he can winnow several times without losing his strength." He frowned to himself. "Theo's magic could soothe hearts, bring others peace. Ironic, isn't it?"

Mera cleared her throat. "How did Corvus find you?"

"He shared a mind link with Theo, much to my own surprise." Leon's face wrinkled as if he was about to cry, but he took a deep, steadying breath instead. "Corvus tried to stop the bleeding, but there was nothing he could do. Our magic can't heal."

Understanding fell over Mera, almost crushing her. That was the reason Corvus' fingerprints had been stamped around Theodore's neck. He wasn't trying to kill him; he was trying to save him, and in his despair, he'd nearly choked his brother to death.

"The way Corvus howled when he realized Theo was leaving us..." Leon drifted off in sorrow.

"Your brother was holding Corvus' necklace when we found him," Mera carefully reminded. "Did you place it in his hand?"

"Theo tore it off by accident when he urged Corvus to flee. It was his last word... 'Run.'" He shook his head, coming back to himself. "Corvus winnowed out of there faster than I could blink."

Leon might not have wanted to implicate Corvus at first, but he hadn't removed the necklace from Theodore's hand either.

"I was left there, watching life ebb away from a brother I'd sworn to protect," he went on, his gaze lost. "A brother I helped raise."

Maybe that was when Leon snapped. When Bast's big brother died and gave way to the mad king.

"You faked the attempt on your life," Mera pointed out to

him. "You murdered an innocent fae to incriminate your brother, and still, Corvus didn't tell on you."

"Of course. He's my blood." As if it was that simple. "Besides, the servant's family will be well looked after. Vinci's sacrifice wasn't in vain."

"And Benedict's?" Mera nodded to the unmoving Night Prince near the pond.

Leon didn't turn to his fallen brother, almost as if seeing him had become physically painful. "If he'd drugged himself senseless as he was supposed to, he might've forgotten he saw me hiding the dagger. I trusted Ben to keep quiet, but I suppose twins will always be twins." His face morphed into a beastly scowl. "He went behind my back and told you the truth. Therefore, he had to die."

"Not really," she countered casually. "Ben wanted to take the fall for you. He confessed to the murders and asked me to arrest him, as he told you he would when you were crowned. If only you believed him... but you grew paranoid, didn't you?"

"Lies," he snarled.

No point in trying to argue with a mad fae.

"Mera, where are you?" Bast's muffled voice popped in her head again.

That same force from before pushed against the base of her skull, but it quickly vanished.

Odd.

"Did you kill your father just to get the throne?" She pushed.

Leon raised his head to the moon. It graced his crown and features, dimming the pink glow of his skin, making the monster before Mera seem nearly angelic. Yet he still gripped his sword tightly, the blade coated in Benedict's drying blood.

"Father told me he would make Corvus king. He hated

me for taking care of my brothers when he wouldn't. Hated me for being better than him at everything." Leon shook his head like he was buzzing away a hundred bees. "He said Corvus could handle the crown's weight. That I was too soft." A single, loud laugh escaped his lips. "I proved him wrong, didn't I? Rest assured, my brothers will forgive me, Detective. They love me, and I love them. We'll meet in Danu's prairies on the day of Argeddon."

"You Night Princes have a strange way to love," she grumbled.

Poseidon in the trenches, this would kill Bast. Of all his brothers, he loved Leon the most. Leon who'd blown on his wounds when he was little; Leon who gave him lemon pie when their father wasn't looking. Leon who struck a deal to save Stella; Leon who always cared, who always gave and never took.

Until now.

A ruthless veil fell across the new king's face. When he snapped his fingers, a crowd of guards burst from the inner porch that surrounded half of the courtyard.

They'd been there this entire time?

"Arrest him," Mera ordered, hoping they would remember that they worked for Hollowcliff first, and the Night King second.

Well, no such luck. The guards kept watching her and Leon without reacting; merciless statues in the night.

Maybe if she threatened him... Quickly, Mera pulled up her dress, fetching the gun strapped around her thigh. Clicking the safety off, she aimed at Leon.

"I see why Bast likes you," the king chuckled. "Try your best, Detective." He tapped his forehead. "One bullet is all you need."

She wanted to, she really did, but Leon was Bast's big brother, even if he'd gone completely mad. Besides, his magic would probably shield him from the bullet—if what he'd said about his darkness forming strong barriers was true.

Mera threw her gun aside, knowing it was useless.

It was pretty obvious she wouldn't leave with her life. She could never beat a powerful fae like Leon, plus some thirty Night guards, in their own playground. Even with her macabre and waterbending, it might be a stretch.

Mera would give them the fight of the century, though. Tonight, she died not as a human. Not as a lie.

Tonight, she died free.

As a waterbreaker.

"Bast is a detective," she stated as the siren soared underneath her skin, twirling and dancing within her veins. "Whatever happens here, he'll never stop digging."

The pond's water stirred, but the faeries didn't seem to notice.

"Don't worry. I'll tell him Ben killed you, and I killed him in return." Leon waved his hand around the courtyard, showing her the guards. "I have plenty of witnesses. Indeed, I'll be hailed a hero in Hollowcliff; no. In all of Tagrad."

For a mad fae, he could be incredibly lucid sometimes.

"Corvus will talk," she argued.

Leon frowned at her with a certain pity, his lips pursed. "No, he won't. He's my brother, Detective."

He was so certain, and yet, Corvus had been willing to be imprisoned just to take Bast away from the island. He'd wanted *Bast* safe; not Leon. Which was mind-boggling considering he hated her partner.

Corvus would always be an enigma to Mera. All of the Dhays would, for that matter.

The Night King raised his sword. "I'll make it quick. I'll grant you this mercy, as I did with Theo."

"There's still hope." Mera insisted, trying to reach out to

Bast's loving brother, the fae who must still be in there, drowning in nightblood. "You can redeem yourself, Leon."

"I killed my father and two of my brothers." His beady eyes glinted with tears, a mountain of pain inside them. "I can never come back from that."

He raised his sword, and Mera fixed her battle stance, lifting her fisted hands.

Her siren thrummed through her veins as dread spread across her chest. If she died today, her only regret was not telling Bast about her feelings for him; feelings she didn't understand or accept, yet kept burning inside her.

"Danu in the fucking pra—," Bast's voice echoed in her mind before a void swallowed the space next to her, and then out he came, nearly stumbling over his feet.

CHAPTER 27

AT FIRST, Bast thought Master Raes had lost his mind.

The old fae had pulled him into a weapons room filled with swords hanging from the walls, adorning the entire space.

Inside it, none other than *sarking* Corvus himself waited for them, wearing a white suit awfully similar to Leon's.

Stupid really, to have a meeting between assassins in a room full of weapons, though Bast didn't think about grabbing one before jolting at his brother. Master Raes held him back, however—remarkable how the old sag remained in prime shape.

"Listen to him!" his mentor yelled as he pushed against Bast, blocking his path. "There's more at play than you think, youngling!"

"He's a murderer!" Bast roared, stretching his arm toward Corvus, his fingers eager to squeeze around his brother's throat.

"That may be," Corvus stated quietly, "but I didn't murder Father and Theo."

Lies. They had to be.

A sense of helplessness suddenly hit Bast, though the feeling didn't come from him. It came from the dormant mind link he'd stablished with Mera when he had released the Faeish in her mind.

He stopped struggling against Master Raes, his jaw hanging. "Kitten?"

Fear overcame her helplessness, but Bast couldn't tell what scared her, not unless she opened her side of the link.

"Let me in!" he shouted through their bond, hoping she would listen.

She didn't—how could she?—but the strangest thing happened. Bast *saw* Leon's blurred image through Mera's eyes. It faded in and out, but it showed him enough. Big Brother's pitch-black eyes, and his sword drenched in dark blood.

No, no, no...

Finding a limp form lying in the darkness, Bast gasped in horror when he realized who it was.

"Ben!" he yelped, but the images disappeared, leaving nothing behind.

Corvus stepped back, tears glistening in his eyes. "Don't you say it." His brother's Adam's apple bobbed. "Don't you dare... "

Bast heard his own heartbeats, felt the frantic rising and lowering of his chest. Warmth slid down his cheeks, and he realized he was crying. Wiping away his tears, he swallowed dry, trying to focus beyond his grief.

Big Brother had murdered their father, which honestly, Bast could forgive. The problem was, Leon hadn't stopped at that. He'd killed Theo like a pig at the slaughter, and now he'd hurt Ben.

And Mera was alone with him.

Reading her mind, or seeing things through her eyes without her permission, should have been impossible with a normal mind link. Emphasis on 'should'. Incredible really, that Bast had seen as far as he did. Maybe their connection was stronger because she was his...

It didn't matter. Not now.

He couldn't explain why it happened, he just needed to get to Mera.

"Ben wanted to take the fall for you," her voice echoed in Bast's mind. Torturing silence followed, until her words tuned in again. *"If only you believed him... but you grew paranoid, didn't you?"*

Halle fuchst ach, she shouldn't poke a beast with a short stick, especially one such as Leon.

"Mera, where are you?" he pushed through the link, but he couldn't see their location.

He caught the sound of waves in the distance, which probably indicated the eastern side of the castle, but the possibilities were too many. He couldn't even tell if Mera and Leon were indoors.

Bast kept trying to connect with her, until the image opened to him; a glimpse as fast as an eyeblink, but it was enough—a neon garden with a pond in the middle, underneath the night sky.

The royal courtyard. And it was filled with guards.

"She's surrounded and alone," he muttered to Master Raes and Corvus.

Regret swarmed upon his partner, filling Mera with a longing for things she would never have. Bast knew that sensation well.

It walked hand in hand with death.

His heart lodged in his throat, and he struggled to form rational thoughts. The possibility of what Leon could do to her crashed against him, swallowing his common sense and replacing it with sheer panic.

Could he get to her in time?

Not from here.

"Danu in the fucking pra—" A strange force swallowed him from behind, immersing Bast in a darkness with glittering stars. It felt both cold and warm.

He floated inside it for a split second until a slit cut through the dark, showing him the courtyard on the other side. At once, he was pushed through it, nearly toppling over as he came stumbling onto the garden. The gateway of night and stars behind him disappeared.

Mera stood beside him, shock and surprise filling her green eyes. "Bast? You winnowed?"

"You're all right," he assured himself, thanking God, Danu, or whatever deity out there, for keeping his partner safe. Steadying his breathing, he stood straight. "Oh, kitten..." Bast pulled her into his arms, silently swearing he would never let go of her again.

Mera hugged him back. Her body trembled against his, her fingers digging against his suit. "Thanks for coming, partner," she croaked.

A brief moment passed before she suddenly glared at him, stepping back. "Wait a second! You created a mind link with me without my permission!" She slapped his chest. "You dickwart!"

He grinned playfully. "A smart dickwart, you mean."

She shook her head, but kitten couldn't hold the smile that broke through her perfect lips. "Smart, and sneaky, too."

The air cracked and whipped as a circle of foggy mist, joined by a patch of night and stars, popped in the space between them and Big Brother.

Yes, Leon stood there, at a distance and on the edge of Bast's vision, but he couldn't bring himself to face the monster he'd seen in Mera's mind again, not yet. Besides, Leon had made no motion to attack. *So far.* The guards around them also watched in silence.

Raes stepped out of the mist, standing on the right. The light-gray freckles on his skin matched the color of his eyes, his blue flaming suit flickering against the night.

Corvus came out of the darkness on the left. The neon canary patterns twirling around his body made it seem like the sun glowed underneath his skin.

They must have followed Bast's winnowing trace here. Also, they had brought gifts from the weapons room—three swords to be exact, plus a couple of daggers.

Raes threw one sword at him, and he caught it midair by the handle.

Wielding a blade against Leon felt horribly wrong. Bast's heart ached, yet he had no choice.

Well, no avoiding the inevitable.

He turned to Big Brother, and all of Bast's relief from seeing Mera safe vanished. He stepped forward and in front of his partner, protecting her.

Ahead, his brother stared at them with balled fists, pain and rage making a strange mix in his face.

How he resembled Father...

"Hello, brothers," he snarled through clenched teeth.

CHAPTER 28

A PART of Bast wanted to leave with Mera and forget Leon had lost his mind to the nightblood. Then again, Ben was lying right there on the grass, as if he was a crumpled piece of paper. Not a whiff of magic flowed from him.

Bast's throat knotted, his eyes pricked with tears, but he stifled the indignity of crying again. First Theo and now Ben. *Halle*, his brothers were dropping dead like flies.

Leon's eyes were the problem. Not pink and gentle, but merciless and pitch-black. Bast had grown used to seeing those eyes in his father, Corvus' face, even in Ben's sometimes, but not in Leon's.

Never in Leon's.

Big Brother resembled one of Danu's devils, not the giving and caring fae who'd practically raised him.

"What have you done, Leon?" Corvus asked from Bast's side, his focus on Benedict.

Leon scowled at him. "You foul traitor. You led them here."

"Technically, I didn't." Corvus pointed at Mera. "You can thank the detective for that. I simply contacted Master Raes,

C.S. WILDE

because I feared you'd hurt our brothers." He nodded at Ben's limp form, the pain in Corvus' semblance resonating with Bast's own. "For Danu's sake, Leon! I told Ben to stay away, but the idiot didn't listen... "

"Ben is dead because he betrayed me!" Leon spat. "I raised you all, and you keep betraying me!"

Bast's jaw set, a bitter taste going up his mouth. Big Brother had given so much, so freely. He didn't deserve what his own body did to him.

"You're not used to the wilderness of nightblood," Bast stated carefully, stepping forward while ignoring the crowd of guards facing them from the porch. "It has always been stronger with Corvus, Ben, and I, but you can control it. Let us help, brother."

Leon chortled, as if he had just told him a funny joke.

Bast wouldn't say they excelled at controlling their wicked instincts either, but at least they hadn't murdered their own kin.

"The nightblood took you by surprise," Corvus added, "We can fix this."

"Fix this?" His beady eyes widened. "I killed Theo and Ben! How do you suggest we fix that?"

He had a point.

Leon's attention suddenly drifted to Mera, his eyes narrowing. "How did you tell my little brother we were here?"

Bast stepped to the left, shielding his kitten once again from Leon's line of sight. "I made a mind link with her without her consent."

"You set a link with the detective against her will?" An amused smirk cut across Leon's lips. "A one-sided link can only happen if there's love on both sides." He turned to Corvus. "Don't you find it interesting, brother?"

Bast frowned at the *shig* next to him. "What's that supposed to mean?"

Corvus didn't answer. He simply stared at Bast and Leon with utter horror.

"When you left for the continent, Corvus fixed a link with your mind," Leon explained.

Bast's throat might've morphed into sandpaper. Scowling at Corvus, he raised one finger. "You fucking—"

"I undid it once Father stopped sending assassins after you." He scratched the back of his neck. "It was a safety measure. Don't make a big deal out of it, *baku*."

"It *is* a big deal!"

Corvus had violated his trust, which didn't surprise Bast. What horrified him was that he'd succeeded in creating the link. Which meant that deep down, after all the bad blood between them—*literally and figuratively*—they still cared for each other.

It made no sense.

Kitten might've been right. Maybe he and Corvus were incredibly similar.

Maybe they both had a weird way to love.

Bast still pointed at Corvus, a strange mix of rage and shock thumping in his chest. There was so much he wanted to tell that *malachai*, but all he did was stand there with his mouth half-open, the words stuck in his throat.

"Gentlemen," Master Raes snapped, his attention fixed on Leon and the guards surrounding them. "Will you pay attention to the matter at hand?"

Even in his madness, Big Brother was smart. He'd been trying to distract them.

Maybe he'd been doing that since they were kids.

Was that the reason Bast never had a proper relationship with Corvus? Because Leon had always been the knight in shining armor; the great good that made all other goods pass by unnoticed?

Bast's entire past slipped between his fingers, crumbling to dust. Turning to Corvus, he found the same doubt in his canary eyes; eyes that hid a world of things underneath. In them, Bast also found an apology, the same two words that rung repeatedly in his head.

Felenue, broer. I'm sorry, brother...

Leon nodded to the guards, and they slowly began stepping down the porch, which meant a head-on fight.

He, Master Raes, and Corvus could jump off the cliff to take the battle to the sky, but that would leave Mera unguarded.

Not an option.

Pushing his link with her, Bast connected their thoughts. *"You good with a sword?"*

"Top of my class."

He handed her his blade, his focus fixed on the approaching guards, who had stopped in a half-circle around them.

Bast's night and stars should be enough to handle their opponents. Besides, he couldn't bring himself to use a sword against Leon, even though he should.

"Avoid using your akritana's powers," he added. *"We can't risk Corvus and my master finding out."*

"Will do." Fear thrashed behind her clear green eyes. *"Bast, you must defend yourself, and if that means hurting these guards, so be it. I just want to avoid a—"*

"—massacre, I know." He winked at her. *"I'll keep Yattusei in check."*

The smile she gave him beamed with pride and joy. Bast wished he could spend the rest of his days making her smile like that.

"You have the disadvantage." The mad king who had

taken over his big brother raised his hand, and the guards unsheathed their swords. "Surrender, and I might spare you."

Corvus chortled without any amusement. "Like you spared Ben and Theo?"

"Have it your way, then." Leon lowered his hand, his lips curling.

The guards rushed forward, bellowing battle cries as the mad king charged from ahead, his furious glare locked on Bast. Pitch-black flames sprouted from the royal blade, and Bast froze, his heart ached. For the first time in his life, he didn't know what to do in a battle.

Well, he did, of course.

Fight. But he didn't want to fight against Leon.

Please, not Leon.

Master Raes rushed forward and met his brother's blade before he got to Bast. A wall of guards soon blocked the space in between them, and Bast could barely see Leon and his master anymore.

Something hit him from behind, and he realized Corvus and Mera had slammed their backs against his, forming a triangle. Corvus raised a shield around them, which slowed down the mass of fae lunging at them, but shields weren't his specialty.

Two guards suddenly slipped through the spot on Bast's left, and his endless darkness swallowed him from inside, filling him up to his head. His fangs pricked his tongue as he willed his power onto the two faeries.

Bast's night consumed the guards' feeble shields like fire burned through paper, and they howled in pain as their skins began blackening; horrid howls that clanged awfully like music to him.

"Partner!" Mera shouted at the same time she plunged her blade into an incoming Sidhe's foot, then punched her opponent senseless.

243

Ah, yes...

He regretted his promise to her, but he couldn't take it back now.

Once the pain rendered the guards unconscious, he let go. They fell, crumpled on the grass, frostbite blackening their skin, but it was nothing a good healer couldn't fix if they got there in time.

More soldiers pierced Corvus' shield from the left. His brother's night wrapped around their wrists and ankles, holding them in place before he slashed deep. Unlike Bast, he left no survivors.

If an opponent goes down, make sure they don't rise.

Leaving the guards alive might bite him in the ass sooner rather than later, but Bast did it for himself, for the detective he wanted to become, and most of all, he did it for Mera.

Soldiers rushed at them and soldiers fell. Kitten had already pierced two guards on their chest and stomach, all in non-vital spots that rendered them unconscious from blood loss.

A slow death, but a death that bought them time.

Mera used the macabre, too. Through their link, Bast felt its bloodthirsty magic thrumming in her core. Yet, she used only enough to slow down the guards, maybe make the weakest of them faint. Surprisingly, the fae themselves had no clue they were losing to an *akritana*.

The things she could do under the radar...

Where two guards fell, however, four replaced them. Also, Corvus' shield had begun fading rapidly.

From in between the battling faeries, Bast found Leon punching Master Raes unconscious, then flinging him away.

The old fae's body landed close to Ben's.

Leon grinned wickedly at Bast. He was coming for him, but *halle* if Bast would let him close to Corvus and Mera.

"Protect her!" he ordered Corvus before charging

forward, pushing the guards away with two walls of darkness that burned them to the touch.

"You asshole!" Mera yelled, but he'd already left them behind.

Pulling the power from his core, Bast shot a raging storm of night toward Leon, but his brother raised a shield just in time.

The courtyard shook as Bast's darkness engulfed the mad king and a part of the castle behind him, a giant wave of magic that destroyed everything in its path.

It came with a price, of course. Using this burst of power drained his energy, but Bast didn't stop; didn't waver. He couldn't kill his big brother, but incapacitating him shouldn't be an issue.

He only hoped his night storm would do the trick.

Stones rumbled inside his uproar of darkness and stars, the sound of things crumbling thundering around him. When his knees buckled and his mind felt awfully light, he had to pull back.

It was either that or losing consciousness.

Retreating to his core, Bast's darkness revealed a path of singed grass and scorched trees that led to a giant hole searing the courtyard's marbled façade, straight through half of the castle.

His brother stood proudly before the wreckage, not a scratch on him.

Halle...

"My turn, little brother," Leon announced with a blood-thirsty grin.

He shot a burst of night and stars toward Bast, who pulled another storm from his core, even if it pained him.

Sweat beaded on his forehead as the raging forces clashed violently, booming into the sky. Clenching his teeth and ignoring the pain that pierced through his body, Bast knew he couldn't hold on for long. His magic already quivered against Leon's.

Winnowing, plus his previous attack, had taken a giant toll on him. He had no choice. He had to find a weapon.

Soon.

As if on cue, his gaze caught a sword lying on the grass to the far left.

The royal sword.

Master Raes must have disarmed Leon during his earlier sparring, yet Bast couldn't reach the weapon and keep defending himself. The mad king's power was too fucking strong.

In one strike, Leon's darkness pierced through Bast's, flinging him to the left, until his back slammed against one of the stone arches that faced the ocean. The sound of his skull cracking against the hard surface reverberated through his body.

Bast fell on the grass, his mind spinning as the stone arch behind him gave in, and plummeted into the roaring waves below.

Coughing, he saw stars from the corners of his eyes. He tried to focus his blurred vision, only to find Leon smirking at him. Instead of finishing him off, the mad king pivoted on his heels and charged at Corvus and Mera, who had their hands full with the remaining guards.

No!

A line of night burst out of Bast's palm, zapping forward. It wrapped around Leon's ankle, pulling him back, but the bastard was fast. Instead of tripping over, he spun midair, letting the whip's pull take him to Bast.

As the mad king smashed against him, his scaled beige wings flashed into existence. Leon punched Bast's chin so hard, he sent him into the air. He didn't stop hitting him, throwing Bast higher with each strike, until he grabbed him by his lapel and pulled him down in a loop.

Bast crashed with his back on the grass, Leon's heavy body immediately landing atop him.

Everything went black for a moment, and when he came to, the mad king was sitting astride him, punching Bast relentlessly as battle sounds rang faintly from the distance. His wings had disappeared.

"I told you to go!" Leon yelled, tears streaming down his cheeks as he struck him again and again.

The strikes didn't break Bast. He could barely feel them anymore. The fact that Leon drew them, on the other hand…

"Bast!" Mera screamed from inside a crowd of guards.

That snapped him out of it. His darkness burst from him in a pulse, flinging Leon away.

Shakily forcing himself to his feet, Bast turned to Corvus. "Protect her!"

"I'm trying, you *baku*!" his brother countered while he punched and slashed at incoming guards.

"I'm fine!" Mera grumbled as she sent a guard to the ground. "Bast, watch out!"

Too late. Leon kicked him in the back, sending him to the grass once more. Yet, Bast slid his feet underneath him, tripping Leon and bringing him down with a harsh thump.

Throwing himself atop his brother, Bast punched his face. "Wake up!"

His fist slammed into the mad king's face nonstop, each blow cutting into Bast's heart. "You have to be stronger than the nightblood!"

Another set of punches followed. Maybe if he thwacked Leon hard enough, the mad king would turn back into his brother. Maybe it would exorcize his madness.

In response, Leon's magic burst from his core, pushing Bast away with a sharp impulse.

Balancing himself over shaky legs, Bast watched him stand. A trickle of blackened blood streamed down the mad king's nose, but Leon wiped it away, leaving a dark smudge on his upper lip.

"You want to be king! After all I've done for you!" the mad king bellowed before propelling himself forward with his power. His foot harshly connected with Bast's chest.

As he stumbled backwards, Bast realized that if he hadn't gone to the continent, Leon might not have gone mad. If he had been there, by his side, as Leon had always been by his... Guilt dragged him under, stealing his breath.

Big Brother was too far gone, but Bast couldn't kill him. Not when he was to blame, not when he could have avoided this if he'd stayed with Leon.

Yes, Bast had failed his brother, but he wouldn't fail him again, even if it meant losing his own life.

The fight in him faded while Leon went on, punching, kicking, and yelling. His knuckles smashed into Bast's face, chest, and stomach nonstop.

At some point, Bast tasted his own blood. It trickled down the edge of his mouth, joining a stream that flowed from his brow thanks to a wound on his forehead. But he didn't react.

"Fight!" Leon gnarled as he attacked Bast. "Fight, Sebastian, or so help me Danu!"

He didn't.

Leon kicked his upper arm with the strength of a wrecking ball crashing through a wall, snapping the bone in a loud crack. Molten pain pierced through Bast's body and he held back a howl so mighty, his throat might've turned into raw flesh.

The pain waned quickly, though.

Too quickly.

A continuous ringing took over Bast's ears, his mind

feeling remarkably light. His consciousness might fly away at any moment.

He fell with his knees on the grass, and a sting swam up his thighs, yet it faded as fast as it came. Breathing got harder with each passing second.

Perhaps, that was the only way to save his big brother. Maybe Leon would realize how mad he had become if he finished Bast.

Maybe his life was the price for his brother's sanity.

Did Theo think the same before Leon slashed his throat?

"Fight, Bast!" Mera's voice rang in his head.

"I'm sorry, kitten."

This was Leon, the fae who protected him from the bullying of Corvus and Benedict. Leon, who'd been proud of Bast his whole life, when there wasn't much to be proud of. Leon, who'd been more of a father to Bast than the Night King himself.

His brother's fist pounded against his face, and Bast's mind spun, his ears zinging.

It was the oddest thing; through his link with Mera, he could feel her unleashing something inside her.

Her akritana.

"Don't," he ordered, and surprisingly, she listened. *"Don't doom yourself over this. He will come back, kitten, you'll see."*

"No, Bast! You have to fight him!" she begged, a cry in her tone.

Yet, he couldn't.

He wouldn't.

The next second, Leon found a night dagger on the ground next to them. Gripping it fiercely, he raised it.

"I *will* do it, Bast!" His hands shook, his beady eyes pleading and in pain. "Fight me, little brother!"

Coughing blood, Bast tried to lift his shoulders in a shrug, but they were as heavy as led. Taking a deep breath, perhaps his last, he stared at Leon.

Come back...

The mad king yelled as the dagger went down, but before he finished the killing blow, a blade burst through his chest from behind.

Glaring at the sword sticking out of him, Leon dropped the dagger. "I-ironic." He smiled to himself.

His nightblood drenched the blade, tainting his white clothes with a deep, blackened red. It slipped from the corners of his mouth, too.

Leon fell to his knees, revealing Corvus behind him.

"I'm sorry," Corvus mumbled, "but you were going to kill our little brother." He yanked the royal sword from Leon's chest, throwing it away as if it burned his hands.

Instantly, the battle around them stopped.

"You're all under arrest!" Mera yelled to the few guards still standing, though her voice rang faintly in Bast's ears.

"He's alive!" Master Raes shouted.

Ben!

Relief spread through Bast's chest, but it only lasted a moment. Leon collapsed with his back on the grass and stared at the moon, his mouth opening and closing like a fish out of water.

Bast wasn't ready. Danu in the fucking prairies, he couldn't lose Leon.

Dropping to his knees, Corvus hid his face behind his palms, his body shaking with restrained sobs.

At the sight, Bast awkwardly crawled toward him. Breathing was futile, moving was impossible, and still, an arm wrapped around his brother as he hugged Corvus for the first time since they'd been born.

"Brothers..." Leon stretched his blood-soaked hand to them, and they placed themselves on both sides of his body.

With whatever strength he had left, Bast brushed a bloodied lock of hair away from his big brother's face. The gentle pink of his eyes, eyes Leon had inherited from their mom, returned.

He was back.

Bast's wounds hurt, but not nearly as much as the pain of losing another brother.

"I'm sorry, Bast," Leon wheezed. "Don't remember me this way..." Turning to Corvus, he took his hand. "You'll be a great king. Father was right."

"I don't want the stupid crown, you *baku*," Corvus sniffed.

"But it is yours, and I'm thankful for that."

Clearing the tears from his voice, Bast caressed Leon's cheek with his good hand. "Ben is alive."

A relieved smile cut through his lips. "Tell him I'm sorry. I wasn't myself... I... I'm so sorry," he whimpered. His gaze suddenly locked on the moon, surprise filling his features. "Theo?"

Leon exhaled deeply, but didn't inhale again.

Bast and Corvus kneeled there, motionless. Shock and sorrow coursed through Bast's veins, and a sob escaped his lips as he closed Leon's eyes.

His focus drifted to the crown resting atop the dead king's head. It was splattered with blood, either his own or Leon's—Bast couldn't tell, nightblood looked all the same.

Leon wanted the crown to prove their father wrong. He wanted it so badly that his need triggered the madness, a story too familiar throughout the Night Court's history.

That damned, fucking crown... always that damned, fucking crown.

Removing it from Leon's head with his right hand, Bast stared at Corvus. His brother nodded in approval.

Bast's teeth grinded as he forced himself up, his bones feeling like they'd turned into broken glass. His left arm hung limply beside him, and he faintly remarked the pain, but it was nothing.

Nothing compared to what he felt right now.

He faced the broken stone arches that showed the vast ocean below, the moon shining atop the dark surface that stretched into the horizon. Perhaps, Leon and Theo were there now. Together, beyond the silvery path of the moon, deep into Danu's realms.

Bast didn't believe in the after-life, but the idea his brothers went on, somehow brought him peace.

"Until we meet again," he muttered.

Closing his eyes, he took a deep breath, then flung the crown into the raging waters.

CHAPTER 29

BLACK AND SILVER bands hung across the palace's halls and corridors. Up in the throne room, the combination draped from the domed ceiling, and it hung in curtains next to the open arches circling the space.

Black and silver; night and stars.

Night for Leon's funeral, stars for Corvus' coronation, since both would happen on the same day.

Mera glanced down at the silvery top of her dress, then checked her dark skirt. Night and stars, the honoring of both brothers. Most Sidhe who crowded the throne room dressed with the same colors.

The sky today was brutally blue, not a cloud in sight. Sunlight ventured through the arches, glittering against the silver ribbons.

A beautiful summer day that didn't fit the severity of the events.

Mera found Seraphina Dhay sitting near Benedict, who still recovered from his wounds in a wheelchair.

The healer had said Leon's blade missed Ben's heart by an

inch. A killing blow, granted, but one that hadn't ended him immediately. Not like the wound which killed Theo.

Mera believed Leon had done it on purpose, and maybe it was wishful thinking, but she didn't care.

Seraphina's eyes were red and puffed, yet she sat straight and proud, like the queen she was.

Approaching, Mera bowed to her, and then Ben.

"The song of demise caught up to Leon," the Night Queen stated to the open air, barely registering Mera's presence. "Nightblood sings to us all, day in and day out."

Offering Mera an apologizing glance, Benedict leaned closer, taking his mother's hand. "We resist its call, Mom."

"Until the day we grow tired, like your brother."

Swallowing dry, Mera searched for Bast, aching to check on him. If he ever grew tired, she would be there to help him find his way back.

Always.

"Bast is with Corvus," Benedict explained, noticing the worry in her gaze.

Suddenly, trumpets blasted around them, startling both Mera and Seraphina.

The crowd turned to the dais at the far end of the room.

A fae wearing an elegant black suit embellished with silver twirls stepped up to the throne, his manner regal and filled with deference. If it weren't for the wickedness in his yellow eyes, she wouldn't have recognized Corvus.

Bast followed after him, carrying a red pillow with the new crown—a simple white gold circlet.

The healers in Lunor Insul lacked Stella's skill, but they'd fixed Bast's arm and his other wounds in time for the coronation. Mera shuddered at the memory of him screaming as the healers snapped his bone in place, then welded it together with their magic.

'He's fine now,' her siren assured. 'More than fine, actually. Yum!'

That horny bastard…

She wasn't wrong, though. Her partner wore a shirt the color of the moon underneath an onyx suit that fit him all too well. His loose hair waved over the left side of his face, which was the style he chose for formal occasions.

Bast looked perfect, but even when he wore his messy man-bun he was still a thing to behold.

Technically, an event such as a coronation shouldn't be tainted by the sorrow of a brother's burial, at least according to the court's advisors. Yet, Corvus had been adamant on having both on the same day.

"So I never forget how I got here," he'd explained pointedly. "So that he will always remain a part of it…"

The advisors disagreed, of course. They claimed Leon should be buried in shame; that he was a traitor to country and fellow faeries. Thankfully, Corvus wouldn't listen, and neither would Bast. He fully backed up his brother's choice, perhaps for the first time in his life.

"While we're on it," the future king added, "I fully reinstate my brother as Night Prince. Sebastian Dhay is disowned no more."

His advisors' glares were priceless. Two of them even resigned.

Corvus might be an asshole, but he was starting to grow on Mera.

Silence fell upon the throne room as Corvus kneeled before Bast. This was it; the moment where he would gain the crown he never wanted.

"May you govern with Leon's heart and Theo's kindness." Her partner's deep voice echoed throughout the room. "Above all, may you govern with your strength, King of Night."

Bast set the crown on Corvus' head, and the throne room

exploded in applause, followed by loud clamors of "Long live the king!"

Not long after, a procession of family and close friends quietly followed down the mountain, taking Leon's body to the courtyard where he'd drawn his last breath.

Bast and Corvus carried the open casket alongside Master Raes, and some of his assassins. Benedict's chair rolled beside his brothers, completely propelled by magic, while Mera followed not far behind with Seraphina Dhay, who had coiled her frail arm around hers.

"I had a nightmare once," Seraphina muttered, her fingers digging onto Mera's skin as she stared ahead mindlessly. "A wolf burst from inside my son, and killed everyone in Tagrad. Fae, witch, human, shifter or vampire; none escaped. Their bodies laid scattered across the land, their flesh ripped, their blood sipping into the ground... but that wasn't enough for the wolf."

Trembling, her fingers dug deeper into Mera's arm. "Even when the entire world burned around him, it wasn't enough."

Swallowing dry, she patted Seraphina's hand. "It was just a nightmare. Leon can't hurt anyone now."

The Night Queen frowned at her, as if she didn't make any sense. "Leon wasn't the wolf... Bast was."

The drop of a drum. A slap to the face.

"It doesn't mean anything," Mera assured, mostly to herself as prickly, icy dread swam down her spine. Clearing her throat, she nodded decisively. "I won't let nightblood take over him, I promise you."

"You can't save him, dear." Seraphina focused on Leon's casket, a whimper stuck in her throat. "No one can."

The procession went on without a sound until they reached the courtyard, where a pyre had been set up.

Bast, Corvus, and Raes laid Leon's body atop it, then stepped away. The former king held the royal sword to his chest, the same blade which had ended his life.

Leon had died brutally, and still, he seemed so peaceful.

Politely letting go of Mera, Seraphina went to the front, where Benedict sat on his chair, not far from Karthana and her father.

Corvus stood near the pyre, his manner stoic and grand as a guard handed him a torch.

"Hey, partner." Bast's voice startled Mera when he came up behind her.

"Hey." She let out a relieved breath because he wasn't a wolf, which didn't make any sense, but she was relieved nonetheless. "You okay?"

"Not in the slightest." Taking her hand, his fingers intertwined with hers. "I will be. Eventually."

Would he?

"Ae wahnala wu tu, broer," Corvus began ahead, facing the pyre. "I thank you, brother. I miss you, brother. The infinite night has called you. Danu in the prairies, receive him."

"Danu in se campin, het im nut," the Sidhe around them repeated. So did Bast, even if he wasn't the religious type.

"May you rejoice in Danu's prairies and feast on her blessings," Corvus went on. "May the beloved you leave behind never forget you. Until the day we meet again."

"Bis se tag we makta an."

Slowly setting the torch into the pyre, Corvus watched the flames burst to life, soon swallowing Leon.

As fire crackled and his brother burned, Bast grasped Mera's hand tighter, his focus trapped on the blazing pyre, his body quivering. Her hand hurt, yet she wouldn't complain.

She wouldn't let go.

The intense heat prickled Mera's skin, but eventually, it waned.

Most fae slowly left for their homes, but the royal family, with Raes and Karthana, stayed there until Leon became a pile of ashes that blew into the wind.

Mera observed Corvus, hand in hand with Karthana as he watched his brother leave them. Not as lovers anymore, not as betrothed, but as friends.

It felt oddly right, somehow.

"Corvus looks well," she noted. "I never thought I'd say this, but he might become a good king."

"He tortured me my whole life, yet he saved me when I most needed him." Bast quietly studied his brother. "Corvus loved Leon, and he stuck a blade into his chest... for me."

"He made a choice." Mera shrugged. "He chose you."

"But did I deserve it?"

Corvus' pointy ears twitched, and Mera wondered if he'd heard Bast. Gently letting go of Karthana, he approached them.

"*Malachai*," the Night King addressed her partner. "I believe you owe me an apology."

"What?"

"You accused me of Father's murder during the enchanted wine incident." Turning to Mera, Corvus put his palm on his chest in an apology that felt less than heartfelt. "You also promised to apologize; gave me your binding word, actually. You do remember that a broken promise can be quite painful, don't you?"

Bast pushed Corvus' chest playfully, but where his manner had been awry and mistrusting with him before, now it was soft. Kind.

Grateful.

"You could always lift the promise, King *Dickwart*."

"What would be the fun in that? Also, *dickwart?*" He

turned to Mera, amusement shining behind his golden irises. "Is that a thing humans say? It's awfully graphic."

She waved carelessly. "Certainly paints a picture, doesn't it?"

With a chuckle, Bast tapped his shoulder. "Fine. I'm sorry, brother."

"There you go. Wasn't so hard, yes?" He winked at Bast, bowed at Mera, and then returned to Karthana's side.

As she and Bast slowly descended the mountain, a severe silence filling the space, Mera figured some light talk might make him feel better. "So, how does our mind link work?"

Gaping at her, he blinked slowly. "You don't want me to remove it?"

"At first I did, but it came in handy back at the courtyard. I figured we should give it a try for a while."

"Should we?" He gave her a soft smile. "Hmm, now that you mention it, our link does differ from the norm. Emotions flow through the bond, but thoughts are something else entirely, unless there's permission. And still, I could hear what you did, and see blurred flashes of what was going on. Which is why we might need to work on your mind blocks."

"Ah, so you'll teach me how to protect my thoughts from your nosy self? How kind, Detective Dhay."

Raising one eyebrow at her, the most wicked grin cut across his face. "I'm a giving fae, kitten."

'Damn right,' her siren cheered.

A furious blush rose to Mera's cheeks as she remembered that time at the precinct, and those skilled fingers of his, his blazing kisses...

Her siren purred.

Down girl!

They walked together for a while, until Bast led her to the base of the island, arriving into a deserted beach.

"You want to go for a spin?" He nodded to the lazy waves ahead. "No one would know. It's the king's private sanctuary, but Corvus never liked swimming."

Had Bast brought her here because of their link? Because he sensed the need that slept inside her? The ache to break water again, the longing that was always there, ignored and shoved deep into the depths of Mera's soul? Or perhaps, her partner simply understood her better than she'd assumed.

Hard to tell which.

Mera watched the opaque blue that turned turquoise where it met sunlight, yearning to dive in. Inhaling the familiar salty tang of home, she recalled how amazing it felt to dash into the waves.

Pure freedom, in every sense of the word.

Those memories, those sensations, they called for her right now. Taking off her high-heel sandals, she went ahead, feeling the fluffy sand underneath her feet. The waves had nearly reached the tip of her toes when Mera halted.

"There's nothing I wouldn't give for a swim," she admitted wistfully, not knowing exactly why she'd stopped. A strange sensation thumped in her chest, a sort of sixth sense that warned her of... something. *Nonsense.* She was probably scared of touching ocean water after so many years. "I'll take the offer another day, partner."

"As you wish."

Stepping beside Mera, Bast stood with her for a while, watching the waves caressing the shore.

"So, what's next?" she finally asked.

He nodded to the ocean. "That."

Poseidon.

Someone using the alias had impregnated Sara Hyland, and basically glamoured the Summer King's son into killing her. Someone who was a waterbreaker; someone who had survived the forbidden zone's death spell.

Someone like Mera.

"We can't go to our captains without concrete evidence," she reminded him. Besides, Mera didn't want to worry Ruth until they had a strong lead. "It's going to be hard digging into this while we're solving new cases, though."

"Hard, yes. Impossible?" Bast took the back of her hand and kissed it. "I doubt it."

Smiling, Mera brushed a strand of silver hair off his face, tucking it behind his ear. "I suppose we've done impossible things before."

She shouldn't be this close or intimate with Bast. It was a terrible idea, but after all they'd been through, just once, Mera wanted to forget what was right and let go. Kiss him, for maybe five seconds, without wondering about the consequences.

Stepping closer, Bast set a hand over her hip, a tantalizing grin on his soft lips. "Onto more pleasant matters, then..."

He bent down to kiss her, and Mera leaned forward, ready to take those five seconds, enjoy them as much as she could, when a glint in the far left caught her eye.

Sunlight shone against a shiny object at the base of a big rock.

"What's that?" she asked.

"Nothing," he grumbled without even turning, his focus solely on her lips.

Yet, that instinct from before shrieked inside Mera, its warning bells reverberating through her bones. "Bast, something isn't right."

That snapped him out of it. Nodding, he turned to the rock and stepped closer. She followed after him, but when she spotted the object, she nearly fell back.

Her eyes had to be playing tricks on her.

She held Bast's arm, stopping him from getting any closer to the water.

C.S. WILDE

They weren't alone.

"Is that…" His question died midway, because, yes.

Yes, it was. Right there, half buried in the sand.

Even with strong tides, that thing could have never reached the beach in such a short time.

Mera looked around frantically, scanning the ocean's surface as she tried to catch a whiff of magic coming from below.

Nothing popped out, yet the sensation someone watched them lingered.

"Sea faeries gave the crown to the Night King millennia ago, so he'd keep it safe until the day of Regneerik." Charles Grey's voice rang in her mind as she arrived at the rock.

Bending down, a chill ran down her spine as Mera picked up the Crown of Land and Sea.

This was *his* doing.

Poseidon was out there, trying to throw her off; trying to scare her. She couldn't see him, couldn't feel him, but Mera had never been more certain of anything in her life.

Gnarling at the peaceful waters, she closed her fist.

"Let the games begin, asshole."

∼

Find out what happens next in TO KILL THE DEAD

Oh, and if you enjoyed TO KILL A KING, do consider leaving a review. They make an author's day!

You can also join the Wildlings to keep up to date on all things C.S. Wilde, and to get a FREE copy of BLESSED LIGHT, an urban fantasy romance novella.

AN EXCLUSIVE GIFT

Join the Wildlings to keep up to date with the latest on C.S. Wilde and participate in amazing giveaways. Also, you'll get a FREE copy of BLESSED LIGHT, an urban fantasy romance novel!

Just go to **subscribepage.com/kateam**

Be sure to check out C.S. Wilde's bestselling Urban Fantasy Romance series,
BLESSED FURY
Out now!

Thanks for reading!

Choose which book you want next!

Ratings help me determine which series I'll prioritize, so if you can't wait for the next book in this series, leave a review and show your love.

I never leave series unfinished, but your input will determine how quickly I'll start working on the next book. That's right: YOU get to choose which books come next by leaving a review.

Yay!

Another aspect that helps me decide which books come next is sales. So if you acquired this book through piracy, make sure to buy your copy. Piracy is not only a crime punishable by fines and federal imprisonment, but it also ensures that no more books in this series will be written.

Piracy ruins books. It ruins authors too. And that's not cool at all.

Keep up to date with the latest news and release dates by joining C.S. Wilde's mailing list

And if you want to discuss all things Mera and Bast, join the Wildlings or follow C.S. Wilde on Facebook!

ABOUT THE AUTHOR

C. S. Wilde wrote her first Fantasy novel when she was eight. That book was absolutely terrible, but her mother told her it was awesome, so she kept writing.

Now a grown up (though many will beg to differ), C. S. Wilde writes about fantastic worlds, love stories larger than life and epic battles.

She also, quite obviously, sucks at writing an author bio. She finds it awkward that she must write this in the third person and hopes you won't notice.

For up to date promotions and release dates of upcoming books, sign up for the latest news at www.cswilde.com.

You can also connect on twitter via @thatcswilde or on facebook at C.S. Wilde.

You can also join the Wildlings, C.S. Wilde's exclusive Facebook group.